Murder in Meadowbank

A Meadowbank Mystery

Margaret Alty

Published 2011 by arima publishing

www.arimapublishing.com

ISBN 978 1 84549 495 7
© Margaret Alty 2011

Printed and bound in the United Kingdom

Typeset in Garamond 12/16

Swirl is an imprint of arima publishing.

arima publishing
ASK House, Northgate Avenue
Bury St Edmunds, Suffolk IP32 6BB
t: (+44) 01284 700321

www.arimapublishing.com

Chapter One

Saturday afternoon in the market town of Meadowbank; the time when many of the residents were either in a semi-comatose state after a prolonged lunch and too many glasses of wine and stretched out on their sun loungers or, a few like Simon Grant, having discovered to his annoyance he had run out of cigarettes, pulling up in front of the stationers in the square and wondering for the hundredth time why he lacked the will power to stop smoking.

The woman was still there when he came out of the shop; standing at the bus stop, an over-large bag on the pavement beside her and one which reminded him of those textured carpet bags which he had only seen in old movies. He had never seen her before and the fact she was there, obviously expecting a bus to come along, proved she was new to Meadowbank. She was quite beautiful in an Isadora Duncan sort of way, but it was more than that; she exuded not only an air of serenity, as though nothing would ever really get to her, she was totally different from any other woman he had seen before and certainly would never expect to meet in his profession. He was all too accustomed to the pouting and petulant models who often made his life as a photographer an absolute nightmare. She was about his own age, he guessed, mid to late forties, but there was a timelessness about her, although her appearance evoked a sixties' style: from the rich dark auburn hair piled up in an untidy knot at the top of her head to the long emerald green embroidered two-layered skirt. Her skin was creamy pale and as he walked towards her he noticed the sprinkling of freckles on her face and bare arms.

'Hi,' he said, 'you probably don't realise it, but there won't be a bus along for at least another hour.'

'Oh, really?' her voice soft, with a faint trace of a Scottish accent, 'I hadn't realised, but it doesn't matter. I can wait.'

'Are you going as far as Stockbridge?'

'No,' she smiled up at him, making him suddenly conscious of his height; he felt he was towering above her, 'only to the Lodge.'

'You must be the major's new tenant.'

'Major Tilsly, yes, that's right. How did you know?'

'In Meadowbank,' amused by her bewildered expression, 'as you will no doubt soon discover, people are never happy unless they know everything which is going on. A bit perplexing I suppose to any newcomer, but I'm told they do get used to it. In time.' Simon added. 'Anyway,' he went on, 'we'll be neighbours. I live at the Watermill, only a few hundred metres away from the major's place and it will be no problem to give you a lift.'

'Well –' she hesitated, deep blue eyes solemnly appraising him.

'– Sorry,' he interrupted her, 'I should have introduced myself. Simon Grant.' he said.

'And I'm Eliza. Eliza Brent.' placing a small cool hand in his. 'And thank you, I would appreciate it if you could drop me off there. It was silly of me, I should have found out about the buses and then I could have taken a taxi.'

'You may have had a problem there also.' he smiled, 'At this time of the afternoon, especially at the weekend; they are, for some inexplicable reason, a scarcity.'

'It's obvious I have a lot to learn about Meadowbank.'

'You won't find it too difficult,' he reassured her, taking the bag from her and placing it on the back seat of the Renault and opening the passenger door for her. Within seconds they were leaving the market square, stopping at the traffic lights before taking the Stockbridge road out of the town. The journey took less than ten minutes and as he drew up outside the gates to the old manor he felt a quick stab of regret the time had been so brief. Although they had said little, having her seated next to him had had a strangely and totally unique affect on him. Most women, certainly the ones he knew, would have talked non-stop, inconsequential stuff most of it, but it would seem his new neighbour wasn't like that. 'Here we are.' he said, switching off the engine.

'Thank you so much,' she said, taking out a small bunch of keys from her shoulder bag. 'I don't get my car until Monday, but I didn't want to waste any more time hanging about in the hotel. I just wanted to get settled in.'

'That's understandable,' Simon said, dragging over her travel bag and passing it to her, 'I'm sure I would have felt the same. Look,' he added, 'here's my card. I only live a short distance away and if there is anything you need, don't hesitate to give me a call. By the way,' he called out to her as she turned away and walked over to the gates, 'Eliza? An unusual name. My Fair Lady?'

'Hardly,' she laughed; a throaty chuckle, 'but my mother was madly in love with Rex Harrison!'

'At least your surname isn't Doolittle!'

'No, I was spared that, I'm happy to say.' she said and then she was gone, although he waited until he saw her walk the short distance to the front door, making sure she was able to get in alright, before driving off.

The Watermill, or the mill as it was called locally, had been Simon's home all his life. Re-designed by his father in the fifties, he only had a few old photographs taken before the conversion had been made to show him what the building had once been like. It had not functioned as a watermill since the beginning of the century; during the Second World War had been used as offices for army personnel and since those days, although rumours had spread through Meadowbank from time to time of wealthy, invariably American, investors being interested, all of which had come to nothing, the property had remained empty, deteriorating rapidly, until his father driving along the same stretch of road caught sight of it hidden behind a tangle of shrubs and bushes and immediately saw the potential. Not as some ultra-modern and exclusive residential apartments, but as a family home and this was what he had done.

Innovative and imaginative, he had created, without losing any of its original charm, an interesting, spacious and comfortable residence.

The whole of the ground floor was, now he had the mill to himself since his parents had left England for their new home in the Bourgogne region in France, devoted to his gallery. Simon's work, covering more than twenty years, lined the white-painted walls: photographs; all of them simply framed and incorporating countries he had visited – the dense dark green of the Amazon jungle, the plains of Central America, the rugged and hostile terrain of the Highlands of Papua New Guinea, the cascading interior of Victoria Falls, the undulating sands of the Sahara and many more. Most of them in colour, but his pride and joy, a section devoted to black and white photographs, each of them abstracts where the use of colour would have been superfluous. Prisms of light streamed from coloured glass panels in the centre of the ceiling, bathing the whole area dramatically and he knew as the day progressed towards evening so would this effect change, subtly and adding different dimensions to what he had spent a long time in perfecting.

A stripped pine staircase led up to the living quarters which, once again since he had taken the mill over, he had made alterations. The loft-style living room, wall-length sliding windows looked out on to the River Test and, further over, the flat water meadows. His kitchen, modern and functional and adjoining the living room was something else he had changed. Replacing his mother's scarlet painted cupboards and marble work tops, Simon had chosen simple primary colours, easy to live with and ones he didn't think would date: chrome fitments and for relief, a touch of the Mediterranean in the turquoise and white floor tiling. From here, the original sash windows faced out towards the high beech hedge which shielded the mill from the main road.

Tossing his car keys on to the kitchen table, he took out a can of lager from the fridge and thought about the woman he had just met. Eliza. An unusual name for, he was certain, an unusual woman and he looked forward to seeing her again. He opened one of the windows to let in some air, took a deep sip of his beer, when the telephone rang.

'Simon? Reginald, here. Hope I'm not disturbing you?'

'Of course not, Reginald,' it still seemed odd to call the major by his Christian name, but a few years earlier he had insisted, 'you're in luck. I've just got in; ran out of cigarettes.'

'Time you gave up that habit, my boy!'

'Don't I know it.' Simon grinned, knowing full well the major used to be a heavy smoker himself and even now liked nothing better than indulging in one of his pungent cigars.

'Anyway,' he went on, 'didn't phone you up to give you a lecture. I need a little company.'

'Yes?'

'Or I should say what I really need is to talk to someone who will know where I'm coming from.'

'Alright, give me fifteen minutes and I'll be with you.'

'You're a good friend, Simon, but do say if you've got something more important to do.'

'No, it's okay, I might go out for a meal later but it's still too early.'

'Good.'

'By the way,' Simon said quickly before the receiver was put down. The major was not in the habit of prolonging telephone conversations. He always said what he had to and that was that, 'I met your new tenant a short while ago.'

'Did you, by Jove!'

'You sound surprised.'

'Don't know why I should be. I'd forgotten she would be arriving this weekend.'

'You haven't met her then?'

'No, I left all that to the agents, can't be bothered you understand, but I'm assured by them she is quite acceptable. What do you think, Simon?'

'Charming. I think you will like her, Reginald.'

Simon decided to walk to the Old Manor, rather than take the car. He followed the footpath from the mill which ran in a straight line parallel to the Stockbridge Road. There was something about this time of the year, the beginning of July when the hedgerows smelt sweet with honeysuckle reminding him of those other days when as a boy he had trudged along the very same path, looking forward to spending the day with the Tilslys. More than thirty-five years ago now. How old had he been? Ten, eleven. The same age as Colin. He hadn't seen him for a long time, ridiculous really he thought, approaching the gates to the manor, but then he supposed not all that surprising. They had both chosen totally different careers; Colin, after university, going into finance while he, never having any aptitude for figures or the prospect of being confined to an office had gravitated to photography. A far more precarious profession, but he had been fortunate, he had broken through the tight barrier of competition and he was reasonably content. He wondered what Nanette was like now. Colin's sister. Incredible to believe she would be in her forties and, as with Colin, he had lost touch. He had been invited to her wedding, it must have been fourteen or fifteen years ago, but he had been out of the country at the time. Somewhere in South America, Peru, perhaps, or had it been Brazil; he couldn't remember, it was so long ago. And Wendy. She had been something else. Some years younger, she had not been like either of them. She had been a dreamer, living in a world of her own, disliking anything remotely physical, always the one lagging behind the three of them, but never really happy unless she was stretched out under the horse chestnut tree at the bottom of the orchard, or on wet afternoons on one of the window seats in the library, reading. Always reading. He had never known anyone who could devour so many words, apparently oblivious to whatever was happening around her. Quite simply, she just did not notice. Reading was Wendy's world. The major had told him she was living in Hong Kong, working predictably in the publishing business. In fact, where else?

There was no sign of Eliza Brent as he walked past the lodge, although he noticed all the windows were wide open. Probably needs quite a bit of airing; the place had been empty for some time. Strains of something classical floated out from the back of the building, following him up the remainder of the drive to the front door of the manor. The door was open and he knew he would be expected to go in, just as he had always done and, as expected, he found him in the library, a carafe of red wine in his hand as a greeting.

'Good to see you, Simon.' he said, brandishing the carafe, a smile creasing the still-handsome face which to Simon never seemed to change all that much. He must be over seventy now he thought, accepting a brimming crystal glass, but he looked younger. Perhaps the new lady in his life had something to do with that, recalling the stir of interest in the town when news of the major's impending marriage became known.

'You sounded worried on the phone, Reginald.'

'To be truthful, Simon,' he said, raising his glass, 'I believe I am more annoyed than anything else. You see,' he went on slowly before taking a sip, 'my engagement to Maureen appears to have upset the family somewhat.'

'They don't approve?'

'Afraid it isn't as simple as that; they want me to draw up a pre-nuptial agreement.'

'Ah.'

'You know what I'm getting at, don't you?'

'I think so,' Simon said, choosing his words tactfully, 'something to do with the age difference?'

'Got it in one, dear boy, as I knew you would. Mind you, even if Maureen had been a mere couple of years younger and not the twenty-odd, I think their reaction would have been the same.'

'So, let me understand what you're saying,' Simon went on, instantly filled with distaste. He had always had an abhorrence for the now commonly held belief that children expected, as their right, to inherit, far less to go so far as to put pressure on a parent, because that was what it sounded like, 'your family want this agreement to be made out in their favour in the event of anything happening to you?'

'Correct.'

'But, Reginald, you don't have to do this. None of them can force you.'

'Of course not, Simon, but it makes the whole situation damned unpleasant. Don't get me wrong, I'm not unduly concerned about my own feelings, but it's Maureen I'm thinking about.'

'Of course. Have you talked to her about any of this? She might just sympathise with their concerns.'

'The thing is, my boy, I'm very much afraid you could be right. Maureen is a nice woman. I don't mean that to sound so ineffectual, but she is. A lovely woman, in fact. She's had enough to put up with in her life; her husband dying, leaving her with a young daughter to bring up. I have no intention of putting her through any of this – this,' he paused, moving impatiently across the room, the glass of wine still in his hand, 'crass display of out and out bloody greed!'

'I do understand how you must be feeling,' Simon sympathised, 'but I don't see an easy solution.'

'No. It isn't often I'm stymied,' the major admitted, refilling both their glasses, 'but there is one thing, Simon,' he went on, putting the carafe back on the table, 'somehow, and I don't at this moment know how, I am going to make it clear to Colin, spell it out to him if I have to, that I'm not going to be browbeaten. He's calling in later,' he added, 'no doubt to try and talk some sense into the old man.'

'What about Nanette and Wendy?'

'So far, Colin has been acting as chief spokesman, but he's told me that Nanette feels the same way. They want a slice, Simon, not to put too fine a point on it. Vulgar, eh?'

'And Wendy?'

'Ah, Wendy, well no. According to Colin she doesn't want to know. He's somewhat miffed about that I think.'

'So it is hardly a full consensus of opinion, is it?'

'No, that's true enough. Wendy has always been the odd man out, never has been in the least materialistic, don't know who she takes that from. Her mother I expect.'

'So, what are you going to say to Colin? Send him away with the proverbial flee in his ear?'

'If only,' the major laughed harshly, but with little humour, 'Colin might be the front man, but it's that wife of his. I bet you anything she's at the back of this conspiracy because that is what it seems like to me. She has high ideas that lady, also some extremely expensive tastes. I have a sneaking feeling Colin may have overstretched himself financially, always was a bit of a smart arse; tried to knock it out of him, but by the time he went to university knew I was wasting my bloody time!'

'And Nanette?'

'Do you know, Simon, I cannot remember when she was last in touch. Alright, she has a family now; they're living in London, probably no interest in making even the odd visit. Mind you,' he smiled above the rim of his glass, 'she soon changed her tune when she heard about Maureen! That shook her alright.'

'I don't expect they ever thought you would re-marry.'

'Complacency, Simon. Should have been written in as one of the deadly sins! Once you think like that, you can, at least in my experience, only expect disaster and quite frankly you bloody well deserve it!'

'Well, whatever you say, Reginald,' again selecting his words with care, 'all of this is hardly complimentary to you, is it?'

'What, you mean me popping my clogs?'

'I suppose I do.'

'As far as they are concerned, Simon, whether it was next month or five, ten years from now, there would always be Maureen and, quite frankly, that is what they cannot stomach!'

'Difficult.'

'Perhaps or perhaps not, my boy, but I have a few home truths to impart to Colin. For once in his life he is going to find I am no longer prepared to give him any handouts when he's made another miscalculated deal, also, and I know this is going to affect him more than me not agreeing to this bloody pre-nuptial piece of nonsense, there is the question of my art collection.'

'Yes,' Simon said, wondering where he was leading and remembering years ago being shown his collection, one the major had spent a good part of his life putting together and he did not need to be an expert to recognise most of it was probably quite priceless, 'you still have it here then; in the manor?'

'Yes,' the major leaned over and once again refilled his glass, 'but not for much longer. I've already made arrangements for it to be transferred to the Tate. It has taken me some considerable time to reach this decision, but the truth is, Simon, it has become a bit of an albatross. I can't remember when I last looked at it, lost interest I suppose, so there is really no point keeping it here. Also,' he added slowly, 'it has begun to attract attention to a number of private collectors and this is beginning to concern me.'

'In what way?'

'Well, I've had a few calls recently from people who may be genuine in that they only want to view the paintings, but quite honestly, Simon, how can one tell. I just have this uncomfortable feeling about them. I regret now agreeing to that last review for the Sunday Times, I don't know whether you saw it or not. About three months ago, a four page spread in one of their supplements?'

'I did, yes. I thought it was splendid, actually.'

'To you, Simon, but then you're an honest man. No, it was a mistake giving the collection and I might add, its exact whereabouts, so,' he sighed, 'far better that others can visit a reputable gallery like the Tate and get the pleasure. Also, I wouldn't sell to individuals, don't want it to be split up, you see. That's one of the conditions I made with the gallery, that I will be donating it in its entirety.'

'And Colin doesn't know?'

'No, he has no idea, but he will tonight.'

Simon left shortly after, trying as he walked back down the drive, to rid himself of a feeling of unease and one he couldn't exactly explain to himself. He had known the family for so long, he had taken them all for granted and it was not until now, the essence of what the major had told him virtually ringing in his ears, did he begin to analyse them, to try to decipher what was behind these undercurrents. The Colin he had known did not sound the same person, or Nanette either if it came to that. As for Wendy, she was the only one who appeared not to have changed. Could people you had grown up with alter so much he wondered. Never having had brothers or sisters, the Tilslys taking their place, he didn't know. Over the years, the major had mellowed slightly although Simon did not think other people in Meadowbank would agree with him. As a father he had often been away and when he came home on leave had little time for his family, even his wife had been forced by his strength of character, often domineering, to step back until latterly, as he tried to remember her; a slim wraith of a figure, always in the garden, always on her own, a vague expression hiding what was really going on in her mind. Eventually, and once again he had been out of the country, she had, or so it seemed, given up and died and hardly anyone in the town ever mentioned her name and probably by now had completely forgotten she had ever existed.

Passing the lodge, Simon wondered if Eliza would consider it an intrusion if he were to call and ask her if everything was alright. He really felt in the need of some light conversation, something to lift the depression which he was feeling, but about to lift the latch on her front gate, he saw there was someone outside, sitting on the small terrace at the back of the building. She had company and what was so unusual about that he thought. It could even be her husband; he hadn't noticed whether she had been wearing a wedding ring, but in any case, an attractive woman like her, there would bound to be a man somewhere in her life and what more natural that he should be here. Looking away, and stifling an unwarranted feeling of disappointment, Simon reached the end of the drive and stepped on to the footpath back towards the mill.

Chapter Two

Eliza was not pleased to see her ex-husband walk round the side of the lodge to where she was sitting, having just opened the bottle of Muscadet she had brought with her from Meadowbank. In fact, she was appalled and not fooled for one minute by his glib explanation. This was the first time she had seen him since the divorce over twelve months ago, although, as he had spent a good part of that period in Brixton prison in south London, any meeting would need to have been arranged and, apart from having nothing to say to him, she had no wish to see him.

Reluctantly, and hoping it wouldn't encourage him to stay too long, she offered him some wine and when, predictably, he accepted followed by promptly making himself comfortable in one of the rattan chairs, she went inside to fetch another glass.

There was no way, she thought, having found out she had moved to Meadowbank he had the remotest interest in her well-being. Steve was an opportunist, quick to take advantage of any situation which happened to present itself. It had taken her a number of years to finally realise this and accept she had made a grave mistake in marrying him. She should have known better and listened to well-meaning friends who had repeatedly tried to warn her. The signs of his dishonesty had been there alright, but she had mentally brushed them aside. She knew now, when it no longer mattered, he had been a young offender in what had then been classed as petty crime: stealing from shops and market stalls and, even before he had been old enough to have a licence, breaking into cars parked in the streets and driving them around the town before abandoning them. Later, when these activities began to pall, he gravitated to large scale robberies, the last one of which had back-fired, resulting in a prison sentence. She still found it difficult to rid herself of the unsavoury fact of having been married to a man with a prison record.

'So, Eliza,' he said as she came back with a glass for him, 'this is your new abode. You don't think it might be too much of a back-water?'

'No, I think it will suit me fine.'

'I can't see you settling here, though.'

'Can't you?'

'No, I can't. Not quite your scene somehow.'

'Steve,' she said, looking across at him and wondering what she had ever seen in him. But the young, impressionable Eliza had been quite different from the woman she had become. He was still good-looking, the straight blond hair without any sign of grey, but she noticed changes which she was sure had not been there before. His eyes, a clear blue, lacked any warmth and the mouth, thinner, and here she noticed the first signs of aging, the finely etched lines on either side. She tried to find a word to describe him, the way he appeared to her at that precise moment and she could only come up with one. Calculating. That was it. She felt everything he had said to her so far had been thought out in advance; this visit was no friendly call, 'this is my new life you're talking about,' she continued, her eyes never leaving his face, watching now for any change in his expression, 'and quite frankly, I don't believe it should concern you.'

'Okay, point taken,' he said, mockingly raising his glass, at the same time looking out across her terrace to the sculptured lawns of the manor, 'very nice,' he nodded, 'Major Reginald Tilsly must be worth a bob or two. Has he invited you over for tea yet?'

'I haven't met my landlord, Steve,' trying to keep her tone casual, not rising to the bait. It was obvious he had done his homework.

'Really?' raising his eyebrows slightly, his head on one side, 'you do surprise me. I thought he would have wanted to show you around the stately home.'

'I rented through the estate agents, quite normal in a situation of this kind I would have thought.'

'Not very neighbourly though,' he murmured, taking a deep sip of wine, 'especially as I was reading the other day about his art collection, quite priceless apparently, and one of the largest private collections in the country.'

'Really?'

'He isn't all that security-conscious, is he, if what he has in there is so valuable.'

'What do you mean?'

'Well,' he said, 'for starters, the main gates were wide open with, as far as I could make out, no alarm fitted. I parked outside, but I could have easily driven straight up the drive to the house, whose main door and most of the windows on the ground floor were open. I could then have walked inside and I bet no-one would be on the threshold to stop me!'

'Not everyone is like you, Steve.'

'Only stating the obvious.'

'Steve,' she had had enough, and she recognised with a sinking feeling at the pit of her stomach where he was coming from, although surprised at his crassness. Did he really believe she could be so naive? After all this time, surely not. 'I am not at all interested in what you're telling me; also I find this conversation distasteful. If you don't mind I have things to do. Incidentally,' she paused for a second, 'how did you know where to find me?'

'Quite by chance as it happens,' he drawled, making no attempt to get to his feet, 'I bumped into one of your old colleagues the other evening. Can't remember his name. Toby something.'

'Toby Steed.' she supplied, not wishing to hear any more and longing for him to leave. Toby was an inveterate gossip, they had never got on well and he had been quite scathing when he learned she was going to branch out on her own.

'That's it. Toby Steed. He had just come from your farewell party and told me you were burying yourself in the Hampshire countryside. When he mentioned you had rented the lodge on the Tilsly Estate, well, I thought I really must come and have a look.'

I bet you did, Eliza allowed the bitterness to creep into her thoughts. How fortuitous to learn she would be living in a place where, quite unwittingly, she could be of use to him. He disgusted her and more especially assuming she would not have the wit or intelligence to recognise his machinations. She didn't want to hear anymore.

'Okay,' he grinned lopsidedly, finishing off his wine, 'I'll be off. I can tell by your expression I'm not welcome.'

'Back to London?' Why on earth did she ask him that? Goodness knows, she couldn't care less where he was going, just that he went.

'Not yet,' he said, 'thought I might hang around for a couple of days. Country life may have some appeal after all to this city boy.'

*

The evening was warm and humid and Eliza left her bedroom window open, although closing the ones at the front of the building. She was struck by the absolute stillness as the light eventually began to fade, but as she prepared for bed she slowly began to distinguish other sounds; the rustle of leaves on the beech trees bordering the drive, and somewhere, further over to the right where she knew the River Test ran, the gurgle and chuckle of water and in the distance, perhaps close to Simon Grant's property, an owl, his call plaintive and sharp in the gathering darkness. She had switched off the small bedside lamp when she heard the shouting. It was coming from the manor, where light from a French window on the ground floor, streamed across the lawn, dramatically highlighting a clump of shrubbery close to the main door. And, then, just as suddenly, it stopped and once again the gardens resumed their mantle of quiet serenity and even the owl had decided to call a halt, perhaps frightened by the sudden interruption to his nocturnal foraging. Tired now, it had been a long day and seeing Steve again had disturbed her, she must have fallen asleep almost immediately.

It could only have been around two or three in the morning when she was abruptly awakened by a car's engine. At first, her mind confused by sleep, she couldn't make out where it was coming from, then realised it had to be out on the main road. Not switching on any lights, Eliza, barefoot, padded over to the window and for the second time that night peered out into the darkness. The engine had been cut, followed by the soft thud of a car door being closed. The driver, impossible to tell whether a man or a woman, had started to walk up the drive, passing below her bedroom window until becoming hidden from view by the trees. Apart from two carriage lamps on either side of the front door, the manor was now in darkness. Whoever it was did not emerge again. This could be perfectly innocent she thought. He could have gone round the side of the building. A member of the family perhaps. Anyway, it was none of her business. She had only recently arrived after all and knew nothing about the family. But, as she went back to bed she could not help thinking that something was wrong. People did not make visits in the early hours of the morning and silently make their way unannounced, not to the main door, but to another entrance. And why leave the car outside the grounds? She tried to stay awake, waiting for him to return, but in spite of her concern, sleep eventually took over and when she finally awoke, around eight, the sun was pouring into the room with the promise of another warm day.

Chapter Three

Sunday morning. The Abbey bells had stopped ringing, the people of the town already shuffling into their usual pews and, depending on how long they had lived there, determining exactly where: the older residents, those born and bred in Meadowbank, merely by their self-declared status decreeing as their right to sit at the forefront of the ancient church while the others, incomers as they were called by the less charitable, still having at least another twenty or thirty years to justify their existence and not having a great deal of choice, positioning themselves at the back and creating, although not necessarily by design, a large void between the two groups. But that morning, the first Sunday in July, with every indication the good weather was going to continue, none of the congregation had any idea that very soon the taken-for-granted peace of their town was about to erupt and bring them together in a way they never thought possible.

Peter Taylor, not a churchgoer, unfastened the shutters of 'The Salmon's Rest' restaurant, relishing for a brief moment being outside. He always liked this time of the day. Danielle was firmly ensconced in the kitchen issuing orders left right and centre to the petit-chef as she liked to call him and to Joan, their latest waitress who had only been with them for a couple of weeks; all of which meant Danielle was not verbally attacking him. He could not help wondering as he leaned against the brick wall, feeling the warmth through the thin cotton of his shirt, just how long this one would last. They had only had the restaurant for eight months and young Joan was their sixth waitress. Nobody stayed very long working for Danielle. Her standards, while not only being extraordinarily high, bordered on the unreasonable and, at times, hysterical. But, and this was something he had to admit, she was an excellent cook, repeat bookings proved that. She had trained in Paris, a shrewd, although ruthless, businesswoman and, when she felt in the mood, pretty good in bed too. But, he thought sourly, taking out a crumpled pack of cigarettes from his pocket, these occasions were becoming less and less frequent. Why the hell he wondered, and not for the first time, had he married a French woman, but after six years of marriage, he still did not know the answer.

Danielle le Breton, as she was then, could never be described as beautiful, but she was strikingly elegant in a sleek, albeit unapproachable, way which in the beginning he had found irresistible. Pint-size, slim, short shiny black hair with a Mirelle Mathieu fringe. She had been an only child, her parents approaching middle-age when she was born and from what little she had chosen to tell him had led a pretty lonely childhood, spending probably too much time reading, not the usual schoolgirl books, but the French classics and most of those romantic fiction. Danielle, he had discovered quite early on, found it difficult to differentiate between fact and fiction. What may have started as harmless fabrication, embroidering the actual facts about some everyday occurrence, would often develop into an out and out lie, and then, realising she may have gone too far, always effortlessly extricating herself with an exaggerated shrug of her slim shoulders.

Danielle was always right and if you knew what constituted towards a relatively calm and non-confrontational life, also if you had any sense of self-preservation and wanted to survive relatively unscathed in the marriage stakes, Peter had learned to agree, to go along with her and, so far, he had managed this fairly well. While at times during those quiet moments, before the day had begun, he did regret marrying her, he was not entirely unhappy. Although Danielle would never admit it, she was like him. Neither of them was concerned how they appeared to others. He was well aware they were not popular in Meadowbank. Most of their time was spent in the restaurant, making no effort to join in the community, so it was hardly surprising that as a couple they had made few friends. As for himself, he neither liked nor disliked the people he met each day, but for her it was different. There was no end to her tirade of gripes and criticisms and no-one was immune. If it was not the customers it would be the staff and poor Joan was currently first in the queue.

It suddenly occurred to him that the square was unusually busy for that time of the morning. It would be another half hour or so before the church service ended, but small groups of people had started to form, first there were six or seven of them, but during the time he'd been standing there the numbers had swelled. By now, there must be about thirty people and the odd thing was, although he was relatively close to them, he could not hear one single word of what they were saying. There seemed to be a peculiar hushed silence pervading the place. This was abnormal he thought, instinctively moving forward towards them. Brian Morrison, he saw, had opened the doors of 'The Market Inn' and catching his eye strode across the square, meeting him half-way.

'What's going on?' he asked him.

'You obviously haven't heard then.'

'Apparently not,' he frowned, 'what's happened?'

'It's Major Tilsly,' Brian said quickly, lowering his voice, 'he's been murdered.'

'What! How?'

'He's been shot, it must have happened some time during the night.'

'An intruder?'

'No idea,' Brian said, 'and it's too soon for even the police to know that yet.'

'I didn't think anything like this happened in such a respectable town like Meadowbank.'

'Don't you believe it; probably Meadowbank is no different from any other town. Mind you,' Brian went on, shaking his head, 'he did have that art collection. Perhaps there was a break-in. Oh, I don't know. I'm getting just as bad as everyone else around here, speculating and jumping to conclusions. Leave it to the police, I say.'

'How did you hear about it?' Peter asked him, more out of curiosity than anything else. Major Tilsly had been no friend of his and the fact he would no longer be around did not concern him one iota. He had not liked the man. Although he had often been standing next to him at the bar in 'The Market Inn', not once had the man made any attempt to get into conversation, treating him as yet another loathed outsider. Peter had once overheard him talking in his loud upper-class voice to one of his snobbish cronies, describing him as that smart-arsed cockney. This had hurt, especially as everyone else in the pub had heard him as well. So, he concluded, the fact that someone had taken it upon themselves to end the old fart's life, was just tough luck or good riddance, whichever way you wanted to look at it.

'You probably know already how quickly news travels here,' Brian was saying, breaking into the bitter thoughts, 'well, Melissa's aunt works at the manor and unfortunately she was the one to find him. Not very pleasant for her as you can imagine. She was in a terrible state when she phoned us. It's going to take her a while to recover.'

'I'm sorry to hear about that,' Brian murmured, 'but, to be honest; I won't be shedding any tears over the demise of Major Reginald Tilsly.'

'I know he wasn't everyone's cup of tea, Peter, but he did have his good points, you know. And in spite of what you thought of him, he is going to be missed in the town. He and his family go back generations and they have owned the manor for longer than anyone here can remember. It's a dreadful business.' he said sadly, moving away and walking back to the pub.

Well, well, Peter thought, watching him cross the square, acknowledging as he passed them, a group huddled together in the centre beside the stone statue of one of England's ancient parliamentary figures, all is not what it appears in sleepy Meadowbank. A murder. This was going to shake them out of their insular complacency.

'Where the hell have you been, Peter?' Danielle's first words when she saw him. 'We'll be opening in about fifteen minutes and the bar hasn't been stocked up yet! I suppose I am meant to do that as well. All the time it is *moi! moi! moi!*

'Calm down, Danielle, it will take minutes only. I did most of it earlier he added, 'when you were still asleep.' Unruffled and as usual allowing her words to flow over him.

'You haven't spent the last hour in that kitchen trying to instil some system and that new waitress! She'll have to go, Peter. She really will!'

'Just as you say, Danielle.'

'Well, I do say! Unless there is a significant improvement she'll be out that door quicker than any of her predecessors!'

'You haven't heard about Major Tilsly.'

'What, that awful person. As I have been stuck in here since the moment I got up this morning, how could I? What's he done?'

'It isn't what he's done,' Peter explained, 'it's what someone else has done. He's been murdered.'

'*Mon Dieu*! Tell me this isn't true, Peter!'

'Brian Morrison has just told me and it looks as if the news is all over the town already, judging by the number of people out there. I've never seen the square like it, not even on a week day.'

'I just knew it was a bad decision to come to this parochial *Anglaise* market town. I just knew it! If it wasn't difficult enough trying to introduce to their uneducated palettes food they would not have dreamed existed, we are living with a murderer in our midst!'

'That's a trifle harsh, wouldn't you say? Our customers aren't all entirely without culinary knowledge, even of your calibre, my darling.'

'Don't bloody patronise me, Peter.'

'I'm not, but have you thought this – this latest development might prove good for our business. You know what people are like –'

' – don't I just,' she interrupted, 'all busybodies, liking nothing better than a good gossip, tearing each other to shreds.'

He let the irony of that remark go unanswered and spent the remainder of the time before they opened getting the bar ready, hoping she would leave him alone, but no such luck. Danielle remained where she was; both hands on her hips, glaring at him, the brown eyes flashing in a way which he knew meant trouble.

'I mean it, you know, Peter,' she said, 'you know I am not happy living here. In fact, if I need a facial, a manicure or even a professional haircut I have to drive the fifteen miles into Winchester and even then their abilities fall below what I have been accustomed to.

'Give it time, Danielle,' placating now; it wasn't the first time since they had arrived in Meadowbank she had made this particular speech, 'we haven't been here twelve months yet. At least let us stay long enough to break even and then I promise we'll seriously consider packing up and going back to London.'

'Is that a promise?'

'Danielle,' he sighed, 'I never break a promise. If I say I'm going to do something, you should have realised by now that I do it!'

Chapter Four

Eliza first realised there was something seriously amiss, when, having taken her coffee out on to the terrace just after nine that morning, a police car, followed by a dark blue van, drove at speed up the drive and with a screeching of brakes, setting her nerves on edge, came to an abrupt halt in front of the manor. Her coffee forgotten, she stood up, moving over to the edge of the terrace, not that there was anything to see once the police officers had clambered out and gone inside. She did not have long to wait. Ten, fifteen minutes, when two of them emerged and walked briskly towards the lodge and, as if by radar, over to where she was standing.

'I'm sorry to disturb you, madam,' one of them said, showing Eliza her warrant card: Chief Inspector Brenda Masters, she read, 'but Sergeant Ash and I would like to have a word with you, if that is possible.'

'What's wrong?'

'Perhaps we could go inside?' adroitly side-stepping the question, the Chief Inspector suggested, cornflower blue eyes appraising her, 'Better than out here, I would say.' she added, putting the card back into the top pocket of her shirt, an identical shade of blue Eliza noticed. She was young and pretty with short blonde hair brushed smoothly back from her face. She was, Eliza guessed still in her thirties, while the sergeant was considerably younger and she could not help noticing the way he was standing; a few steps behind her, every line of his thin frame, his whole presence, in fact, exuding tenseness, as if he was forcing himself into a role he was not yet familiar.

'Of course.' Eliza said, taking them into the lodge. She cleared the stack of papers she had been working on earlier to the far end of the kitchen table and asked if they would like some coffee, but the Chief Inspector, speaking for both of them, declined with a brief smile.

'How well did you know Major Tilsly?' she asked once they were seated.

'I didn't know him at all,' Eliza answered slowly, not missing the use of the past tense and, bracing herself for what was going to come next, she took a deep breath, 'I only arrived here yesterday afternoon. I arranged the lease through the estate agents in Meadowbank, so I didn't meet him.'

'And your name is -?'

'Eliza Brent.'

'You're married?'

'Not anymore,' Eliza said, aware, although she no longer wore her wedding ring, there was still a faint white line remaining, 'I was divorced a year ago.'

'So, you are living here on your own?'

'Of course. Are you going to tell me what has happened to Major Tilsly?'

'Yes, Miss Brent, we are. He's been murdered,' nothing subtle about this woman Eliza thought; no gentle approach, no attempt to lessen the impact of what she must realise would have a shocking effect, 'and he was found this morning by his housekeeper when she arrived for work.' she concluded.

'How did –' Eliza faltered for a second, not really wanting to hear anymore, but of course she had no choice, '- how did he die?'

'He was shot, Miss Brent. At point blank range.'

'But,' and again she faltered, finding it impossible to grasp the reality of what she was hearing. The manor was on the edge of a small market town in the depths of rural Hampshire. These things did not happen. But she knew they did; you only had to read the newspapers to learn that crime was not discretionary. It could hit anyone anywhere, and at anytime. 'why? Did someone break into the manor?'

'Why should you think that, Miss Brent?' she asked and, as if by some signal, Sergeant Ash pulled out a small square notebook and began to make quick jottings, not looking up as he wrote, but keeping his head down, his full concentration on what he was doing. No eye contact there Eliza thought dryly. The man was like a robot. A perfect example of what she had always thought a young police officer in his position, very much at the beck and call of his superior, would be like. And a woman. Even in these enlightened times when sexual prejudices were taboo, it could well be a problem for him.

'What else could I think?' Eliza said, 'I'm sure, judging by the size of the estate, the major is, I mean, was,' she corrected herself, 'wealthy. Also, I've heard he owned a priceless art collection. Surely people like that, Chief Inspector, must always be a vulnerable target to the unscrupulous?'

As soon as she had mentioned the collection she realised she may have made a mistake, but, she reasoned, it was probably common knowledge in the neighbourhood. She had never heard about it until Steve told her and with this thought, not that she had forgotten, only placed it firmly at the back of her mind where it belonged, was the fact Steve had been here yesterday, had gone to some lengths to tell her what he had learned about the major. And could still be in the area. She tried to dismiss the snakelike threads of suspicion. Steve may have spent a good part of his life carrying out robberies, some no doubt more profitable than others and most of which he had got away with, but she was positive he was no murderer. And, as far as she knew, he never carried a gun. She remembered a conversation she had with him some years earlier, at a time when he had stopped pretending to her that he was the squeaky-clean husband she had believed, that he did not believe in firearms. "A mug's game, Eliza," he had said, "once you are on the way down that nasty spiral, there is never any turning back." No, whoever had killed Major Tilsly it had not been Steve.

'It is possible you are right, Miss Brent.' the Chief Inspector said, 'However, this is something which will eventually be revealed once we have started our full scale enquires. Meanwhile,' she continued quickly, 'there are a few questions we would like to ask you. Also, I would add, this is a purely informal interview.'

Really! Eliza thought cynically, managing to prevent herself from raising a disbelieving eyebrow. With the sergeant sitting there silently between them, diligently writing up his notes? But, she tried to rationalise, they were only doing their jobs, forcing herself to relax but unable to get rid of the unpleasant feeling that this so-called informal interview was becoming more and more like an interrogation. Chief Inspector Masters was clever, there was no doubt about that; she would hardly have risen to the position she was in otherwise. And deciding there was nothing she could say in response, Eliza remained silent.

'You say you arrived at the lodge yesterday afternoon,' she said, 'I didn't see any car, but perhaps you hired a taxi.'

'I do have a car,' Eliza told her, 'but it won't be delivered until tomorrow. I decided, having sold up my flat in London, I wanted to get down here as soon as possible.'

'I see. And when was this?'

'On Friday.'

'Where did you spend the night?'

'In Meadowbank, at the King's Arms Hotel and after collecting the keys from the estate agents yesterday, I came straight out here.'

'You still haven't said how you got here, Miss Brent.'

Good grief, she was like a terrier! She was not merely sharp. She was razor sharp. Eliza could not remember meeting anyone before, especially so young, who was quite so tenacious. Perhaps this explained the sergeant's manner. Poor man was probably a nervous wreck, worried in case he would say or do something wrong.

'I had hoped to get a bus, but apparently they are few and far between out this way at the weekends, so I accepted a lift from one of the local residents.'

'Who was?'

'Honestly, Chief Inspector,' she said, trying to keep the impatience from her voice, 'is all this information so important?'

'I can assure you, Miss Brent, every piece of information we can glean is crucial in a murder enquiry.'

'I understand,' Eliza stifled a sigh, she knew when she was beaten, 'it was a Mr Grant.'

'Simon Grant?'

'Yes, he owns the watermill, further up the road.' Eliza told her reluctantly. Simon is really going to thank me for supplying them with that.

'I know him,' the Chief Inspector said, permitting Eliza the luxury of another smile, 'and last evening, Miss Brent,' she went on, 'did you leave the lodge; go back into Meadowbank, perhaps?'

'No,' Eliza said, 'I didn't go anywhere, besides I was tired. It's been a hectic couple of weeks, packing up and making all the necessary arrangements to move.'

'And you were alone all the time? No visitors? You weren't invited over to the manor?'

'No,' her mind by now beginning to work overtime and realising it was at this point she would have to mention Steve's visit or remain silent, 'Major Tilsly, or if it comes to that, no-one else from the manor got in touch with me. Actually,' she went on, 'I didn't expect them to.'

'I see,' she said quietly, those eyes looking directly at her as though she could read her mind, 'no-one from the manor you say, but perhaps someone did call. A friend maybe, to find out how you were settling in.'

'I have no friends in the district, Chief Inspector,' Eliza said, 'at least not yet.'

'So,' she persisted, 'you actually spoke to no-one from the time Simon Grant brought you here to this morning when we arrived here. Am I right?'

'Someone did call, quite unexpectedly as it happened.'

'Yes?' she prompted, no change in her expression, as though uncannily it was what she had been waiting for.

'Steve, my ex-husband. He was in the area, had heard I was moving into the lodge and came here on the off-chance of finding me in.'

'Your ex-husband?'

'Yes.'

'Were you surprised to see him?'

'I was, yes.'

'What sort of terms are you both on, Miss Brent?'

'The divorce was amicable; we have no problems in talking to each other, that is when we have to.'

'Yesterday, Miss Brent, how long did he stay?'

'Not long. Twenty minutes or so, enough time for him to have a glass of wine.'

'And afterwards. When he had gone? What did you do?'

'I spent the remainder of the evening pottering about, unpacking, made myself a light supper and went to bed, shortly before ten, I think it was.'

'There are only a few more questions, Miss Brent; we don't want to take up too much of your time.'

'That's alright.'

'This house, the lodge,' the Chief Inspector said, 'is relatively close to the manor.'

'It is, yes.'

'If there had been any unusual noises last night coming from there, you would have heard them, wouldn't you?'

'As a matter of fact I did hear something.'

'Yes?'

'A man's voice, rather loud.'

'How loud?'

'Well, he was shouting.'

'When was this?'

'Just as I was about to go to bed. My bedroom is at the back overlooking the manor and I could hear quite well, but it didn't last for long.'

'How long?'

'No more than five minutes.'

'You didn't hear anything else?'

'No.'

'Are you sure?'

'Of course, although there was something. It was much later on; I had been asleep and the sound of a car pulling up on the road outside woke me.'

For the first time Sergeant Ash looked up at her, his head on one side, reminding her of an eager puppy waiting for a tasty morsel to fall on the floor at his feet. Chief Inspector Masters leaned forward slightly in her chair, impatiently pushing back a loose tendril of hair and obviously waiting for enlightenment.

'I looked out of the window,' Eliza went on, 'but it was too dark to see very much.'

'But what could you see? The driver, perhaps?'

'I think it must have been,' she answered, trying to remember what exactly she had seen; she had been half asleep and it had been dark, 'I heard a car door closing and then saw someone walking up the drive. He came past my window but I didn't see him again.'

'So, it was a man?'

'Oh, it was impossible to make out whether it was or not. I suppose I just assumed it was, but I could have been wrong.'

'Your terrace, Miss Brent,' she said, 'faces directly towards the manor. Does your bedroom have the same view?'

'Yes, it does.'

'So, if I'm right, you should be able to see the front door of the manor?'

'I can, especially as the outside lights were on, but he didn't go anywhere near the front of the building.'

'What time was this?'

'I can't be certain, but I reckon around two or three o'clock.'

'And what did you do then?'

'Sorry?' genuinely puzzled; it was becoming increasingly difficult to keep up with her, impossible to fathom out her train of thought, also, Eliza had the distinct impression the woman was trying to trip her up in some way. Only an impression, but it was a strong one.

'Simply that.' the Chief Inspector said, 'Did you wait up, standing at your window, hoping perhaps to see the driver going back to the car or –'

'– I went back to bed,' Eliza interrupted, 'As I've said, last night was my first night here and I didn't know the major or any of his family. I don't even know how many people live there, whether he lived on his own and, quite honestly, I considered it to be none of my business.'

'I see,' she really did have an irritating habit of repeating herself Eliza thought, 'and the fight you overheard?'

'I didn't say it was a fight. A raised voice, shouting, that was all. Again, it was none of my concern.'

'True. Well, Miss Brent you've been very helpful and I hope we haven't taken up too much of your time, but before we go I would like to ask you something.'

'Yes?'

'You've told us you were woken by a car's engine.'

'I was, yes.'

'Yet,' the Chief Inspector, terrier-like, went on, 'you didn't hear the sound of a gun being fired?'

'No, I didn't.'

'Odd.'

'I don't think so. It could have had a silencer.'

'That is a possibility of course.' she admitted, 'Do you have any knowledge of firearms, Miss Brent?'

'None at all.' Honestly, she thought, if the situation wasn't so awful she could almost find the question amusing. 'I know as much as anyone who watches thrillers on the TV, Chief Inspector.'

'Of course.'

As she spoke, she rose to her feet, her 'shadow', once he had put his notebook away, following her. They had only been with her for less than half an hour, but it felt much longer. Perhaps living in the country, time did have this ability to stretch itself out, although never in her wildest dreams when she made the decision to leave London did she think on her first morning in her new home she would be involved in a murder enquiry!

'Oh, Miss Brent,' the Chief Inspector said quickly, pausing in the open doorway, 'after your divorce did you revert back to your maiden name?'

'I did, yes.' And don't blame me, Steve, she thought, stifling another sigh, it's not my fault you took it upon yourself to come here yesterday. So, I'm afraid, inevitable as it will be, you will have to extricate yourself from this one!

'Would you be good enough to give us your ex-husband's surname?'

Eliza almost felt sorry for the Sergeant as, caught off-guard, he started fumbling for his notebook, seeming to have some trouble finding the stub of a pencil before resuming his puppy-dog look.

'It's Blackwood,' Eliza said, watching as he deliberately and carefully wrote out each letter: S T E V E N   B L A C K W OO D

'And does he live in London?'

'Yes, he does. You want his address?'

'Please.'

'He has a flat in Bayswater Gardens, number thirty-three,' Eliza told her, 'but if you're thinking of trying to get in touch with him, he may not be there. He told me he intended to spend a few days in the area.' As soon as the words were uttered she regretted them. Why did she say that? The woman really did excel in extracting information.

'Do you expect him to come back?'

'I've no idea, but I wouldn't think so.' Metaphorically crossing her fingers and waiting for the inevitable response.

'I see.' Chief Inspector Masters said.

When they had gone Eliza poured the now undrinkable coffee down the sink and re-filled the cafetière. There was now more activity outside and she saw the Chief Inspector and the Sergeant drive past her kitchen window, turning left out of the estate. Probably on their way to the watermill, although she supposed only to be expected. They would need to verify the truth of what she had told them and wondered what it must be like to have a job like theirs, having to suspect the worst of everyone.

Not wanting to look across towards the manor, she took her coffee instead into the lounge. It was a light cheerful room, a low-beamed ceiling, white painted walls and a bow-shaped window overlooking the neat square of garden at the front. The gates, she noticed, had been left open. Presumably they would be back.

The death of Major Tilsly, a man she had never met, had not yet had sufficient time to register with her, but as she stood at the window, both hands clutching her coffee mug, she experienced a feeling of unease, imagining what must have happened during the hours she had been asleep: a short distance away, less than two hundred metres, someone had carried out a cold-blooded murder. And they say London is a dangerous place, the cynical thought occurring to her, making her shiver in spite of the warm morning. At least in cities people had cultivated a built-in awareness by avoiding those areas which had a reputation for muggings and other all too common everyday offences. But here? It seemed not only incongruous to her, but infinitely shocking and this was what she was finding so difficult to take in.

She recognised the silver grey Renault as soon as it turned into the drive and pulling up outside the lodge. Simon Grant. To actually see someone she knew, although not well, in what was fast becoming an alien place if she allowed it, acted as an immediate fillip to her flagging spirits, more so when, spontaneously, on seeing her at the window, he waved to her.

'I hope you don't mind me coming over, Eliza,' were his first words as she opened the door to him. 'but I didn't think it was a good idea for you to be on your own.'

'You've heard then?' she said, taking him into the lounge.

'Yes,' he answered, putting a hand on her arm, 'I've heard. Absolutely tragic.'

'How well did you know him?'

'In recent years I came to know him fairly well. You see,' he went on, 'I grew up with the Tilsly children with all the freedom imaginable. Supervision wasn't in plentiful supply. Both my parents were totally absorbed in their work and the major was seldom at home during that time.'

'I understand,' Eliza said quietly, 'this is going to be a dreadful shock to his family.'

'I know.'

'I had a visit from the Chief Inspector a little while ago; perhaps they called to see you. They wanted to know how I got here yesterday. I've been trying to tell myself it is only their duty, but well -'

'- it is, Eliza, but I know exactly what you mean. And yes they did come to the mill and although they didn't stay long they made me feel the same. It's an odd thing living in a place for most of your life and knowing practically everyone. I've known Brenda Masters since we were kids, although she is a lot younger, but I remember her at school. Long blonde pigtails which some of the boys used to take great delight in tugging.'

'She's quite awesome, isn't she?' Eliza remarked, trying with difficulty to imagine the woman who had spent the last thirty minutes subjecting her to a bombardment of questions, as a child; a young girl, running around the school playground, but it was impossible.

'Yes, but from what I hear she's pretty good at her job. I'm sure she'll get to the bottom of what's happened.'

'I hope so.'

'Has this made you nervous,' he asked, 'being here on your own, I mean.'

'I haven't had time to think yet, but I don't think so. I don't see why I should be.'

'A good point,' he smiled gently, 'and a sensible approach. Most women would have vacated the premises by now.'

'I'm not like that,' she returned his smile, 'I'll cope.'

'Good, however, I meant what I said earlier. I thought you might appreciate some company, perhaps have lunch with me. We could go to 'The Salmon's Rest' restaurant, it's in the square. You may have noticed it.'

'I did, yes and I would like that very much. I don't think I could settle down to doing anything constructive today.'

'That's settled then. We can go now if you're ready. We can have a drink first in the pub; it will help you to get the feel of the town.'

Chapter Five

'The Market Inn' was not merely busy as one might expect on a warm Sunday morning, but packed to overflowing with customers, glasses in hands, standing outside on the cobbled pavement.

'My goodness,' Eliza said as they approached, 'is it always like this on a Sunday?'

'It's a popular pub,' Simon said, 'but I have to admit this is exceptional.'

'Because of what has happened, do you think?'

'I would say so.'

There were no empty tables and throwing her an apologetic smile over his shoulder he led her up to the far end of the bar where they managed to squeeze into what seemed to be the only available space. Eliza looked around with interest: oak beams permanently blackened by years of wood smoke; a wide open fireplace which, in the days before smoke-free zones had ever been heard of, would she was sure, during the long winter months, have held blazing logs, crackling and spitting sprays of glowing embers on to the stone-flagged floor and would have been the only warmth for customers coming in out of the cold. Old framed hunting prints immediately caught her attention, also the copper warming pans and gleaming horse brasses and hanging above the bar, beer tankards: pewter, pottery and glass. She liked what she saw. Eliza had never lived in a town as small as Meadowbank before; in fact, had seldom visited the more rural parts of the south of England and while realising it was very much still a novelty, felt she would have no difficulty in adapting to what was going to be a totally different lifestyle.

'What would you like to drink?' Simon asked her.

'A glass of white wine, please.'

'Right, I'll try to catch Brian's attention.'

'He's the landlord?'

'That's right; when he eventually reaches us I'll introduce you and to Melissa too, that is if she is able to break away from serving for a couple of minutes. That's Melissa over there,' he added, pointing towards an attractive red-head, her cheeks flushed with the effort of trying to deal with many thirsty customers at the same time.

Eliza watched the man now making his way over to them; he was exactly how she believed a country town landlord should look: tall, almost six foot, about the same height as Simon, but where Simon was slim, he was of a much heavier build; broad-shouldered, but by no means overweight and gave her the impression he might very well enjoy the good things life had to offer: wine, a rich burgundy naturally; country cooking and convivial company. A genuine host; no doubt born into the hospitality business.

'Morning, Simon,' Brian Morrison said, 'I wondered if you would be in this morning. And, I can tell by your expression you've heard the news.'

'I have, yes.'

'Melissa's aunt found him, you know. Poor woman, she was in a state when she telephoned us earlier. She had already called the police and was waiting for them to arrive. I guess it's going to take her a while to get over the shock.'

'It's going to take those who knew the major some considerable time as well.' Simon said, 'Brian,' he went on quickly, 'I'd like to introduce you to Eliza Brent. She's come to live in Meadowbank.'

'Hello, Eliza,' Brian smiled at her, reaching across the bar to shake hands, 'you've moved into the old lodge, haven't you?'

'Don't look so alarmed, Eliza,' Simon intervened quickly before she had a chance to say anything, 'he's not clairvoyant, but what you have just experienced is an example of the Meadowbank grapevine! I can assure you if you live here long enough you are in danger of catching it!'

'Now, now, Simon,' Brian said, 'give me some credit, please. We all knew the lodge had been rented out and by a lady,' he added, nodding at Eliza, 'and I just put two and two together.'

'Okay,' Simon laughed, holding up his hands in mock surrender, 'and for once two and two actually added up to four!'

'This hasn't been a very good start for you, has it?' Brian said, becoming serious again, 'but I hope you'll be happy living here.'

'Thank you,' she smiled at him, 'I believe I shall.'

'Good, now what would you both like to drink? These are on the house, Simon; to welcome you to Meadowbank, Eliza.'

Brian poured their drinks; a lager for Simon and a wine for her. There was a sudden flurry of customers demanding replenishments, but it was not long before he was back.

'I was talking to Peter Taylor earlier,' he mentioned, 'and, as expected, he was his usual caustic self.'

'Peter was never too fond of the major,' Simon said, 'I think the pair of them got off on a bad footing not long after he and Danielle moved into the town.'

'I know,' Brian said sourly, 'talk about a bull in a china shop. I honestly don't know why the pair of them decided to come here, far less invest in the 'Salmon's Rest'.

'You have to admit they run a good restaurant though.'

'From what I've heard, I'm sure you're right, but look, Simon, they just do not fit in here and quite frankly, as far as I can see, neither of them have made the slightest attempt to do so.'

'Perhaps they won't stay long,' Simon said, 'I know Peter is a fairly insensitive sort of guy, but surely, eventually he's going to realise he's made a big mistake in trying to settle into such a small community.'

'Nor the stuck up madame, either!'

'By that, I presume you mean Danielle,' Simon chuckled, turning to Eliza, 'you must think we are a pair of old gossips, but the two we're talking about have, in a matter of months, managed to upset quite a number of people in the town.'

'And we're going to their restaurant for lunch?'

'Don't worry, I guarantee you will enjoy your meal.'

'It seems incredible,' Brian was going on, automatically wiping the bar in front of them, 'to think only on Friday evening - you were here, Simon - the major made his announcement to us all.'

'I know,' Simon smiled sadly and once again turned to Eliza, 'you see, the major surprised us all that night by announcing his engagement. I don't think there was one single person in Meadowbank who had expected that. He hadn't mentioned to me he had intended to re-marry and I had often been in his company over the last few months.'

'Oh, he kept it very much to himself,' Brian said, 'and quite honestly, I don't blame him. Maureen is a lovely woman and she would have made him a good wife.'

'You've met her?'

'Yes, she came in here with him a couple of times, but I just thought they were friends, I never realised there was more to their relationship. I suppose that was why it was such a surprise when we heard.'

'What's happened is not going to be good for the town,' Simon remarked, taking a sip of his lager, 'once the news reaches the press, I mean.'

'Inevitable,' Brian shrugged, 'not to mention when the holiday season gets under way. Of course it will be good for business,' he went on, 'but I feel the same as you, Simon, having lived here for so long, we need to stick together. I certainly don't relish the idea of being some sort of peep-show for the sensation hunters and you can mark my words, there will be plenty of them.'

'Quite,' Simon agreed, 'by the way, that guy over there, Brian, I haven't seen him in here before. Do you know him?'

'Not really,' Brian said, 'he's not exactly what you would describe the talkative type.'

Eliza had already noticed him, sitting on his own in the corner of the room with his back to the open window. He had a half-drunk glass of lager on the table, which periodically he had picked up, but only taking desultory sips. An unopened Sunday newspaper also seemed to hold little interest for him. For a fleeting and disarming second he reminded her of Steve. In appearance they were not in the least alike, but he had the same shut-in look she had often seen on Steve's face and one which she had come to recognise as his ability to single-mindedly concentrate inwardly, totally unaware of his surroundings. Private thoughts: never shared with her.

'Just passing through, apparently;' Brian explained, 'he booked in here at the end of last week. From the Far East. Singapore I think, but I'm not sure. Melissa took the booking.'

'A loner.'

'In this business, Simon,' Brian smiled, 'you get them. Good at blending into the background, but never joining in. That's obviously the way they want it. Good looking chap though, wouldn't you say, Eliza?'

'To some, I'm sure he would be,' she smiled across at him, not missing the twinkle in his eyes; he was teasing her, 'but too closed in on himself, also too aloof. Not my type of man at all.'

'Sensible woman,' Simon chuckled, 'well, Eliza, if you've finished your drink shall we go and eat?'

They stepped out on to the pavement again and, if anything, there were even more people out there than before.

'No chance of me introducing you to Melissa,' he said, 'perhaps the next time you're in it will be less hectic.'

'Is she married to Brian?' she asked him as they walked across the square to the restaurant. Melissa could be no more than in her early twenties, a good fifteen or more years younger than Brian.

'No, they've been together for a while now and although he's never said as much to me, I think it is rather a sensitive subject with him after the failure of his marriage. He's a good guy, Brian; he deserves some luck in his life after what he went through with his ex-wife.'

'That's too bad,' Eliza said, 'I liked him.'

'Also,' Simon smiled at her as he opened the door to the restaurant, 'he runs an exceptionally good pub!'

Walking into the 'Salmon's Rest' was a revelation. Eliza, going by the name of the restaurant, had expected to see swathes of fishing nets cradling coloured floats which always reminded her of translucent bubbles; lobster pots and all the usual paraphernalia associated with a fishing theme, but instead, this was a complete contrast: a heady mix of French chic and the romance of Italy. Split-level and spacious, two-toned honey hued floor tiles; walls painted deep red and mustard and softly illuminated by concealed ceiling lights. Royal blue earthenware pots filled to the brim with orange and yellow geraniums had been placed on either side of double glass doors leading out to a walled courtyard; more geraniums, tubs of begonias, marguerites and marigolds – a gorgeous and brilliant splash of colour. Circular wrought-iron tables and chairs with red and white checked tablecloths and matching cushions took up most of the floor space, the total effect pure French. Inside the restaurant, a shelf unit displayed hand-painted china plates which Eliza recognised as being typical of those she had seen many times in Italy. There was only one picture: an oil painting, again the vibrancy of the Mediterranean reached out to her: in the forefront, a stone archway, shallow crumbling steps leading down into an orange grove and in the distance the sea stretching out to the horizon.

A young waitress showed them to their table, pulling it out slightly to enable them to take their seats on the cream leather banquette, before handing them the menus.

'What a delightful restaurant, Simon.'

'You approve?'

'Very much,' she said, 'I can almost feel the heat bouncing off the walls, also, if I stepped through the old archway in the painting and walked along that dusty path towards the orange grove I'm sure I would be able to smell the fruit.'

'I don't suppose you expected this in Meadowbank.'

'No, I didn't. I don't mean to sound patronising; I'm really more surprised by their choice of name.'

The 'Salmon's Rest?'

'Yes, it sounds so typically English.'

'There's always been a restaurant here, at least as long as I can remember,' he explained, 'and it was always called the 'Salmon's Rest'. I suppose Peter and Danielle saw no reason to change it. A good talking point though, wouldn't you say?'

'Definitely.' opening her menu, intrigued to find out what was on offer. There were a number of fish dishes and yes, they did have salmon and noticing, another surprise, it was printed in both English and French.

'Some might say a trifle pretentious.' he remarked, watching her reaction.

'Not really,' she said, 'it probably makes Danielle feel more at home.'

They gave their order, both deciding to start with the melon and Parma ham with 'a gentle sprinkling of ginger', followed for her by the salmon cooked in a hollandaise sauce, Jersey potatoes and fresh garden peas and for Simon, the pan-fried chicken breasts, with a pepper sauce, sauté potatoes and haricot beans.

'Good choice,' he said, once their order had been taken and a bottle of Sauterne opened, 'I wouldn't be too surprised if the salmon doesn't come from the River Test.'

'Of course. I remember the estate agent telling me about the salmon leap near here.'

'Yes,' he smiled, raising his glass to her, 'that salmon leap is actually more or less at the bottom of my garden. Nanette Tilsly was particularly good at catching them. Quite illegal, of course.' he added.

'Why, didn't your parents own that stretch of river?'

'They did, but when it came to the salmon, my father had to make annual returns, as I have to now, telling the authorities how many have been caught. I suppose they don't want the species to become extinct.'

'I hadn't realised,' Eliza replied thoughtfully, 'how living in the country could be so very different.'

'Yes,' he agreed, 'as you say, different, certainly from the lifestyle in the city, different rules also, some written and some not.'

'I'm beginning to understand what you mean. It's going to take a bit of re-adjusting.'

'And do you think you will, Eliza?' he asked, looking at her over the rim of his glass.

'Eventually, after a few hiccups, I probably will. At least I hope so. I've wanted to get out of London for a long time, but,' she hesitated, 'the opportunity never seemed to present itself until after my divorce and then I had the space I needed to sit down and think things through properly, how I wanted to spend the rest of my life and where. It was a big step, but I knew if I didn't give up my job and make an attempt to start up my own business, I may regret it later.'

'It couldn't have been easy, though, actually carrying out your decision, I mean.'

'It wasn't, but I had already built up some good connections and with a couple of firm contracts, I decided to take the plunge.'

'And what is it you do? No,' he smiled quickly, 'let me guess.'

'Go on,' she said, enjoying herself. Simon was easy company and had that gift of listening; a rarity. 'guess.'

'It has to be something artistic.'

'You're warm.'

'You said you had resigned from your job; perhaps you're a graphic artist?'

'You're getting warmer,' she laughed, 'go on.'

'I give in.'

'So soon,' she teased, 'very well then; I design jewellery.'

'And now you plan to work from home?'

'That's right. I'll have to make regular trips up to London, but, for the main part, I'll be here.'

'You don't think you'll find it lonely, working on your own?'

'I don't think so,' she said thoughtfully, 'it's something I have wanted to do, but I suppose I lacked the courage before. Well, you know how it is, Simon, I'm sure. Various factors, by that I mean people, relationships, events, can carry you along in one direction and it becomes more and more difficult to step aside and make the final break.'

'I know what you mean. I've been lucky,' he went on, taking another sip of wine, 'although I started off my career in a very mediocre way, working for a local firm of photographers, my parents gave me the chance – and the money I might add – to go freelance and well, I can't complain.'

'So, you're a professional photographer?'

'Got it in one!'

'And you work from home?'

'Mainly yes, I do weddings, christenings, special events and some catalogue stuff which I don't particularly enjoy, all that sort of thing, but then they're my bread and butter. My real interest is for the more abstract side of photography. And this has involved a fair amount of travelling.'

'What exactly do you mean by abstract?'

'Black and white. I photograph practically anything in fact and have over the years built up a reasonable gallery.'

'Which you exhibit at the mill?'

'That's right. I don't intend to come out with the crass line, Eliza, of asking you to 'come up and see my etchings', but if you are interested I would like to show them to you.'

'I'd like that,' she said, 'this will be an entirely new experience for me; I've never known a professional photographer before.'

'Well,' he said, 'I hope you won't be disappointed. They are not to everyone's liking, but I think you will agree the setting for them at the mill is pretty impressive.'

The Parma ham with the melon was delicious, the ham moist and just the way it should be, the melon also, not over-ripe. The girl had taken their plates away when Eliza looked up to see a petite, dark-haired woman walking towards them whom she guessed was Danielle Taylor. Slim to the point of being thin, navy-blue linen shift, sleeveless and cut a mere fraction above her knees. Her hair; straight and cut ultra-short. Not beautiful, or even pretty, but definitely striking and so very Parisian. Why was it, she wondered, so many French women exuded the immediate effect of being well-groomed, having just that moment stepped out of the beauty salon. Everything about her was honed to perfection, from the shiny black bob to the low-heeled black patent shoes. Uncharitably, she couldn't help but feel that a great deal of effort had gone into creating such an appearance.

'Simon, 'ello,' she said, 'it is good to see you.'

'Hello, Danielle,' he said making to rise, but she lifted a hand, small; nails perfectly manicured and painted a pearly pink.

'There is no need. Perhaps you will introduce me to your companion.'

Eliza did not miss the curious, slightly surprised look on her face as she underwent her close, verging on rudeness, scrutiny. She was well used to this sort of reaction and Danielle's was no exception. Eliza was not fashion conscious; she lacked both the interest and the dedication to emerge looking the way a twenty-first century woman in her forties was expected to look. She preferred clothes in which she felt comfortable, enjoyed the softness of fabrics which flowed and breathed with her and had no wish to be stereotyped. She had once overheard some friends of Steve's talking about her and saying, their words well above a whisper: 'Well, she's an artist and you know what artists are like!' It had been some years ago and she had felt offended by them, but had learned to build up her own personal shell and now it didn't concern her what people thought. Today, she was wearing a dress she'd had for a long time: pale lilac Indian cotton, ankle-length, with broad lace panels in a deeper shade and she loved it. Her hair, always unruly, she had clipped back at the nape of her neck with a heavy silver clasp she had found in one of the tiny side streets off Carnaby Street in London.

Simon introduced her, repeating, as before, that she had recently moved to Meadowbank from London. Danielle Taylor's response, while not wholly unexpected, given what she had already heard about the woman, struck her as a little odd.

'You have chosen to live in this, this – Oh, Simon,' she struggled to find the word she was looking for, her dark brown eyes narrowing, 'this neck of the woods, that's it, isn't it?'

'If you wish to describe Meadowbank in that way, Danielle.' he said, a small smile hovering.

'I do! So, Eliza,' she went on, her whole attention on her now, 'you do realise you are making a very big mistake. *Une grande erreur*! What do you intend to do all day?'

'Eliza has her own business,' Simon helped her out; 'she's a jewellery designer.'

'Oh,' a little deflated, but only momentarily Eliza thought, amused herself by now, 'you are an artist!'

'That's right, I am,' Eliza said, 'but I think you also must be artistic, Danielle, that is if you are responsible for the design of this lovely restaurant.'

'I have never thought of myself like that before, but I suppose I am. Totally wasted, of course, with the residents of this town!'

'Thanks, Danielle.' Simon by now unable to keep the smile from spreading.

'Oops, sorry, Simon! I didn't mean that to sound quite like that, but surely you must know what I mean. And now,' she continued without pausing to take a breath, 'we have a murderer in our midst! Goodness knows what our clientele is going to be like. They will be pouring into this town in their droves! I shudder to think about it!'

'Wow!' Eliza gasped after Danielle, with an exaggerated shrug of her shoulders, had left them.

'She is a bit heavy going,' he said, 'but you can't say you weren't warned.'

'Why is she like the way she is, I wonder.'

'I have no idea, but all I know is, she is one very unhappy woman.'

'She does seem to be – I don't know. I suppose what I am trying to say is she seems so out of place here, in spite of the superb surroundings. It isn't everything, is it?'

'You mean you might try to make an environment to suit you, but if everything else is out of kilter, then, it just doesn't gel?'

'That's exactly what I do mean.' Eliza said, 'Perhaps we should change the subject, shall we, Simon? Tell me about your friends, the Tilslys. Do you still see them? You mentioned Nanette.'

'Yes, she was a real tomboy, but unfortunately as these things happen sometimes, I've lost touch with the three of them.'

'That's a shame.'

'It is,' he agreed, 'Colin; he's the eldest, is the same age as me, forty-six. Nanette is a couple of years younger and Wendy, the 'baby' will be thirty-eight now. She's living in Hong Kong, working for a publishing house over there.'

'And is she married?'

'No, but the other two are. Colin; mind you I haven't seen him for years, although he only lives in Winchester, married a girl he met at university soon after he graduated and never came back to the manor to live. He didn't visit his father very often after that and from what the major let drop I think there was always a clash of personalities there.'

'And Nanette, the tomboy?'

'She married a guy called Alan Jackson; he works for one of the major financial consultancy firms in London, but like Colin, Nanette didn't pay many visits either.'

'So the family wasn't all that close?'

'I suppose not,' Simon said slowly, 'I don't know why. Perhaps it had something to do with their father never being around much when they were all growing up. Each of them learned, in their own separate way, how to be independent.'

'You haven't said anything about their mother.'

'I can scarcely remember her and if I do it is only as a vague memory. She used to spend most of her days in the garden, a shadowy, dreamy kind of figure; she just seemed to drift about. I do know she spent a lot of time on her own, which was probably not a good thing. I don't remember any friends visiting her, but perhaps that was the way she preferred to live. But then she died, she couldn't have been all that old. I've been trying to work out how old I would have been when we heard about her death. I think it must have been at least ten or fifteen years ago, but to my shame, I can't remember.

'And the major?' intrigued, it sounded reminiscent of a bygone age, long before Simon and the Tilsly children's time: the stately home, a husband who spent too much time away, a wife, an unfathomable ethereal figure drifting around and three boisterous children running unchecked through the estate, completely impervious to what was happening in the background of their young lives. And now, she thought sadly, the mainstay of that family had gone. Murdered. No wonder the town was in a state of bewilderment and shock. She was beginning to understand now Brian Morrison's reaction to the news. And here she was, newly arrived, hoping for a trouble-free life!

While Simon ordered coffee, Eliza excused herself to go to the ladies which she had already noticed was up a short flight of stairs at the rear of the restaurant. On the landing and passing an open door a telephone was ringing, followed by the sound of the receiver being picked up and then a man's voice. She had no intention of eavesdropping, but having reached a door which elaborately informed her in copperplate script that this was the one she wanted, she could not help but hear the start of what to her could only be a one-sided conversation: 'Oh. It's you.' A brief pause. 'On the midday news, was it? ......Yes, we've heard about it, in fact I don't suppose Meadowbank has ever known a day like this one. The place is buzzing. So? Why the phone call?' another pause, equally as short, 'The answer to your question is the same as you damn well should realise by now. No, I am not open to negotiations of any kind. You know the score ....' at this point the person at the other end must have interrupted him, but she didn't want to hear anymore.

It was not what she had heard which disturbed her, but the tone of the man's voice, the deliberate and precise way he had spoken. Whether there were any sinister connotations or not, one thing was certain, it was no friendly chat. The door, she noticed as she went back downstairs, was now closed. Sliding into the seat beside Simon she could not get the incident out of her mind.

'You look worried, Eliza.' Simon commented, looking at her. She never had been any good at hiding her feelings, but normally she would have dismissed those few disjointed words as not only being out of context, but inconsequential and not her concern, but these were not normal circumstances. Less than twenty-four hours ago a man had been murdered in this town and unless it was a burglary which had gone tragically wrong or premeditated murder, someone must, she had already worked out for herself, know something. It was possible anything out of the ordinary could have some relevance. Simon was still waiting, an expectant smile on his face but, when she told him, his expression slowly changed as he listened without interrupting until she had finished.

'I'm probably making too much of it all.' she said with an apologetic shrug.

'I don't know,' he said slowly, obviously mulling over what she had told him, 'that would have been Peter Taylor of course.'

'Can you be sure?'

'I think so; he came down into the restaurant a few moments ago. In fact, I fully expected him to come over; he usually does, but instead, he went straight into the kitchen, banging the door behind him. He didn't look too happy, if the scowl on his face was anything to go by.'

'I suppose it must have been him, then.'

'Yes, mind you, Eliza,' Simon added, 'he's an odd person. I would say suffers from mood swings and from what you overheard it sounds as if someone has more than ruffled his feathers.'

Chapter Six

Some hours earlier Colin and Rachel Tilsly were having breakfast; their youngest daughter, Polly, was staying with a school friend over the weekend which meant they could have the whole day to themselves, free from having to ferry a demanding fifteen year-old from one venue to another. Rachel, in particular, was looking forward to them trying out a newly opened restaurant in town, having heard glowing reports and, more importantly, that anyone who was anyone was going there, the in-place in which to be noticed. Apparently.

Colin was reading the 'Sunday Times', but only half-heartedly, selecting pieces of news at random and trying not to dwell on the worries which had, over the past few weeks, become like toothache, all too insistent and which eventually would have to be resolved. Last night's confrontation with his father had only exacerbated them, bringing that day of reckoning even closer. He had deliberately left the business section un-opened. It remained in the same pristine condition as when the paper-boy had pushed it through their letterbox. The unpalatable memory of the drastic drop in shares he had recently purchased with the utmost of confidence that their price would, as had been widely predicted, soar and when, within hours dropped to an all-time low of twelve per cent, was still too raw.

Rachel, as she always did each Sunday morning, was idly flicking through the Culture Magazine with, it would appear, nothing more important on her mind than to avidly read about the successful and super-glamorous lives of people he knew he would never have heard of. As he watched her over the top of his newspaper he wondered what her initial reaction would be when he told her quite bluntly that they were broke. Technically insolvent. Unable to make the proverbial ends meet. Their expenditure far exceeding their income.

Take your pick. There would be no way of prettying it up, making it sound less dire. She probably wouldn't believe him, indeed why should she; he had never been in the habit of talking to her about his work, also she had never shown the slightest interest, even in the early days when they were first married. She wasn't that sort of woman and, in many respects that had not been a bad thing. It had meant he had the freedom to make all their financial decisions, also to speculate on the market. She had taken everything for granted: the indisputable fact he was senior partner of Tilsly, Roberts and Hutton, Chartered Accountants, with prestigious glass-fronted premises in the centre of Winchester; their large Georgian town house on which there still remained a substantial mortgage; two top-of-the-range cars, bought earlier in the year with a couple of bank loans; Polly's school fees as a weekly boarder and monthly payments for their other two daughters: topping up Hilary's grant at the London School of Economics, Sally's fees at the Guildhall School of Music and Drama, not forgetting the rent for their Chelsea flat. The list was endless, cuts would need to be made; it was deciding where and how to make them which was going to prove difficult.

The telephone in the hall rang, instantly putting a halt to his mental anguish, and Rachel, tossing her magazine on to the table, said she would take it.

'Probably the girls.' she said going out of the kitchen.

'Bit early for them I would have thought.' he called after her, checking the time on his watch, only eight-thirty. They would, he was pretty sure, still be sound asleep; he had never known any of his daughters, since they reached their teens, to emerge much before midday on a Sunday.

'It's Mrs Thing, Colin.' Rachel said, coming back almost immediately and standing in the open doorway.

'Who?'

'Your father's housekeeper, I never can remember her name, far less pronounce it.'

'What does she want?' but as he spoke he knew instinctively there must be something wrong. He could not remember Mrs Plenderneath ever phoning before.

'She didn't say, but she sounds dreadful.'

Colin's hand was shaking as he finally replaced the receiver. He leaned heavily against the wall and tried to take in what the woman had told him. She had been barely coherent at first, but he had managed to get her to calm down and eventually she had. He had already got the gist of it anyway. His father, that larger-than-life, indominatable figure, was dead. Murdered. She had found him lying on the floor at the bottom of the stairs. A hundred thoughts were flying through his brain, none of them making any sense. Of course, there had always been the risk of a break-in with all those paintings. He and Nanette had told him often enough, but typically he had brushed away their concern. His father had always known best. But he had not been a stupid man. He would never have confronted anyone, especially if they had been armed; he would have telephoned the police. That would have been his way; Colin was positive about that. His father was ex-military; he would never have done anything on impulse. Unless, the thought suddenly occurring to him, it had not been an intruder, but someone he knew. It did not add up, but in any case, he was now dead and with this realisation another one, and one which made him feel ashamed, but it continued, insidiously, to creep into his brain and once there, settled, refusing to budge. Now, there was no longer the need to be concerned about their inheritance, that would be intact, the way it should be, except of course for his decision to donate the collection. But, Colin entertained the idea; perhaps there could be ways of over-ruling that; he was his father's eldest child, his only son, which to Colin meant he was the chief benefactor. The shock was gradually beginning to wear off now; there were things to be done. Nanette would have to be told and then there was Wendy. What time was it he wondered in Hong Kong. Was it seven or eight hours ahead, not that it mattered, he would have to call her.

'You were a long time, Colin,' Rachel said, glancing up from her magazine, a fresh mug of coffee by her elbow, 'what was bothering the old dear?'

'Do you think you could pour me a coffee, Rachel,' he asked, sitting down heavily on the chair beside her, 'and then I'll tell you?'

'Colin,' she gasped, 'you look awful!'

'Pour me some coffee, please, Rachel.'

'I'll get you a brandy; that will you do you more good.'

He watched, without really focusing, as she busied about in the kitchen, taking a glass from one of the cabinets, breaking the seal of a new bottle of brandy and pouring out a generous measure.

'Take a sip, Colin. Come on.'

He did as he was told, instantly feeling the warmth of the spirit flow through him, helping, easing the unbelievable tension and then he told her; as much as he knew and she listened, her fingers pressed involuntarily across her mouth, her eyes wide with shock as the impact of his words reached her. When he came to the end, exhausted and taking another sip she still did not say anything, just sat there.

'Rachel,' he coaxed, gently pulling her hands away, 'it's your turn now,' and without even filling another glass, placed his own up to her lips, watching as she tried to sip.

'Oh, Colin,' she said at last, 'what can I say? It's terrible. Terrible.'

'I know.'

'Murder.' she whispered the word. 'Because that's what it was, wasn't it?'

He nodded, persuading her to take another sip, not much this time, but enough to bring the colour back to her cheeks. He had been afraid she was about to pass out, but no, she was alright and even managed a tiny sad smile as she handed the glass back to him.

'And to think,' she said quietly, 'you only saw him last evening. It is just so – so unbelievable.'

'After what's happened, Rachel,' he said, 'I'm not too proud of the way I handled things last night. We had quite a heated argument, you know. Oh, he didn't lose his temper, but I'm afraid I did.'

'You have absolutely nothing to reproach yourself with,' she said quickly, sounding more like her old self now, 'okay, he refused categorically to have an agreement drawn up and that was that. You told me last night, Colin, how stubborn he was being, but that was the way he was. I suppose we should have known better than to ask him to do it.'

'It doesn't make me feel any better though.'

'Look, he was alive and well when you left, wasn't he?'

'Of course. In fact he told me to buzz off and not to come back again until I could keep a civil tongue in my head.'

'There you are then, so don't be so hard on yourself.'

'That's all very well, but once the police hear I was there they are bound to jump to conclusions, especially if they find out about the row we had.'

'Why should they? Mrs –'

' – Plenderneath.' he assisted.

'Yes, well, she wouldn't have been there at that time in the evening, would she?'

'True.'

'So, who would have seen you then, or if it comes to that have overheard you?'

'The woman who's moved into the lodge; she was there.'

'Oh, I didn't know she had arrived yet.'

'Neither did I until he told me, but she must have been in because there was a light on upstairs. I noticed it when I drove past the lodge and that room faces directly across to the library. We were in there and both the French windows were open.'

'I think you're worrying needlessly, I really do, Colin. Just say, she had overheard you, wouldn't she also have heard –' stumbling over the words, her mouth beginning to tremble again, '- I mean,' she went on slowly, 'the gun going off. Surely she would have heard that.'

'It's possible, but Rachel, until we know what time this happened, we don't know whether that will be in my favour or not.'

'The police are not stupid; they will hardly go around suspecting the first person they think of!'

'No,' he admitted, 'but I think the sooner I get over there, find out who is in charge of the case, the better.'

'Are you going to phone Nanette? It's best she hears from you, Colin.'

'You're right; I'll do that straight away.'

'What about Maureen?'

'Maureen?'

'Your father's intended, darling. Surely you haven't forgotten about her!'

'Believe it or not, but I had. Besides, I hardly know her; I'll leave that to the police.'

The conversation with Nanette was predictable. His sister was easily the most placid and laid back person he had ever known, also the most prosaic, or so he had always thought. While there was no doubt the news had shocked her and, Colin thought cynically, penetrated her normal air of what he always described as complacency, it had not taken her long, three minutes at the most, to make an extraordinary précis of what it would now mean to them all. Their idea of persuading their father to draw up, far less sign, a pre-nuptial agreement, was now no longer necessary. In other words, their inheritance was intact. He did not think any less of her. Nanette was, in spite of that soft facade, one tough cookie. She was certainly no less materialistic than he was, not an attractive characteristic, but there it was. They were, he thought, very similar.

'Well, Colin,' Nanette was saying, 'it's obvious to me someone broke in last night; let's face it, he only had the minimum security, it was a gift to anyone determined enough, also to learn about that collection. I have lost count over the years the amount of articles I've read about it and that last extravagant spread in the 'Sunday Times' was most informative; photographs of the manor, the lot. You have to admit,' she went on relentlessly, scarcely pausing for breath, 'it was only a matter of time before someone took advantage; we've discussed it often enough.'

'That's true,' he agreed, 'but it's early days, Nanette, we don't know what happened or whether it had anything to do with the paintings.'

'Perhaps not,' she put in sharply, 'but it seems obvious to me.'

'I saw him last evening, you know.'

'Did you? Well, you did say you were going to have another go at him, try to make him see sense. So, Colin, what transpired?'

'Nothing. I lost my temper, called him a stubborn old fool and then left, that's all.'

'Oh dear, it doesn't bode very well for you, does it? I hope you can prove exactly when you did leave the manor?'

'My dear and trusting sister, as to that I don't honestly know whether I can or not, besides,' he added, wondering why he was going to such lengths to prove his innocence to her. At the same time the unsavoury thought crossed his mind that if he couldn't convince his sister, what chance did he have with the police. 'he was shot, Nanette, and never once in my life have I ever as much as held a gun in my hand, far less fire one!'

'For goodness sake, Colin, cool it. I'm not accusing you. There was an intruder; Dad confronted him and that was how it must have happened.'

'It may have, I don't know and at the moment I don't believe anyone does. That's for the authorities to sort out.'

'True,' Nanette admitted, 'so what now?'

'I'll have to go over there, of course, speak to the police, but first I had better try and get in touch with Wendy.'

'This is going to hit her hard.'

'I know.'

'She was dad's favourite; I think she reminded him of mother. At least that is what I've always thought.'

'Nanette, we need to talk.' Colin said, impatient to bring the conversation to an end, but more anxious now to talk to Wendy. Nannette had not been wrong. Wendy would be devastated when she heard. Already, before he had even dialled the number of her apartment in Hong Kong, he was anticipating and dreading her reaction. She had not been born with the hard shell of Nanette and himself; she was over-imaginative and in his opinion far too vulnerable, susceptible to anything, however unimportant, which happened around her, too easily upset. Apart from Rachel, whom he loved unquestionably, although at times they often seemed to be living on two entirely different planets, the love he had for his younger sister was something else. He had, from that very first moment, early in the morning he remembered, when his father had taken him into the main bedroom at the manor to be shown his new baby sister. That memory had stayed with him. Even more poignant than seeing his three daughters soon after they were born; that moment looking at the tiny baby in his mother's arms was the most memorable one.

'Do we, Colin?' Nanette, her voice too shrill, bringing him back.

'What?'

'Need to talk.'

'Of course we do.'

'I honestly don't see what we have to say. Now, I mean. Everything should be perfectly straight forward. Thank goodness, he hadn't married that woman!'

'I haven't told you yet about what he'd decided to do with the collection.'

'What?'

'He told me he was donating it to the Tate Gallery.'

'I don't believe this! Why on earth would he have done such a thing, Colin? Why?'

'He didn't elaborate and, quite frankly, I was in no mood to pursue it. It was his personal collection after all; I suppose he could do what he liked with the paintings.'

'Colin Tilsly!' forcing him to pull the receiver away from his ear. So much for her armour of complacency he thought wryly. '*His* collection! So, it may have been, but you don't believe he bought every single painting with his own money, do you? Colin, he didn't *have* any money, apart from his army pension of course. Surely I don't need to spell out to you who paid for them.'

'Mother?'

'Who else? You surprise me, Colin, you really do. I don't know whether you are being deliberately obtuse, but I thought you knew this.'

'What you are saying —' pausing, finding it difficult to formulate the words which he knew were distasteful, '- it belongs to the family.'

'Exactly.'

'We would have to prove it you realise, Nanette.'

'We will,' she said, 'good grief, Colin, the manor didn't even belong to him, only through marriage. It had been in mother's family as far back as I don't know when!'

'All the more reason why we should meet, then. Can you and Alan make it down here later on today? I'll need his input as well.'

'Not possible. He won't be home until tonight; he's on another of his management awareness courses in Brighton this weekend.'

'Well, when can you both get here, then? Tomorrow?'

'I don't know Colin. I really don't. I can't see Alan getting any time off this week and, of course, being the holidays we have the boys to consider.'

'Just do your best, Nanette. Phone me tonight, okay? We really need to be together on this,' he added, 'with or without Wendy's agreement.'

Chapter Seven

The metallic blue BMW was back again Eliza noticed the following morning, parked alongside the police van which had remained there all night. The BMW had been there when Simon had brought her home the previous afternoon.

Her own car, a new Ford Fiesta, had been delivered earlier, shortly after nine, followed by the carriers with her boxes. Apart from clothes, books, art equipment and materials, plus a few treasured possessions; paintings and ornaments, all of which she'd had for years, she had brought little else from what she now thought of as her other life. After the final break with Steve she wanted nothing tangible to remind her of a period she would much prefer to forget. There was, she decided, something pleasantly therapeutic about making a fresh clutter-free start, erecting her easel and positioning it exactly as she liked it. She had, on her first visit to the lodge with the agent, already decided on the room she would use as a studio: upstairs, at the end of the narrow landing; small, but with a window running the width of the room, east-facing and with an uninterrupted view of woodland which, presumably, separated the estate from Simon's land. The light, she was finding, as she carefully and methodically arranged drawing paper, sketch pad, pens, pencils, coloured inks, art magazines and books on the table and shelving, was excellent and was exactly as she thought it would be each morning, preferring to do her design work then; the afternoons she would spend on the tedious tasks: correspondence, faxes, accounts and any telephoning she needed to do, but she had no choice. The business was still very much in its infancy and it would be some time she reckoned before she would be able to afford to employ anyone to help out, even part-time.

Towards the end of the morning, glancing from her bedroom window, it looked as though the police were making preparations to leave; the blue and white barrier tape around the front of the manor had been removed, rolled up and was now being placed inside the van. She hoped they were going, although she did realise they had their tasks to carry out and to them, no doubt, this was all routine, but to Eliza, watching them, she could not help visualising the scene which would have greeted them when they first arrived the day before, also a near-hysterical housekeeper to contend with. She would not have made a good policewoman, far too vivid an imagination, she thought, turning away from the window.

The next and important thing she had to do she decided, going back downstairs to the kitchen was to make a shopping list. The few basic essentials she had brought with her on Saturday were by now depleted. Also, she wanted to stock up the fridge with enough food to keep her going for the rest of the week and this would have to be done today as she had already planned tomorrow would be her first working day.

Her mobile rang as she was leaving the lodge. Steve. Not totally unexpected and she took a deep breath and waited for the tirade which she was certain was going to come.

'Eliza,' no niceties, straight to the point, 'thanks a bundle! You do realise I spent a good part of yesterday afternoon being interrogated by the police!'

'I didn't, actually,' play it cool she told herself, knowing from past experience it was the only way with him when he was angry, 'are you back in London?'

'What the hell does it matter where I am?'

'I just wondered, that's all. You did tell me you were going to be in the area for a couple of days.'

'Ah! I see what you're getting at,' he sneered, 'after kindly informing them, you're now wondering how they managed to find me so quickly, eh?'

'I'm not wondering anything, Steve,' she said quietly, 'and quite frankly I see no purpose in this call.'

'Well, I do! Why the hell did you have to tell the police I had visited you on Saturday afternoon?'

'Because they asked me if I'd had any visitors.'

'And you, the good little citizen, promptly told them.'

'I didn't think I had much choice.'

'Don't give me that! Everyone always has a choice, Eliza. Even you. So, why did you?'

'Because I'm honest, that's why. Also, if I had said no-one had been here, they would be bound to have found out.'

'What! In that out of the way place!'

'It may seem like that to you, but there is always someone around and I didn't want to be found to be lying.'

'I see,' the sneer returning, 'covering your back.'

'You obviously know the police are investigating a murder, Steve and I have nothing to hide.'

'And I do?'

'You said that, Steve. I didn't.'

'Don't get smart. They gave me one hell of a grilling, wanted to know why I was in the neighbourhood, but then, having a prison record, I'm bound to be treated like that.'

'I'm sorry about that, but as I've already said, there is no point in discussing this with me any further. I am not interested, Steve. If you have nothing to hide, why should you be so concerned?'

'You'll be telling me next they are only doing their job.'

'Well, they are,' she couldn't resist that, but he deserved it Eliza thought and she'd told him, she really did not have a choice, 'and it might interest you, but I was also questioned. At some length.' she added.

'I wasn't questioned, Liza, I was bloody *grilled*. Anyway,' he went on, 'I suppose now your landlord has been bumped off you'll have to leave the lodge.'

'I wouldn't think so, but then I don't see what business it is of yours, Steve. I am quite capable of looking after myself.'

He muttered something which she couldn't make out, probably some derogatory remark, before switching off. The thought she may have to give up her lease had not occurred to her. But it was far too soon to speculate about that possibility and to seek reassurance from the agents would be pointless as well as insensitive. That could wait she decided, locking the front door behind her and getting into the Fiesta, adjusting the seat and rear view mirror, appreciating the long forgotten newness of a new car; the way the engine effortlessly purred into life and the smoothness of the gears as she moved away from the lodge. At the gate, open as they had been all day yesterday, she stopped to allow a dark green van to turn into the drive, the gold lettering immediately catching her eye as it drew level: "Assessors and Valuers of Fine Arts", reminding her of the major's art collection and how knowledgeable Steve had sounded. Steve again. She was finding it difficult to dismiss him from her mind. Why could he not stay away? What she had once felt for him had gone and there was no going back. Never.

These thoughts, unpleasant and uninvited, followed her all the way into Meadowbank, spoiling what should have been a pleasant first-time experience and even when managing to find a parking space in a narrow street off the square, he was still there, refusing to leave. She would not be the only person wanting to know the real reason why had turned up, she decided; no doubt the police would also like to know.

The first person Eliza saw when she walked into the square; considerably quieter than it had been the day before, was Danielle Taylor. Today, she was wearing white cotton trousers, cut French-style above the ankles, a straight scarlet tunic and soft leather moccasins. Eliza expected only the briefest of greetings and was therefore surprised when the woman stopped to shake hands with her.

'Good morning, Eliza,' she said, the same look of appraisal on her face and shamelessly absorbing every detail of what she was wearing, lingering for several seconds on her earrings: silver filigree circles, a tiny blue parrot delicately balanced in the centre of each of them. They were from her latest 'Blue Parrot' range, not that she would mention this to Danielle. Eliza's job was not to market any of her designs, but she could not resist wearing them and delighting, as now, when they caught attention, 'I am admiring your earrings. They are – they are most unusual.'

'Thank you, I'm glad you like them.'

'Oh, I do. *Certainement*! But, not you understand, exactly my style. I prefer a more classical, more *classique,* style of jewellery.'

'I know what you mean,' Eliza said, amused in spite of her complete lack of tact. Danielle, she concluded was a woman who spoke without thinking, not realising, or if she did, not caring what sort of an affect she was creating.

'We enjoyed our lunch yesterday,' Eliza said, veering her away from the subject, 'my salmon was perfect. Your restaurant must be very popular,' she added, looking across at the 'Salmon's Rest' and noticing the shutters were still closed, 'you're not open today?'

'My goodness, no. It is Monday,' she said, permitting a slight frown to appear on her smooth forehead, 'my one day of rest,' she emphasised, 'although even today I have work to do, planning the menus, ordering and organising my staff. A real trial, I can tell you. Mind you,' now gathering steam, her dark eyes flashing, 'I make no excuses for them. Compared to what I have been used to in Paris, also I have to admit, in London, they fail one hundred per cent!'

How she pitied anyone who was unfortunate enough to work for her. They would never please her and would, Eliza felt sure, invariably fall far short of what was expected.

'I should have realised you wouldn't be open today,' she said in an attempt to lighten her mood, 'I remember how difficult it used to be to find somewhere to eat on a Monday in France.'

'You know my country?'

'Reasonably well,' Eliza said, 'I finished off studying for my art degree in Paris and never could get it into my head you could always buy meat, fish, vegetables and flowers on a Sunday, but these shops were closed on a Monday and that invariably included my favourite restaurants.'

'You interest me, Eliza,' Danielle said, 'I hadn't realised, but you speak French?'

'Yes,' Eliza could not keep the smile from appearing now; the woman was so obvious, also it occurred to her, possibly homesick, 'but not fluently. I got by.' she laughed.

'I simply do not understand why you should want to bury yourself in this place.'

'Oh, I don't see it like that at all. I *am* English and I could never imagine wanting to live anywhere else, no matter how much I enjoyed staying for a time in other countries. I'm rather boring, I'm afraid.'

'I do not think that for one minute,' she said quickly, 'but I am sure you will find the people in this town exceedingly dull! So parochial! All they ever talk about is the weather. And now,' she went on, 'they have something else. A murder! Imagine! In this quiet little town!'

'It's probably given them all rather a shock.'

'I'm sure it has, but they are so – *trop mediocre*! They drive me crazy!'

'But you married an Englishman, Danielle, you must have realised how different we are from the French.'

'*Touché*! How right you are, but tell me; Simon, how well do you know him?'

How forthright and to-the-point these French women can be Eliza thought, reminded again what it had been like during the time she had spent there and had often been subjected to the same kind of conversation. If they wanted to know something, if they had something to say, they just came out with it. And they were so very personal.

'I hardly know Simon at all,' she said, 'we met on Saturday afternoon for the first time and he was good enough to give me a lift to the lodge.'

'I see. A chance encounter?'

'I don't know about that,' Eliza laughed at the idea, 'I hadn't realised the bus service was as infrequent as it is and that's where he found me; standing at the bus stop.'

'You do not have a car!'

'I have now,' honestly Danielle Taylor was unreal. But in spite of her amusement, Eliza could not help liking her. She was refreshing and at least her emotions were on the surface, unlike the type of woman she was used to in London when each nuance of speech was weighed up carefully, adeptly camouflaging what they were really thinking. She thought she could become friendly with her, given time.

'We must have coffee one morning, Eliza,' Danielle suggested, 'it would have to be on a Monday though.'

'I'd like that.'

'On one condition.' she smiled; a secretive cat-like smile.

'Yes?'

'That when we do, we converse only in French.'

'I'll try.'

Half an hour later, her shopping completed and placed in the boot of the car, Eliza returned to the square, walking along the pavement towards 'The Market Inn'. She would have lunch there she decided. Today, she had no intention of cooking, also it may give her another chance to get to know how this town ticked!

Melissa served her, introducing herself and apologising for not being able to the day before. Although not long after mid-day, the bar was already filling up, but far less hectic. Brian was at the far end and waved over to her as soon as he saw her. She ordered from the chalk board propped up against one of the wooden pillars: the Market Inn Ploughman – freshly baked bread, a hearty chunk of mature cheddar and Branston pickle.

'How are you settling in at the lodge, Eliza?' Melissa asked, pouring wine into a glass.

'Quite well, I still have a lot of unpacking to do, but there's no rush.'

'It's a lovely old house,' she said, passing the glass over to her, 'years ago, when I was a young girl, I would often be up at the manor with my aunt and I used to help her with the dusting. At least my attempt at dusting.' she smiled.

She was really pretty; curly red hair, tied back from an elfin-shaped face, but there was a look of sadness in her eyes. What was it Simon had said yesterday; that Melissa and Brian had been living together for some time and how Brian had an aversion to discussing why, although now divorced, they had not married. Something to do with what he had been through with his ex-wife, making him nervous to make that final commitment. Watching Melissa as she moved away to serve a couple who had come in and the spontaneous smile as she greeted them, Eliza wondered what it must be like to live in a relatively small community when practically everyone knew everyone else. For too long she had been used to city life where you could live for years and never speak to or even learn the name of your neighbour. Living in Meadowbank, she smiled to herself, was going to prove to be some learning curve, but in spite of the dramatic start she had every confidence she had made the right choice. Already, she was beginning to feel welcome here, not just the natural friendliness of her new neighbour, but generally. Some of her more cynical friends in London would, she was sure, have disagreed with her, being quick to label these people as over-familiar, but she didn't see them like that. For the first time in years, even before she had met Steve, she felt part of what was going on around her and wondering why she had not realised she had been living in an environment which simply hadn't suited her.

'Will you miss London?' Melissa asked, coming back.

'I don't think so,' Eliza smiled, 'I badly needed a change and as part of that was deciding to branch out and work for myself, London no longer held any appeal for me.'

'I hardly ever go there,' she said wistfully, 'it always seems so glamorous on the rare occasion when I do.'

'I suppose it is a bit like the grass being greener on the other side,' Eliza said, 'but believe me, Melissa, it isn't like that at all.'

'Perhaps you're right. Tell me, what sort of work do you do?'

'I design jewellery.'

'Really! You're an artist? I thought you might be.'

'Is it so obvious?' Eliza couldn't help laughing; there was such a unique freshness about the girl, no side to her whatsoever.

'Oh dear,' she put a hand up to her mouth, 'have I said the wrong thing? I'm always doing that. Brian just laughs at me. Calls them my little gaffs.'

'You haven't said anything wrong. Honestly, Melissa; in fact I take it as a compliment. After all,' she went on, 'I hardly look like a high-flying executive, do I?'

'Whatever they are meant to look like!'

'Quite.'

'What's the joke ladies?' Brian asked coming over to join them.

'You might not get it.' Melissa said, laughing up at him.

'Try me.'

'Well,' she said, 'what does a high-flying executive look like, Brian?'

'You're right,' he grinned, 'I don't get it.'

Chapter Eight

'What sort of a day have you had, Eliza?' Simon asked her. He had wanted to talk to her again, as soon as he had woken up that morning, but he had delayed the moment to phone her until well on to the end of what had been for him, an unusually long drawn-out day. He had gone through the motions of sifting through his mail, writing cheques, making a couple of telephone calls, sorting out a pile of negatives 'National Geographic' had asked him to send in for an article they were running on a lost and forgotten tribe in Papua New Guinea, and during the afternoon, driving into Meadowbank to post his mail; all the time hoping he might see her, either outside the lodge when he passed, or in the town and, when he didn't, feeling ridiculously disappointed. He could not get her out of his mind. She fascinated him. Like a love-sick schoolboy he kept going over and over again the previous afternoon; the disconcerting way those lovely blue eyes had looked at him, the swift gurgle of laughter when he had said something which amused her, all of which he had found delightful.

'I suppose you could say it's been interesting.' Eliza was saying now, bringing him back.

'It's a lovely evening,' he said, 'why don't you come up to the mill and you can tell me what you've been doing? Also,' he added, 'I can show you the salmon leap. Who knows, we might be lucky enough to see one.'

'I'd like that,' she said, 'but I think it's time I returned some of your hospitality, Simon. I've been meaning to phone you today to thank you for lunch, but –'

' – Eliza, please, it was my pleasure.'

She told him she now had her car, assuring him there was no need for him to collect her and he said she could not possibly miss the mill: to follow the road along the brick wall of the estate and when it ended to turn left up the lane for a couple of minutes.

While he waited for her, he took a bottle of Sauvignon from the fridge, opened it and together with a couple of glasses took everything out on to the balcony, arranging the basket chairs to face the river. Seven in the evening, still warm, and apart from the faint rustle from the wisteria threading its sweet-smelling way along the top of the balcony, wonderfully peaceful. He always enjoyed this time of day, especially in early summer with the promise of many more evenings such as this one, before autumn arrived and the chill in the air would force him inside, but now, as he leaned against the rail, feeling the warmth from the wood on his arms, he was experiencing something else. It had been a long time. Too long he thought ruefully, living practically like a hermit. It was not as if he didn't have friends, male and female, but since Annabel's death which had been staggeringly tragic and sudden, leaving him not only bereft, but reluctant to face making another commitment which could, he had believed, fallen short of what he had known with her. Now, perhaps, it might be possible to move forward, but he was not fooling himself; commonsense telling him that the woman he only met two days ago could very well have someone else in her life, recalling the man he had seen at the lodge, but don't assume, Simon, he told himself. Either way. Just lighten up and enjoy the moment.

He saw her from his kitchen window as the car turned in at the top of the lane: strong sunlight reflecting against the canary yellow of the bodywork and watched as it came to a neat standstill next to his Renault. Eliza, sunglasses pushed on to the top of her head, stepped out and waved up to him. He felt his heart give a tiny momentarily lurch. She was utterly stunning and he wondered if she realised the affect she had, not only on him, he was sure. There were women like her he supposed, completely at ease with themselves, quite natural, giving off a spontaneous warmth and not in the least coquettish as so many beautiful women were, at least in his experience, and which he always found not only irritating, but off-putting, making him feel he may as well be talking to himself for all the interest they were showing, unless the conversation did not revolve exclusively around them.

The path, hard-packed gravel, bordered on either side by ankle-high fern and bracken and a spreading blanket of forget-me-knots and bluebells adding a deep and brilliant splash of colour, led them to the humpbacked bridge which they would have to cross before they reached the salmon leap.

'Is it safe?' Eliza asked, placing one foot tentatively on to the old timber.

'It's okay,' he smiled, going in front of her, waiting for her to follow, 'it was built by a master carpenter,' he told her, 'my grandfather. I would have been about eight and he was staying with us. It was shortly after my grandmother died and I think, although of course not then, I was far too young, but I believe he needed to do something positive, something physical and so,' Simon finished, 'hence this very elaborate bridge, totally out of place where hardly anyone comes near and can appreciate the fine workmanship, but,' he shrugged, 'I think it was something he felt he had to do.' the voice of his grandfather coming down to him through the years. He had been told to firmly hold in position one of the rustic side panels and all he wanted to do, selfish little sod that he had been, was to crawl through the nearest hole in the hedge and spend the afternoon playing with the Tilsly kids. 'Come on, Simon,' his grandfather had frowned at him, 'just stand still for one minute, won't you, while I bang this piece of wood in place and stop fidgeting. What have you got, ants in your pants, lad!' and smiling to himself at the memory, Simon picked up a handful of small pebbles and tossed them into the water, watching as they skimmed the surface, 'We used to do this,' he said, 'a mindless occupation, but we found it compulsive, trying to find out whose stones went the furthest.

'Boys.' she smiled at him.

'In our case, not exactly; remember, I told you about Nanette; she excelled, I don't know how exactly, but she did. She really should have been a boy, although mind you,' he went on, 'it was Colin who thought of the great idea, at least we thought it was, of flinging in one of those small lemonade bottles –'

' – you mean,' she interrupted, laughing, 'you actually put in messages?'

'Of course,' grinning at her, 'why else throw a bottle into a fast moving river like this!'

'Why else?' still laughing, but he didn't mind.

'We were young, Eliza, and totally ignorant of anything ecological. I doubt very much if any of us had ever heard of the word, far less understood what it meant.'

'The way you describe your childhood, Simon,' she said, becoming serious, 'it sounds so idyllic.'

'We were lucky, but what about you?'

'Me? Well, like you, I was an only child, but I wasn't fortunate enough to have the freedom you enjoyed, with friends living next door and to live in a kind of Enid Blyton way.'

'Enid Blyton?'

'Oh, being a boy I don't suppose you would have read any of her books, but I thought they were wonderful. 'The Famous Five'; they were children and they had the most marvellous of adventures without any intervention from adults, unless they were villains of course, but they always managed to outwit them.'

'No, I didn't,' trying to remember whether he had ever seen any of her books. He doubted it. He only read books at that age when ordered to at school, and even then with considerable reluctance. Wendy probably did read them though.

'I spent most of my time at boarding school, you see,' she explained, the blue eyes dreamy as though she was back in those days, remembering, 'in Kent. And my holidays were either with my parents in Kenya; my father was with the Diplomatic Service out there, or with my grandparents in Scotland.'

'I see.' he said, thinking that would explain the Scottish accent, only slight, but now and again he could pick it up.

'It's lovely out here,' Eliza said, 'and so quiet and so very, very different from what I've been used to. Even in Africa. I can remember lying in bed, marvelling at the dense blackness and always the sounds; discordant, mostly in the distance and I used to lie there under my mosquito net and try to identify them.'

'I know what you mean.' how refreshing it was to speak to someone who had actually been there, had experienced the same night sounds as he had. Anyone else he had ever met, although many of them had travelled equally as much as he had, had invariably been staying in hotels, the only sounds to disturb their slumber coming from the air conditioners, the whole of the outside world completely muffled.

'Those rooftops over to the left, Simon,' Eliza interrupted his thoughts, 'do they belong to the manor?'

'Yes, they do.'

'I hadn't realised it was so close.'

'Deceptive, isn't it? There is a shortcut which we always used. We shouldn't have done, of course, but the hedge over there. It looks impenetrable, doesn't it, but, I can assure you it isn't. We hardly ever went the more orthodox way; along the footpath linking the two properties, but simply pushed through one of the many gaps, widened, I'm ashamed to say, by the four of us!'

'Country life,' she smiled wistfully, 'it never ceases to amaze me.'

As she finished speaking, continuing to look over to where he had pointed, his eye had been caught by a patch of colour, incongruous among the variegated greenery and which should not have been there. Screwing up his eyes against the glare of the sun which even at that time in the evening, although sinking, was quite strong, he tried to make it out.

Cloth, hunched up, a bundle, but from where they were standing impossible to tell.

'What is that, Simon?'

'I don't know,' he answered slowly, feeling a sudden dryness at the back of his throat. He recognised the material. Grey and white check. A jacket. Old, much worn and once belonging to his father and one he had been reluctant to discard in spite of constant nagging by his mother and then, eventually, and with considerable complaining, he had given in and handed it over to Len Roberts. Len, the local poacher, now quite elderly, but he was still to be seen in the neighbourhood. Condoned, he never did any harm; he caught the occasional rabbit for his cooking pot and more than the odd salmon, but nobody said anything.

'It's a person, isn't it?' she whispered, putting a hand on his arm. 'You think so, don't you?'

'I think it could be. I'm going over to have a look.'

'Shall I come with you?'

'No, Eliza, we could be wrong, but if not, it's best I go on my own. You'll wait here, won't you?'

'Of course,' a tight anxious smile on her face which had grown pale, the freckles standing out in stark relief across her cheeks.

Simon gently released her hand and stepped over on to the grass, walking through the undergrowth, ducking below the over-hanging branches of the willow trees, until he reached the hedge. It was old Len alright. He was lying huddled, his body bent almost double, his head half-buried in the soft earth at the bottom of the hedge and there was no doubt he was dead. He felt a wave of nausea as he looked down at him, at the same time seeing through blurred vision the dark rusty stain on the collar of the jacket. Taking a deep breath, he turned away and walked back to the bridge, taking both Eliza's hands in his.

'Breath deeply, Simon.' she said, squeezing his hands, 'Do you want to sit down for a minute?'

'No, I'm alright,' he looked at her gratefully, feeling her strength flowing through him, 'we have to phone the police, Eliza. I think I know who it is.'

'Yes?' she spoke softly, her face, if possible, even more pale.

'I didn't see his face, but I'm fairly certain it's Len Roberts. It's a well known fact locally that he's been poaching rabbits and salmon between the major's estate and the mill for years, but always people have turned a blind eye; in fact, I've never heard anyone so much as mention it.'

'What do you think happened to him?'

'I don't know, but one thing for sure, his was no natural death.'

'My God,' she gulped, 'oh, no, how dreadful!'

'Come on,' he said taking her arm, 'let's get back to the mill and I'll phone the police. They'll know what to do.'

An hour later, Chief Inspector Masters, Sergeant Ash and the police team had been and gone, the body of the man they had quickly identified as Leonard Roberts, taken away. It was not yet night and the sun, although with less of its former strength, still continued to shine. If Brenda Masters had been surprised to see Eliza there she had shown no sign. Efficiently, questions were asked, notes were made and that was all. Indeed, what else could they have done Simon thought as he watched them drive away.

'A drink, Eliza?' he asked, coming back into the lounge, 'I think perhaps we both need one.'

'I think so,' she smiled wanly, 'what a terrible thing to happen, Simon. Poor old man. He was – he was murdered, wasn't he?'

'I would say so, yes.' He did not want to tell her anymore, about the blood. That would not have been fair and already he was concerned about her. She still looked too pale.

'I wonder when it happened.' she murmured almost to herself, following him into the kitchen, the last of the sun filtering into the room, making what they had so recently seen seem bizarre.

'Forensic will soon know the answer to that,' he said, filling two glasses and handing one to her, 'but there could be a connection with the major's death. Len was lying very close to the hedge, as though he had come through from the estate.'

'It's possible,' Eliza said and he noticed how her hand shook as she raised the glass to her lips, 'he may have seen who shot Major Tilsly. That's feasible, don't you think, Simon? I cannot believe two murders in such close proximity to each other could be isolated incidents.'

'Neither can I.' he agreed, watching her closely. It was more than her pallor; her eyes looked troubled. Something was deeply disturbing her and having more of an impact than what she had heard, and only seen from a distance. She had something on her mind, he was sure of it. Eliza, he judged, was the type of woman who would be unable to hide her emotions, but he didn't want to press her. Whatever it was, and if she decided to tell him, she would; when she was ready.

'I expect you're wondering about my reaction to all of this?' she asked quietly, uncannily reading his thoughts, 'Because,' she went on before he had a chance to say anything, 'I have a ghastly feeling that – how can I put this,' she paused for a second, the blue eyes focused on him, 'that,' she continued with a deep sigh, 'now the police will be continuing with their suspicions of a man whom I rather think was their first suspect for what happened to the major and –'

' – and you know who this man is?' he asked gently, wanting to help her, wanting to take away the anguish.

'Yes, Simon, I do.'

And she told him about Steve, the years she had been married to him and for many of those years not having any idea of his criminal background until, finally, when he was caught and served an eight-month prison sentence, the divorce which followed and how she never expected to see or hear from him again, pausing at that juncture as though trying to gauge his reaction.

'And he did get in touch with you.'

'Yes, he did, but how did you know?' surprise instantly lightening her expression.

'I didn't actually,' he said, relieved to see she was looking better, the faraway look in her eyes had gone and at last the colour was beginning to return to her cheeks, 'I was assuming; wrong of me, I know, but on Saturday when I arrived back here after dropping you off at the lodge, the major rang me, asking me over for a drink.'

'Oh, I see and you probably saw us on the terrace.'

'I didn't see you, Eliza, and this was when I was leaving. I did consider calling in to see whether you were managing to settle in okay, but then I saw you had a visitor. I take it that was him?'

'Yes, it was.'

Eliza then went on to tell him of the keen interest Steve had shown in the major's art collection and that when asked by Brenda Masters if anyone had called she felt she had no option but to tell her.

'You see, Simon,' she continued, 'the chief inspector asked me his name, also his address; she wanted to know if I had gone back to using my maiden name after the divorce which I had, so I suppose it was fairly easy for them to trace him. I had a telephone call from him this morning telling me the police had given him a grilling. His words. He was absolutely furious with me.'

'He had no right to be, Eliza! No right at all.' Indignant on her behalf. What a bastard! Simon wished now he had called in on her that evening and seen for himself what sort of person he was. 'Listen to me,' he said, taking the glass from her and putting it down on the coffee table, and taking both her hands in his. How cold they were. 'I'm not going to ask you whether you think he had anything to do with either of these deaths.

'Even if you did,' she said quickly, looking down at their linked hands, 'I wouldn't be able to give you an answer. I never saw Steve as a violent man, but then for years I didn't think he was capable of being a thief, so I am probably the last person to analyse him. God knows, I feel ashamed enough having been gullible to marry someone who had a police record, never mind considering the possibility he may also be a murderer.'

'Ashamed?'

'Perhaps that's the wrong word,' she said, 'I believe tainted would be a better way to describe the way I feel, Simon.'

'I'm truly sorry you should think like that, but under similar circumstances I may very well have thought exactly the same. Perhaps it is only natural, but don't let it spoil your life, Eliza.'

'I'm trying not to let that happen, Simon,' she said, 'and until he turned up again I did think I was succeeding, but now, well,' gently taking her hands away and giving him a sad smile.

'You may not hear from him again, but if you do and it disturbs you in any way, Eliza, you have the right to complain, officially that is. Harassment, I believe it is called.'

'You're right, although I'm sure he will be receiving another visit from the police.'

'And if he does,' he told her, 'remember it has nothing to do with you. I want you to promise me something, Eliza.'

'Yes.'

'If he does, will you please call me. It doesn't matter what time of the day – or night.' he added.

'You're being so kind, Simon, and you hardly know me. Why is that?' a look of genuine puzzlement on her lovely face.

'Because, and I know we have met only recently, but I want us to be friends and eventually get to know each other better. And besides,' he continued in an effort to make her feel better, but he had meant what he had said and the last thing he wanted was to put any pressure on her. He wanted their relationship to develop naturally and he rather thought she felt the same. 'we're living next door to each other and most of us around here try to help our neighbours as much as we can.'

Chapter Nine

Nanette Jackson or, as she had, even in the early years of her marriage, always thought of herself as Nanette Tilsly, dialled her brother's office number in Winchester.

'What the hell is going on in Meadowbank, Colin?' were her first words after being put through to him.

'What do you mean?'

He sounded tired, but he was not the only one she thought bitterly. He and Rachel were lucky; they had the whole of each week to themselves. They didn't have two boisterous young boys to control while she had a husband who was no help at all. If Alan was not working ludicrously long hours, the remainder of his time was spent on the golf course.

'Haven't you heard the news this morning?' she asked impatiently, unable to envisage how anyone could start their day without automatically switching on their radio or television to find out what had been happening during those sleeping hours.

'I usually do, Nanette,' he said and she recognised the placating tone of voice which he had only fairly recently started to use when he was talking to her, 'but not so far today. I left the house early, having a lot of catching up to do. I've spent the last two days at the manor,' he explained, criticism creeping in with more than a touch of martyrdom, 'going through dad's papers, trying to pacify Mrs Plenderneath who is threatening to leave, coupled with a second session with the police. And tomorrow morning there's the inquest. Anyway, you said you were going to call on Sunday night when Alan got back, but you didn't. Or yesterday either.'

'For the simple reason, Alan didn't come home on Sunday, that's why, and yesterday, well as soon as he got in from work he had to go out again.'

'Don't tell me he's left you!'

'You're being facetious, Colin and it doesn't suit you,' she snapped, 'on Sunday after their course had finished a crowd of them had dinner at the hotel, a lot of wine apparently, and he thought it wiser to spend the night there and drive straight into work the following morning.'

'He phoned you, then?'

'Of course.'

'And,' he paused as though waiting for her to elaborate, 'did you tell him about dad?'

'Naturally, and of course he was shocked, but aren't you remotely interested to hear why I'm phoning?'

'I suppose so, but quite frankly what with everything else, not to mention an appointment scheduled for this afternoon with dad's lawyers, I am finding it difficult to concentrate on anything else, even on work, I may add, and I have one hell of a pile of it waiting for my attention. My urgent attention.' he added.

There were times when her brother could be utterly single-minded and she wondered how Rachel put up with him. With Colin, as it always had been, everything had to revolve around him. Anything else was extraneous and therefore of no significance, but paradoxically, he was easy to understand.

'There's been another murder, that's what.' she told him.

'What! You don't mean in Meadowbank?'

'Closer to home; in that no-man's land between the estate and Simon's place.'

'Hell!'

'It probably was for the poor man,' she said. She had his full attention at last, 'he was found last evening apparently.'

'Shot?'

'Like dad, you mean?'

'Yes.'

'Oh, no, he had been bludgeoned to death, Colin. At least that was what they said on the eight o'clock news.'

'Did they say who he was?'

'Yes, Len Roberts.'

'Not old Len, the poacher!'

'I don't think there are two in the neighbourhood, do you?'

'What else did they say? Did they say when it happened?'

'They didn't say much more, except he was killed around two or three o'clock on Sunday morning.'

'This is incredible, Nanette! I just cannot believe it!'

'I think you will have to, also, you can probably expect another visit from the police.'

'Why the hell should I?'

'Why the hell shouldn't you, Colin? Think about it. They already know you visited dad earlier on Saturday evening. I don't suppose you can prove to them you didn't go back there later. Need I say anymore?'

'I'll ask you one thing, Nanette.'

'Yes.'

'Do you honestly think I had anything to do with what happened to dad, or to Len either, if it comes to that?'

'Don't be stupid. Of course I don't, but then I'm your sister. The police, I would guess, will think quite differently. They are trained to be impartial, otherwise how would they ever be able to get to the bottom of all the flotsam and jetsam of what they have to go through to finally solve a case.'

'Thank you for your confidence.'

'There's no need to take that belligerent attitude. Surely it's up to the authorities to sort out all of this; that's what we pay our taxes for, isn't it?'

'It is so shocking; it really is, but you still haven't told me when you and Alan will be here.'

'No, I haven't, have I,' she said calmly, although she was very far from feeling in the least bit calm. Alan, not coming home when he said he would, had infuriated her, not that she would have admitted it to Colin, and then, last night when he eventually came in, they had hardly spoken. The boys being around had hampered any mention of what had happened and by the time they went to bed Alan had promptly fallen asleep, leaving her with the inevitable and increasingly frustrating realisation she had no idea of whether he would be going with her to Winchester or not. In fact, the few words they had exchanged when they had been on their own he had made no comment when she told him they needed to make a trip to Meadowbank. 'I'm sorry, Colin,' doing her best to be more amenable; after all it was not his fault she was married to a man who showed no interest in what was going on in his own home and little interest either in supporting his wife at a ghastly time like this, 'it's difficult here. Alan is terribly busy; I know that is no excuse, but I promise to try and pin him down when he gets home tonight and I'll give you a ring later. That's the best I can do.'

'Alright,' he sighed, 'I'm beginning to get the picture, Nanette, but even if Alan can't manage away, surely you can. As for the boys,' he went on and she knew he was trying to pre-empt any excuses he expected her to make, 'bring them with you. There's no problem in that, surely.'

'Normally, there wouldn't be,' Nanette answered, 'but I don't think you have thought this through properly. There has now been a second murder, practically in the same place and I do not think it would be a very good atmosphere for them. Also, don't you think the police will be crawling all over the place?'

'That hadn't occurred to me. This is positively bizarre!'

'It is, isn't? You took the words right out of my mouth. By the way, Colin,' she went on, 'before I ring off were you able to get through to Wendy on Sunday.'

'No, afraid not. I only got her answering machine. It was the same when I tried again yesterday. She must be away.'

'You didn't leave a message, then?'

'Nanette, what the hell do you take me for? What did you expect me to say? Dad has been murdered; you had better get the next plane back home prompto!'

'Okay, okay, there's no need to get on your high horse. I didn't mean you to actually break the news to her, but to ask her to get in touch as soon as she could.'

'Well, I didn't.'

'She has to be told, Colin. It could be some days before she hears officially and what about the funeral? Have you thought about that?'

'No, I haven't.' he groaned, and for a second she felt sorry to take such a tough line with him, but the feeling didn't last. It was time he faced facts and started to deal with the basic formalities. After all, he was always pointing out that he was the eldest. So, she rationalised, let him get on with what he should be doing. 'I'll have another go this afternoon, Nanette.'

'Good.'

An unsatisfactory conversation she thought as she replaced the receiver, but then often talking to Colin, especially on the phone, it was like this. She disliked intensely the role he always seemed to force her into; that of the hard-faced and practical woman when she was neither of these. All she wanted from life was tranquillity. Fat chance, she thought, picking up the mail from the hall and taking it into Alan's study. Mostly bills: electricity, gas, telephone, council tax and school fees. Why was it she wondered irritably they all arrived at the same time. Was it a devious scheme thought up by the various authorities to systematically undermine the equilibrium of the twenty-first century householder when, no sooner had one batch arrived, as this one had done, and before the ink was dry on the signature of each cheque, another equally demanding lot would be in the preparation stages for a repeat performance. And so it went on, she sighed. Life should not be as repetitive as this Nanette grumbled to herself, absentmindedly opening the monthly bank statement. It was not as if they were hard up; they always had expensive holidays each year, somewhere warm and exotic. Last year they had spent two glorious stress-free weeks in the Seychelles with not a golf course in sight and next month they would be in Hawaii. Alan earned a high salary from the financial consultancy firm he was with, far more than many of his friends and contemporaries; she had no reason to feel dissatisfied, but it was just the sheer tedium of it all which she found so terribly depressing.

Much later, when she had time to think about it, she was to question why she opened the envelope. She never had before; Alan always took care of the money side of their affairs and she almost put the statement back into its envelope, but it was not the closing balance, much lower than she would have expected which drew her attention, no doubt explained because his salary had yet to be credited to the account, but on glancing down to the various expenditures; all of them familiar, including the numerous cash amounts drawn by them both, one debit stood out. Not their monthly mortgage payment, although goodness knows that was staggering enough, but this amount was high, the date she saw was the first of the month. It was not a credit card payment, neither a cheque payment, therefore she concluded, a tight knot of anxiety beginning to form, it must be another standing order, but she didn't think so. Alan would have told her. Wouldn't he? She had to find out and there was no way she could wait until he came home. She knew she could phone the bank; it was a joint account after all, but she could not humiliate him like that. He would never forgive her. Instead, disliking the way her suspicious mind was working, she opened the top drawer of his desk and pulled out their statement folder, going back for the last twelve months and there it was again, on the first of each month; for one thousand pounds. When did all this start she wondered, but suddenly she was reluctant to go back any further, she had seen enough. Another woman? What else? Slowly, she closed the file, placing it back in the drawer, and putting the pile of mail on the desk as she always did with the bank statement on the top where he would see it as soon as he came into the room.

Nanette went back into the kitchen and, robot-like, filled the dishwasher with the breakfast things and made herself some fresh coffee. She needed time, space on her own to think this through, but it was impossible. She could hear the boys moving about upstairs; their high-spirited laughter floating down to her. She would have to take them out somewhere; the weather was far too good to stay at home all day. She would take them swimming and then somewhere to eat, knowing if put to the vote that somewhere would be 'Burger King', their current favourite eating place. The joys of motherhood she thought with resignation, but then she reminded herself it was what she had wanted and she did love her sons. If only she didn't have to spend so much time food shopping, cooking at regular intervals and perpetually tidying up after them; their cleaning lady did a good job, but she was no super-woman!

She realised she was also suffering from a large dose of guilt. Her father's sudden death had hit her hard, making her face the fact she had seen little of him over the last few years and although they had never been close, not like Wendy and he had been, she felt strangely isolated. No doubt she would eventually snap out of it and come to terms with the way things were now, not as they had been, nor what she had not done. It was too late to make amends for that.

'Come on, boys,' she called up the stairs, 'get your swimming things together, we're going out for the day and, do you think,' she added, knowing she was wasting her breath, 'you could make less noise. I can hear you above the vacuum cleaner!' and you are all giving me a headache she muttered under her breath.

Chapter Ten

Chief Inspector Brenda Masters pulled a fresh sheet of paper towards her and wrote the date at the top right-hand corner, underlining it twice as she always did at the start of each day. Such automatic actions, which she was well aware appeared pedantic to others, allowed her time to think, to mentally sort out her thoughts and put them into some semblance of order.

Meadowbank Police Station had recently undergone a major face lift. Open-plan offices with shoulder-high glass partitions; pine desks and matching swivel chairs had replaced the old regime of utility office furniture. Some of her colleagues, those who had worked there for years, felt uncomfortable with the changes, but not Brenda. She liked to feel part of what was going on and didn't find the constant background noises in the least bit disruptive. Looking up, she saw Sergeant Ash striding towards her work-station, his expression of chronic anxiety firmly in place.

'What have you got there, Ian?' she asked.

'The report from the London valuers. It's just been faxed in.'

'Yes?'

'They say three of the paintings are fakes.'

'Do they indeed.' all her senses immediately on alert. This was just the sort of development she had hoped for. 'I take it, that this wasn't their first valuation?'

'No, ma'am,' he said, 'that was carried out two weeks ago, Tuesday, the twenty-first of June, to be exact, and everything was in order then.'

'Well, I would say that narrows the time down quite well, wouldn't you?'

'I would, yes.'

'I think we need to find out a little more of the major's daily routine. He would have had one, I'm sure. I'd like you to go back there, Ian, have a word with the housekeeper, ask her a few questions, but don't alarm her. We don't want another case of hysterics on our hands.'

'Right; I'll find out whether there have been any visitors recently, shall I? That sort of thing.'

'Fine. We don't know when these forgeries were actually carried out, but whoever did it must be familiar with his gallery, must have known which pictures to target. It could be someone he had shown around or it could be someone who had learned about them. He or she may have had a key; remember, there was no sign of any break-in.'

'I know.'

'There's the fiancée. Nothing much is known about her. I'll go along and talk to her this morning.'

'She works for the same firm as the major's lawyers, I think.'

'Yes, she does, and while I'm there I'll make some enquiries about the will, at least find out the salient points; it may help.'

'Do you want me to get off to the manor now?'

'Shortly, Ian, but that aside for the moment,' Brenda Masters leaned back in her new leather-backed chair, 'let's recap, shall we? We have two sudden deaths and so far we are no further forward.'

'They must be connected, don't you think?'

'More than likely, but I don't want to jump to conclusions. It's important to keep a clear mind. I've known Len Roberts since I was a child; he was always around Meadowbank, mostly where he shouldn't have been. It is possible he may have seen something or someone that night. We now know he was attacked on the estate; he was a poacher after all, and if he had been setting any traps, he could have heard the shot being fired.'

'And somehow he managed to make his way through the hedge.'

'Well, that's right. Somewhat belatedly we've seen the evidence. The man left a trail of blood, for goodness sake. It is a great pity we hadn't been more thorough in examining outside the property, rather than concentrating on the inside.'

'We didn't think to do that, especially after what Miss Brent told us.'

'That's no excuse, sergeant. Talking about Miss Bren; we really should not dismiss her in any of this, you know.'

'You don't think she can be involved!'

'She could be. And by your expression, you obviously don't agree.'

'Bu - t,' he stammered, 'but, Chief Inspector, she and Steven Blackwood are divorced.'

'So they might be, but that fact doesn't completely exonerate her if he has anything to do with any of this.'

'I can't believe she's in cahoots with him.'

'Don't be taken in by a pretty face, Ian. Look, she leased the lodge, came down here from London and moved in on Saturday. The same day her ex-husband turns up on her doorstep. Why?'

'Well, he has a police record,' Ian said, 'perhaps he was trying to have a look round the manor, see how easy it would be to break in.'

'Yes, but remember, nobody *did* break in. And that leads me to anyone who would have a key.'

'Colin Tilsly.'

'Again, a possibility. He would have had numerous chances to switch the paintings; although you would need to be something of an art expert to do that. He would have had needed professional help, but, when you think about it, he did have an argument with his father earlier that evening and we only have his word for it he didn't return to the manor later.'

'That's true.'

'See what I mean about keeping an open mind Sergeant.'

'There's someone else.'

'Who?'

'Simon Grant.'

'Why?'

'He was a frequent guest at the manor; would know his way around the place.'

'A bit feeble. What about motive? Why would he have?'

'I suppose money.'

'But why choose now and I don't think he would be so stupid as to bungle it up the way it has been.'

'The motive would have to be money though, wouldn't it?'

'More than likely. It usually is. And that is why we need to find out about the will.'

'Major Tilsly was about to re-marry.' Ian reminded her, 'I wouldn't think his family would be too pleased about that.'

'Diluting their inheritance you mean?' she asked.

'Yes.'

'Do you know, sergeant,' the Chief Inspector smiled up at him, 'you may have a valid point there. So, let's see what we can achieve today, shall we?'

*

Brutton, Brutton & Brutton, an old established family firm of solicitors, was in the centre of Winchester, halfway along one of the cobbled streets running parallel to the cathedral and tucked tightly between an antique shop and an Italian restaurant Brenda Masters didn't remember seeing there before. She had still to meet Maureen Summers and wasn't sure whether she would be at work or not. Also, she had no idea either of how much the sudden death of the major had affected her, although the woman who came into the waiting room showed no visible signs of being deeply distressed. She struck Brenda as being someone very much in control: late forties, perhaps early fifties, Brenda judged; short dark hair smoothed a little too severely back from a high forehead;

intelligent grey eyes with incredibly long lashes; a slim figure, about her own height, but in spite of this brief assessment she did get the impression that here was a woman well accustomed to whatever life would throw at her. She had that calm aura of acceptance which gave nothing away; her personality was well hidden behind the invisible screen she may have had to build up over the years.

'Mrs Summers,' Brenda introduced herself, showing her the obligatory card, not missing the quick flutter of those eye lashes as she read it before silently handing it back to her, 'there are a few questions I would like to ask you, but first of all, I would like to say how sorry we were to hear about your fiancé's death.'

'Thank you, Chief Inspector.' the voice, low-pitched and matching her personality.

'How long have you worked here, Mrs Summers?' going for the gentle approach, not dismissing that this woman had recently been through a lot and it could be she was adept at bottling up her emotions.

'I've worked for the firm for thirty years;' she answered, 'after I left secretarial college. In fact,' she added with a smile which lit up her face, and for the first time Brenda Masters caught a glimpse of the beauty behind the mask, 'it's the only job I've ever had.'

'A long time.'

'I suppose it is, but I would never dream of moving anywhere else.'

'Major Tilsly was one of your firm's clients, I understand.'

'Yes, he was. As far as I know, he and his late wife had always been our clients.'

'I see,' the chief inspector said, not taking her eyes away from her face, 'and when did you last see Major Tilsly?'

'Last Friday,' she said, 'he had been in to see Mr Brutton earlier and we had lunch at the restaurant next door.'

'The Italian restaurant?'

'Yes, that's right.'

'It's new, I think?'

'Yes, it is.'

'So,' Brenda Masters continued, her verbal strategy already in gear, 'that was the last time you saw him, but did you speak to him after that? On Saturday, perhaps?'

'Yes,' she said, 'he phoned me in the evening, it was about seven o'clock. His neighbour, Simon Grant, had just left; he'd been in for a drink.'

'And how did Major Tilsly sound?'

'Actually, a little overwrought, but he said he was alright and just needed to sort out a few things with his son.'

'And he didn't elaborate?'

'No, he didn't.'

'And you didn't press him?'

'Of course not.' the first spark making its appearance. Was it irritation, Brenda wondered, or did she know why the major had sounded the way he had? Had she asked him? Could she be so complacent, so aloof to what was disturbing the man she planned to marry? 'You see, Chief Inspector,' Maureen Summers explained, 'it was like this; I don't think his family wanted him to get married again, but I found that a perfectly normal reaction. Why should they? Reginald had been a widower for a long time; they had become used to not having a mother, so their dislike of me arriving on the scene was really quite understandable. At least that was the way I thought.'

'Were they openly hostile towards you then?'

'Not at all. I had only met two of his children a couple of times and this was fairly recently, but a woman can sense animosity, a general air of disapproval. Surely you can understand that yourself, Chief Inspector?'

'How well do you know the manor, Mrs Summers? What I mean is, were you a frequent visitor?'

'It may surprise you to hear I have never been there; Reginald and I usually met here; in Winchester, although he did take me to Meadowbank a couple of times, but not to the manor.'

'How unusual.'

'I didn't think so. It was Reginald, the man, I was planning to marry. I really had no interest in any of the material trappings. He understood how I felt. We had plenty of time for that, or so I thought –' she broke off, and for the first time Brenda detected the strain she was under and how valiantly she was making every effort to overcome what could only be grief, but, Brenda rationalised, her job was not to sympathise. That was for others. She had to remain impartial and completely impersonal. What she thought of Maureen Summers was really neither here nor there. This was a murder enquiry she was conducting. A double murder enquiry. And that was the way it had to be.

'So,' she asked, keeping her voice casual, 'you didn't have a key to the manor?'

'I did not.' The second little spark. She was beginning to get through to her and this was what she wanted, but for the moment she felt she had gone far enough.

'Thank you for your time, Mrs Summers,' Brenda said, 'and I apologise if I have caused you any further distress. It wasn't my attention, but we need to get to the bottom of what happened, you understand?'

'I understand.' Maureen Summers said quietly.

Chapter Eleven

'I cannot tell you how distraught we were, Colin, when we heard the dreadful news about your father. I knew him well, for many years in fact. We both went back a long time; to our university days. I will miss him.'

'It was a shock.'

I don't believe I am having this conversation Colin thought to himself. Here he was; sitting in front of the senior partner of Brutton, Brutton & Brutton on a warm afternoon in July when he should really be in his own office, not having this discussion about his father who had recently been murdered. The situation was surreal. He had known Arnold Brutton since he was a young boy; he remembered him spending evenings at the manor playing endless games of chess with his father. My God, he thought, that seems a lifetime away!

'Naturally it's been a shock, Colin. And what about your sisters?'

'As you can imagine, Nanette just cannot take it in yet, but I haven't been able to get hold of Wendy. You know she's living in Hong Kong?'

'I do, yes, your father told me. She's working for one of the big publishing houses over there, I believe. You say you can't contact her?'

'Yes, I've been trying since Sunday, but there's been no reply so far.'

'Does she have an answering machine?'

'She does, but Mr Brutton, I didn't feel it was right to leave a message like this. I would much rather speak to her personally.'

'Understandable, of course, but I rather think you should. She would want to attend the funeral.'

'I know. I'll try again this afternoon.'

'Would you like me to? She may be away, but it is possible she has a friend looking after her apartment and perhaps they could get in touch with her. Everybody, I'm told,' he added with an old-fashioned smile, 'owns a mobile phone these days.'

'I'd be grateful,' Colin said, 'I'm not opting out, you understand, but quite frankly, Mr Brutton I don't know how I would begin to break the news to her. My father and Wendy were very close.'

'I know. I know. So, don't worry about that, Colin. I'm sure you have enough to contend with at the moment. Now, is there anything else I can help you with?'

'There is as a matter of fact,' taking a deep breath; here it is he thought, hoping he wasn't going to mess things up. The last thing he wanted to do was to give the wrong impression. He didn't want Arnold Brutton to think he only had one thing on his mind and that was money. He did, of course, and he wasn't proud of himself. But, desperate times, he told himself, meant desperate measures and he had to make inroads into finding out how his inheritance lay, 'it's about my father's art collection.'

'Ah.' One word. This was going to be more difficult than he thought. The lines he noticed around Arnold Brutton's mouth had tightened and he did not imagine the way his eyes narrowed as he peered short-sightedly at him across the desk.

'When I last spoke to him,' Colin began, already beginning to regret opening his mouth in the first place, 'he told me he had decided to donate the whole collection to the Tate Gallery.'

'That's exactly what he did arrange, Colin.'

'I've been through the papers in my father's desk and I haven't been able to find any evidence of this agreement, not even a listed catalogue of the paintings. Also, not one single invoice stating when he bought them and how much he paid for them.'

'No, you wouldn't, Colin,' Arnold Brutton said, 'because your father lodged all the relevant paperwork with us. Each time he made a purchase, he dealt with one of the main auctioneers and valuers in London and we handled the transaction.'

'Why on earth would he have done that?'

'It isn't all that unusual, you know.' he answered calmly, 'we have a number of clients who entrust their financial portfolios to us and your father was no exception. You may have heard him say many times he had no head for figures.'

'But.' he had to think quickly, he knew he was close to overstepping the line between professionalism and a long friendship, but he couldn't stop now; he had to continue. 'But, Mr Brutton,' attempting a placating tone, 'surely those paintings belong to the family?'

'Belong is not quite the right word, Colin, in relation to the family. They belonged to your father, exclusively.' he added.

'When did he start collecting them, Mr Brutton?'

'Nineteen seventy-five.'

'While my mother was still alive?'

'That's right, yes.'

'But – '

' – allow me to stop you there, Colin, before you say something you may regret. You'd left home by the time your mother died and, as far as I know, you never saw a copy of her will.'

'No.'

'She left the entire estate to your father, Colin, with the proviso that in the event of her pre-deceasing him, he would make adequate provisions for the three of you, which I may say, he did.'

'But –' Colin repeated, and recognising when he was losing; he had been down this particular road too many times in the past not to recognise the signs, painful and familiar as they were. 'the collection; he hasn't bequeathed it to us?'

'No, he wanted to donate it in its entirety and this is included in the will. He has left you all a generous inheritance.'

'There is no way we can contest the will, then.'

'No, there isn't, Colin. Please listen to me, I can see how distressed you are, especially given the manner in which your father died and naturally disappointed over his bequest, but it was his wish and I can assure you it will be carried out. To the letter.'

'I see,' Colin took a deep breath, trying to lessen the tightness in his chest, 'and may I ask what provisions he has made for the woman he had planned to marry.'

'I am sorry, Colin, that is something I am not in a position to divulge. After the funeral, we will all meet. Hopefully, Wendy will be back by then, and I will read out the full contents of your father's will and, incidentally,' he paused for a moment, by now his thin lips set in a straight line and there was no friendly expression on the face he had known for so long, 'Mrs Summers will be with us on that day.'

There was no point prolonging the meeting and after a cool handshake he left the office, walking slowly along the carpeted passageway back to reception. So, this Maureen person was going to benefit after all. By how much he wondered; the thought leaving a sour acrid taste at the back of his throat. The door to the waiting room he noticed was open slightly and he recognised Brenda Masters. My God! That woman is like a snake! What the hell is she here for? And who is she talking to, but he didn't need two guesses to answer that one. The soft and, to him, simpering voice of Maureen Summers, described so succinctly by Rachel on Sunday as his father's intended! Not wanting to speak to either of them, he quickly left the building.

Well, Colin, he thought walking back to where he had parked the car, you well and truly messed that up! Why was all of this being left to him to sort out; the bitter thoughts following him on the short drive home. He'd had every intention of asking that mean dried-up old skinflint for an advance; the very thought making him cringe. That would have been the ultimate in crassness!

Chapter Twelve

Mrs Plenderneath was sweeping the front steps when Sergeant Ash turned up at the manor. Although noticeably startled to see him she appeared calm enough; that stricken, glazed look which had permeated her features on Sunday had gone; now she merely looked tired and there was, he noticed, a wariness in her eyes which was new. He had seen her many times over the years. Melissa and he had been in the same class in junior school and he remembered seeing her aunt waiting outside the railings for the school to finish, but the woman who stood nervously at the bottom of the steps watching him climb out of the car bore little resemblance to that other one who had laughed as Melissa had skipped and jumped ahead of her along the pavement. It had been, he thought sadly, a long time since she had laughed like that. As he had been told, he would tread carefully with her.

'Sorry to bother you, Mrs Plenderneath,' he said, closing the car door and walking up to her, 'but there are one or two questions I need to ask. It won't take too long.'

'That's alright,' managing a smile, perhaps remembering him, although it was unlikely, he thought, walking alongside her towards the back door of the manor; twenty years was a long time. 'I was going to make myself a coffee, Sergeant, would you like one?'

Encouraged, he followed her into the kitchen and hoping it might be possible he could learn something which just may impress the chief inspector; prove to her he was capable of conducting a productive interview, not a silent sergeant hanging on to her every word and, worst of all, feeling he always had to agree with her. Sergeant Ash had no illusions. He knew he had a lot to learn. He did admire Chief Inspector Brenda Masters, but wished he didn't have this continual impression she found him lacking. This was his first murder case and he wanted to conduct his part in the procedures methodically and intelligently. What was it she had said? Don't jump to conclusions. Well, he would try not to, but it was not easy, he grumbled to himself, sitting down at the much-scrubbed kitchen table and taking out his note-book.

'I need to write down a few points, Mrs Plenderneath,' he explained, noticing her nervousness returning; the way the worn fingers plucked at the side of her apron, 'nothing for you to be worried about; it is so I'll remember what we've been talking about.'

He waited while she poured out the coffee, neatly arranging digestive biscuits on a plate, recognising the 'Willow' design which reminded him of some his grandmother had owned.

'What I'm trying to do,' he went on, when she had finally stopped fidgeting and was sitting down across the table from him, 'is to establish Major Tilsly's daily routine. To get some idea of how he spent his time.'

'I see,' she said, 'that doesn't sound too difficult.'

'No, I'm sure it won't be.' he said quietly, 'You've worked for the family for a long time, haven't you?'

'Yes, ever since I left school, that's more than fifty years ago now.'

'So you must know them all very well?'

'Well, I did when the children were young, but you know how it is, Sergeant, especially these days, when families seem to grow apart.'

'I know,' he smiled encouragingly, 'so, only the major lived here?'

'Yes,' she said, 'Wendy was the last of them to leave home and, since then, he's been on his own.'

'They didn't visit him very often?'

'No, they didn't,' a tiny edge of indignation creeping into her voice, 'mind you, Wendy is living in Hong Kong now, but, before then, she used to come down from London most weekends, but as for Colin and Nanette, months could go by when we never saw them.'

'But, they're married, aren't they, with families of their own?'

'True,' she agreed, but with not too much enthusiasm.

'What about visitors, Mrs Plenderneath?' he prompted, arriving at last to the point he wanted, 'Did he have many?'

'Over the last few years, no, although recently there had been quite a few.'

'Friends?'

'One or two were old friends, going back many years, but the others, no. They were only interested in those pictures of his.'

'The art collection.'

'Yes, he was very proud of that, you know, liked nothing better than showing people round, those who were interested, I mean.'

'I've been in the room where he had them of course. A quite splendid collection.'

'I suppose it is,' she said, 'although I think recently he had lost interest in it; he hardly ever went in there.'

'Really?'

'Yes, and then only when someone came to see him.'

'Can you remember anything about these people, Mrs Plenderneath?'

'That's difficult. I'm not sure.'

'Sorry, but for instance, when was the last person here? That might make it easier for you to remember.'

'It was that young man from abroad.'

'Yes?' another gentle prompt, but at the same time trying to keep the flow of ready information in control, not wanting to overlook anything, also to remember the chief inspector's advice.

'He came here twice. Two days running in fact; last Thursday and then again on Friday.'

'How did you know he came from abroad? Did the major tell you?'

'Oh, no, it was Melissa. I'd called in at the 'Market Inn' after I had finished work here on Friday, shortly after six I think it would have been, and I mentioned the young man to her.'

'And she knew who you meant?'

'Yes,' the first smile, 'you see, he was very handsome, he reminded me of that actor, Robert Redford.'

'I see.' Ian didn't really, but he was prepared to wait for enlightenment.

'And,' she went on, 'Melissa had thought exactly the same when she booked him in at the inn'.

'Did she say when that was?'

'Yes, the day before, Thursday afternoon. It must have been after he left here because he called about two; the major had just finished his lunch and I was clearing away, that's why I remember the time.'

'Do you think Major Tilsly was expecting him?'

'I don't think he was; now you come to mention it.'

'And you say he was here again the next day?'

'Yes.'

'And was he expected that time?'

'No, he wasn't. I heard the major swear under his breath, but he made a good attempt to hide his irritation.'

'But he took him into his gallery all the same?'

'Yes, that's right, but Major Tilsly couldn't stay long; he had an appointment in Winchester that morning.'

'What happened then, Mrs Plenderneath,' Ian asked her, wondering if what she was going to tell him would have any significance, 'did this mean the man had to curtail his visit?'

'Oh, no, not at all.'

'You mean he was allowed to stay in the room on his own?'

'Yes, he was there for most of the morning and he left before the major returned.'

'Was this quite usual, giving a virtual stranger such freedom?'

'It wasn't, but in spite of his annoyance at being disturbed I think the major quite took to the young man. He had one of those small computers with him; I can't remember what you call them –' she paused for a moment.

'A laptop?' helping her out.

'Yes, a laptop. Melissa has one, but, of course, I have no idea how they work.'

'Did you actually see him using it?'

'Yes, I did,' she answered, 'I took him in a cup of coffee about eleven and he was sitting at the table and I noticed it was on. He looked very industrious; I hardly liked to disturb him. I thought to myself, he might work for a university or somewhere like that.'

'It's possible,' Ian agreed, his mind working overtime and trying to think the best way to move forward. This visitor may have been perfectly genuine; someone with a keen interest in paintings, whether in connection with his work or for his own personal pleasure, at this stage it was impossible to say, 'and presumably,' he went on, 'he had a case to put his laptop in?'

'Oh, yes. Real leather it was, too.'

'I see,' he said, 'you've mentioned this one man in particular, Mrs Plenderneath,' he said, deciding it was unlikely he was going to glean anything further from her, at the same time trying to curb the thought it could have been feasible during the time he was there on the Friday to switch the three paintings. It sounded as though he only had the one interruption when she took him a coffee, 'but,' he continued, 'were there any other visitors around this time?'

'Well,' she answered slowly, 'he was the only one last week, but there were the two men from the valuers in London. They came here the week before, on the Tuesday and again yesterday morning.'

'Yes,' Ian nodded, 'We heard they were here.'

'Did you?' a look of surprise crossing her face, 'Major Tilsly had already told me they would be returning. Little did I know he wouldn't –' she faltered, her eyes instantly filling with tears.

'It's alright, Mrs Plenderneath;' he said quietly, 'talking about this is obviously causing you considerable distress; perhaps it would be best if I didn't ask you any more questions.'

'No, no, Sergeant,' she answered, wiping her eyes with the corner of her apron, 'I want to do all I can to help you, I really do.'

'If you're sure?'

'I'm sure.' managing a smile.

'So,' Sergeant Ash took a deep breath, not displeased with what he had learned so far, 'in recent weeks there were no other visitors. No more people interested in the major's collection?'

'No, I don't think there were.'

'What about telephone calls?'

'Pardon?'

'Were you in the habit of taking any calls or did the major take them?'

'He always preferred to answer the phone himself, so I would let it ring two or three times and when he didn't answer I did.'

'And can you remember, perhaps recently, any of those calls you took?'

'Not really,' she paused, wrinkling her brow once more as she tried to remember, 'Colin phoned, that was Saturday morning, but no-one else. Not that I recall.'

'Not the young man you've mentioned?'

'No, I don't think so.'

'Mrs Plenderneath,' he went on, 'these visitors you've mentioned, not many it's true, but they are all male. What about any ladies who may have telephoned?'

'I suppose you mean Mrs Summers?'

'The major's fiancée?'

'Yes.'

'Did you speak to her recently?'

'No, I didn't, Sergeant. If she did call, and she most probably did, he would have taken any of those himself. I know the lady works fulltime and perhaps she would phone him in the evenings, and I would have finished for the day by then.'

'And no lady visitors?'

'No,' she said slowly, 'oh, just a minute, how stupid of me, you've just reminded me! He did have a telephone call from that French woman. That was about the middle of last week. I can't remember which day, but it was around six, I was about to leave and I was in the hall when the phone rang so I picked up the receiver.'

'You say French woman? Have you any idea who she was?' he asked, his pulse quickening. Was this important he wondered, or wasn't it?

'Yes, Mrs Taylor; from the 'Salmon's Rest'.'

'You're sure it was her?'

'I'm quite sure. After all, there is only one French woman in Meadowbank!'

And with that enigmatic reply he had to be content.

It was almost lunchtime when he got back to Meadowbank and managing with unusual ease to find a parking place in the square, he walked the few hundred yards to the 'Market Inn'.

'Hello, Ian,' Melissa called out to him as soon as he went inside, remembering in time to duck below the low lintel above the door, 'is this business or pleasure?'

'A bit of both,' he smiled at her. How pretty she was, her hair tied back in a long pony-tail and looking about sixteen! Brian Morrison was a lucky man.

'I thought as much,' she said, 'but first things first, what are you having to drink?'

'Half a lager, please, Melissa and one of your Ploughman's.'

'Okay, won't take long,' she answered, expertly pouring out his beer, 'and the business side, Ian; do you want to speak to Brian?'

'No, not really,' he said, thinking how odd it sounded to his ears to be addressed by his Christian name. There were times, he thought cynically, when he was only known as Sergeant Ash, except for the rare occasion when the chief inspector decided to use it; his true identity forgotten in this town, a town where he had been born and brought up. 'I'd like some information about one of your guests. Apparently, he booked in here last Thursday.'

'I think I know who you mean. Who wouldn't,' she smiled again, 'he was fantastic looking!'

'So I believe,' Ian Ash replied, wishing for a moment he could relax and wasn't on duty, but he was and he would have to put up with it, 'all I need is his name, address —'

'— as to his address,' she interrupted quickly, 'he only gave 'The Piccadilly Hotel' in London. He told me he was over here from Singapore for a few days on business, but I'll get his name for you, Ian, and the registration number of the car,' she added, 'if you think that may be any help.'

'I hope so,' he said, realising it was too much to hope he would get anything else. But he would still have to go through the motions of trying to find out as much about the man as he could. If his name proved a no-no, there was a good chance he would be able to trace the car.

'Here you are, Ian,' Melissa said, coming back to the bar, 'I've written the details down for you. His name was Anthony Appleyard and his car, at least I think he'd hired it; there was a sticker in the back window of a car hire company, but not one I recognised. It wasn't Hertz or Budget or one of the well known ones.'

'And when did he leave?'

'Sunday afternoon, around two o'clock. I was outside serving when he drove off.'

'You didn't happen to notice which road he took, did you, Melissa?'

'Well,' she said thoughtfully, a tiny frown appearing on her forehead, 'he didn't take the Stockbridge Road, that's for sure; I thought he might be going in the direction of Winchester to join the motorway. Sorry, Ian, to sound so vague.'

'There's nothing to be sorry about, Melissa, you've given me enough to be getting on with.'

'Do you know,' she said, 'it was weird, all the time he was here, he hardly spoke to anyone and didn't even sit at the bar.'

'Unsociable guy, eh?'

'Definitely.'

'By the way, how did he pay? By credit card?'

'No, cash.'

Once again, too much to hope for he thought, his spirits dropping a further notch. There certainly weren't going to be any shortcuts here, or lucky breaks either. He had been told in the early days when he was first recruited into the force that police work was, in the main, one hard, often tedious slog, but sometimes perseverance paid off. So, this man: a Robert Redford lookalike by all accounts, had spent three nights at the 'Market Inn', a non-sociable type, preferring to sit on his own as far away from the other customers as he could and paid his bill in cash. And, apart from his two visits to the manor, sketchy though they were, that was all he had. Pulling out his mobile he gave the station a ring and asked them to do a check on the car. And then there was Danielle Taylor to question, but at this point he decided he would wait until he spoke to the Chief Inspector. He didn't want to drop any clangers. From what he had heard around the town she was not the easiest of women to approach and would certainly object to a mere sergeant asking why she had telephoned Major Tilsly. Brenda Masters, he was confident, would be able to handle her. No problem.

Chapter Thirteen

'That man's phoned again today, Peter.'

'What man?'

'He didn't give his name, or I should say, wouldn't! What does he want, do you think?'

'I've no idea. Selling something I expect.'

'He was most persistent.'

'Salesmen usually are, Danielle. They have to be; otherwise they would never sell anything.'

'He didn't sound like a salesman to me.'

'Well, until he phones again and I speak to him, we won't know, will we?'

'There was one thing though which I found puzzling.'

'Yes?'

'We've been married for six years.'

'Yes.' Exercising as much patience as he could manage and wondering where she was coming from this time.

'And not once,' she went on, 'have I ever heard anyone refer to you as Pete.'

'And he did?'

'Yes, he did, so who is he, Peter; somebody from your mysterious past?'

He let that one go. She was goading him. Danielle knew practically nothing about what he had been doing before they had met, but over the years it hadn't stopped her making wild speculations, as she was doing right this minute. She had known the company he had been working for in London, but as far as he was aware, that was all she knew. She didn't know how long he had been with them. Four miserable years, he recalled bitterly, although he had to admit somewhat fortuitously it had turned out reasonably lucrative, but as always in his life, it had been time to move on and marrying Danielle had been a sensible decision. She had recently opened her own restaurant in Bond Street and with her own money, having sold up in Paris. No finance required for Danielle Le Breton, as she had been called then.

'Quite frankly, Peter, I didn't like the sound of him one little bit.' she persisted. Would she never let up, give him some much-needed space to think. It had been many years since anyone had called him Pete and, more recently, only a handful of close friends, if you could describe them as such he thought wryly, and certainly no-one from this back of beyond place.

'Forget it, Danielle. I'm sure it isn't important.'

'Oh, I intend to,' she replied, shrugging her shoulders in that aggravating way she had, 'I have far too much to do. In case it may have slipped your mind, Peter, we have a party of twelve booked for this evening.'

'I haven't forgotten,' he sighed, wishing he was anywhere but in the 'Salmon's Rest', in the middle of this hick town and at the brunt end of the constant naggings and demands of a discontented wife.

He finally escaped upstairs to the room he used as his office; there were a few bills which needed to be paid. He would write out the cheques and, as an excuse, albeit a feeble one, wander across to the post office and then drive up to the 'The Royal Oak' for a quick drink. The last thing he wanted was to get into conversation with Brian Morrison and to hear again his pathetic renderings of the recent events in Meadowbank.

Peter got as far as writing the first cheque when the phone rang. Not wanting Danielle to take the call downstairs, he quickly picked up the receiver.

'The Salmon's Rest.'

'Hello, Pete.'

'What the hell do you want?' instantly recognising the voice, a surge of unease coursing through his brain.

'Tut. Tut. That's a fine welcome for your old friend.'

'You are no friend of mine! Get to the point, man! Why are you phoning me?'

'I would have thought that would have been obvious; surely I don't need to spell it out to you, Pete? You used to be pretty quick on the uptake, in fact the last time we met you were just a shade too bloody quick! To my cost I may add.'

'So?' his heart beat returning to normal. He could deal with this. The way he had always done in the past. A damn nuisance, just when he had managed to achieve a well-earned equilibrium to his life. He did not need this! This intrusion!

'So,' he mimicked, 'to put it bluntly, I want my share, Pete. And, before you say anything, I don't need a crystal ball to tell me you would have raked in a fair amount from that last haul. As I said I want my share. Fifty-fifty. That's what we always agreed, in case you've had a lapse of memory.'

'The situation has changed.'

'You bet it has! I'll give you until Thursday to get the funds together.'

'How much?'

'Now you're talking! A hundred thousand and we'll call it quits.'

'It will take more time to get that much together.'

'Don't give me that! If you don't, the consequences could destroy the nice respectable niche you've made for yourself in Meadowbank, not to mention how the beautiful Parisian will re-act!'

'How do you know about Danielle?'

'I've had a lot of time on my hands recently. Remember? Time to devote exclusively to research and, my word, I must admit I didn't expect to dig up quite so much!'

'Okay.' He had to get him off the phone. Danielle could pick up the receiver at any moment. She would have noticed he was still on the line and by now her curiosity must be increasing by the second. 'I'll see what I can do. Where do we meet?'

'We'll meet half-way. Neutral territory you might say: the M3 service station at Basingstoke,' he went on, 'Thursday afternoon, three-thirty. I'll be waiting for you inside the coffee shop.'

'Just a minute; I won't be able to leave here in time. It's not –' but he had rung off and there was no way he would be able to find him. He had been trapped. Well and truly cornered and this time, he thought grimly, it was going to take more than his in-built ability to extricate himself. He had no choice. He had to go through with it.

*

Nanette thought the day would never come to an end. Her mind had been on overdrive from the moment the boys had clambered into the back seat of the car, followed by what seemed to be a ridiculous pile of gear for a few hours at the pool. The obligatory meal at 'Burger King', where she watched the pair of them wolf down an extraordinary amount of food: hamburgers oozing with tomato ketchup; French fries with more ketchup and as if that wasn't enough to re-fuel them, double portions of vanilla and strawberry ice creams stabbed with two chocolate flakes. So much for the latest trend for healthy eating, but for once it didn't matter. She needed them to be pre-occupied while she mentally hovered on the periphery: this way they were happy. No questions of what shall we do next, mum!

At last, they were home, after stopping off to rent a video for them. She had already determined Alan and she would have this evening to themselves. She'd prepared a chicken casserole and all she had to do was switch on the oven. Hoping the boys wouldn't take it as a precedent during the long summer holiday, she made them a plateful of their favourite sandwiches: Heinz sandwich spread, and told them they could eat their supper in the lounge and get square-eyed watching a re-make of 'Casino Royale'. She knew what they liked to watch; they were still young enough to enjoy the simple, somewhat fantastic chase and inevitable survival of James Bond and it didn't really matter to either of them which actor was playing the part. She was sure, although she had never bothered to ask them, they could not tell the difference between Sean Connery, Roger Moore, Timothy Dalton or whoever! He was James Bond and that was all that mattered to them.

She had opened a bottle of Chardonay when she heard the car pulling up outside the house. He was back. She must try to conduct what she had to say to him as calmly as she could, although as the front door opened, she realised the next couple of hours would not be easy, but whatever happened, whatever his explanation was going to be, she must not lose her temper.

'Hi!' he said, coming into the kitchen. 'On your own? Where are the boys?'

'In the lounge watching another James Bond. A special treat for them this evening, Alan.' she explained looking up at him and with a jolt realised just how much she loved this husband of hers. Perhaps she had taken him too much for granted, focusing too much on the children. But she didn't want to think like this; why should she? Putting herself in the wrong!

'Which one is this?'

'Casino Royale.'

'Ah, wouldn't mind watching that myself,' he said, 'so it's just the two of us for supper, then. Smells good.' he added, going over to the stove. 'Chicken, eh?'

'You're right. A glass of wine, Alan, or would you prefer a beer?'

'Wine, please,' he said sitting down and loosening his tie, 'another stifling day! Far too hot to spend in the city wearing a shirt and tie! We should be on holiday, Nanette, where we could all enjoy splashing about in the sea and you wouldn't have to spend so much time cooking. Next month, eh? I should be able to get away by then alright.'

'I'd like that, Alan.'

'What's wrong, sweetheart,' he asked, leaning forward and covering her hands with his, 'something's troubling you?'

How she wanted to put her arms around his neck and be reassured, but she resisted the temptation. Taking a sip of her wine, she gently put the glass back on the table and took a deep breath, all the time aware of the concern in his eyes.

'I could be making something out of nothing, Alan,' she began, 'but this morning, I wasn't thinking, I opened our bank statement.'

'Ah.'

'I wasn't prying, you must realise that.'

'I know, Nanette, that isn't your way.'

'Well, I expect you know what I'm going to say,' she said, finding it inordinately difficult to spell out her suspicions, to even hint at them, but she had to, 'the withdrawal of a thousand pounds, Alan. Not just for this month, but for several months. You didn't tell me about this, so I –'

'– so you thought the worse.'

'Well, I did, yes. Is there someone else?' she whispered.

'I can put your mind at rest on that immediately, Nanette,' he said, 'there has only ever been you.'

'What's the money for then?'

'I could tell you a lie, you realise that, don't you?'

'I want the truth, Alan.'

'You're not going to like this.' he was warning her.

'I don't suppose I am, but I think I have a right to know.'

'Of course you do.' he sighed, refilling both their glasses. 'First of all, I make no excuses for what I've done, Nanette; I've been extremely stupid. In a nutshell, I used some of our clients' money for my own personal gain.'

'How?'

'It wasn't difficult,' he said quietly, 'too damned easy in fact. These clients of ours entrust their portfolios with us to enable us to either buy or sell shares on their behalf. We, at least a few of us, have direct access to their accounts, but unfortunately, Nanette, I overstepped the mark. Those amounts I speculated with invariably yielded profits and I'm truly ashamed to say I kept that profit, siphoned it off into a fictitious account and returned the amounts I had used back to their accounts.'

'So they were none the wiser.'

'No, they weren't. It's extremely rare for a client to request a day-by-day account of what is happening to their shares.'

'I understand, but what did you do if any of your speculating made losses?'

'That didn't happen often, but when it did I had sufficient funds in the account I had created.'

'Alan,' she said, 'I need to know whether you are still doing this.'

'No, I'm not. This happened some time ago. Six years actually and after a couple of months I stopped because I realised what I was doing was wrong. Also, I was beginning to find it difficult to live with the person I had become. Self-disgust had crept in, Nanette.'

'And this thousand pounds each month? You're being blackmailed, aren't you?'

'Yep. One of my colleagues literally caught me in the act. It was one evening when I was supposed to be working late and he came into the office. I had no idea at the time that he guessed what I was doing. He never so much as gave me a hint, Nanette, so I began to relax, sure that I had got away with it.'

'But you hadn't?'

'No, you see, he left the company shortly afterwards and I thought that would be the end of that, but just over a year ago he got in touch with me and that's when this nightmare really started.'

'And now?' she pressed, appalled at what he'd told her. Alan, her husband, was not a gambler. If it had been Colin facing her across the kitchen table at this moment confessing – hold it here she told herself – her brother, as far as she was aware, never confessed to anything. It wasn't in his make-up, but Alan, a far more sensitive man, one who had always from the very first moment when they had met in a noisy wine bar in Kensington, come across as basically honest. But, she tried to rationalise, this was not the time to judge him, there would be no point. It was so apparently obvious to her that he was already suffering from what he had done. Not last week, nor last month, but six years ago. She thought back to that time: the year of the millennium, when everyone was hyping themselves up to the start of the new century; when parties were being planned, vast sums of money were being spent for fun. And Alan and she had been no different from the rest of their friends. They had held a party, inviting practically everyone they knew and they all required refreshments. And masses of it; their dining room table literally groaning with food she had spent days preparing and she remembered being stunned at how much their wine bill had come to. Perhaps, and she was not reducing in importance of what Alan had been doing around that time, but perhaps knowing about the forthcoming phenomenal expenditure at the end of that year, had triggered off this madness. It was possible. But now was not the time to question him and try to analyse things and deep down she knew she never would.

'Now, sweetheart?' he sighed again, leaning back in the chair, 'He wants more.'

'Greedy.'

'Blackmailers are, I suppose. A great pity I hadn't realised that before giving in to him in the first place.'

'You're not going to pay him anymore, are you?'

'Do I really have an option?'

'I think you do.'

'I always thought I would have to keep paying up —'

'- living with this scumbag hanging over our heads for the rest of our lives!'

'You think I should come clean, don't you. Tell the company?'

'That is one possibility,' she said slowly, not sure what his reaction was going to be, 'but there is another option.'

'Is there?' genuine surprise written across his face as he waited for her to go on.

'Well,' she began tentatively, 'you could stop paying him.'

'Do you know, that never occurred to me.'

'That's because you've been struggling with all of this on your own. But when you come to think about it, what could he actually do?'

'Expose me,' he answered, 'that's what he threatened to do.'

'What, by getting in touch with the company? And how effective would that be? Would they believe him?'

'He also said he would be putting you in the picture.'

'Well, that part is redundant now, isn't it, Alan?'

'True, but —'

'- just say,' she interrupted him, 'just say, if he did tell them, after all this time, do you honestly think they would take him seriously?'

'They might.'

'But, surely they would ask him why he had taken so long?'

'Yes -,' he hesitated and for the first time since this conversation had started, she noticed a change in his expression: that awful dead look of despair was dissipating and she felt encouraged.

'Six years is a long time. Do you think anyone could prove what you'd done? And, have you thought of this, Alan; could they actually prove you had been in any way involved?'

'As to that, Nanette, you're probably right, although by back-tracking they would see various transactions leaving those accounts and then days later being replaced by the same amount each time.'

'Alright,' she was now the practical one, trying to show him there was a different way of looking at things. A position she had never been in before, but then, there had never been any need. Alan was the breadwinner, always had been; he was the one who paid the bills, while she had been quite happy to give up a career and one which didn't particularly satisfy her, to look after the family, 'that aside for the moment.' she went on, 'Blackmail is a criminal offence, isn't it?'

'Of course it is.'

'There you are then, you can always report *him*, you know, Alan.'

'He would know I would never do that.'

'Perhaps. Where does he live by the way? You've never said.'

'I was hoping you wouldn't ask me that.'

'Why?' she gave a quick burst of laughter before covering her mouth apologetically with her hand, suddenly seeing the funny side in spite of the potential seriousness of their situation. And the situation did belong to both of them. She was with him all the way; they would sort all of this out together and there was no doubt in Nanette's mind that it wouldn't be resolved. 'He doesn't live next door, does he!'

'It's not funny, Nanette.'

'I know it isn't, my darling,' she said, getting to her feet and putting her arms around him, drawing his face close to her, aware for the first time how thin he had become. For too long she had been blaming him for neglecting her and the boys, but she had been wrong, realising she was the one who had been guilty of neglect. She had been in danger of wallowing in self-pity; the hard done-by little stay-at-home wife, a role she had willingly created for herself. 'I'm with you on this, you know.'

'You are truly a rock, sweetheart,' he said, 'I don't deserve such loyalty.' his voice muffled against her neck.

'Nonsense,' she said gently, finally pulling away from him, 'we'll manage to sort this out, Alan. Both of us will.' she emphasised, sitting down again.

'Okay,' he said, running a hand through his hair making it stand on end, 'so that's what you think we should do? Put a stop to the payments?'

'I do, darling,' she agreed, stretching out a hand to smooth back his hair, 'so where does this character live then?'

'In Meadowbank.'

'No! I don't believe it!'

'He and his wife bought the 'Salmon's Rest' restaurant about six months ago. He told me he was leaving London, probably thought I would have no idea where Meadowbank was.'

'What a coincidence though.'

'It is, yes, but I'm sure we don't need to read anything significant into this.'

'So, does he know who you're married to; me being a Tilsly, I mean?'

'I'm sure he doesn't. As far as I know he's never seen us together and I only saw him the once after he'd left the company; he'd called me at the office and we met in the pub round the corner. I've tried a number of times to see him, but he's always refused.'

'You could have gone to the restaurant, Alan. He would have had to see you then.'

'I know, but I didn't want you involved, Nanette.'

'And of course neither of us has been to Meadowbank for ages. I feel so guilty about that, you know. I can't even remember when I was last at the manor, it must be at least a year, and now with Dad –'

'– Listen, sweetheart,' he said softly, 'I do know how you feel. We've both been too pre-occupied. Me, with my work and spending far too much time either on the golf course or in the club house.'

'And me, running around like a headless chicken, trying to find hours in the day when I wasn't involved with the boys, all that sort of thing.'

'That's going to change, Nanette. I promise you. I realise I've fallen short of being a father and perhaps more importantly been more supportive to you and now, well –' he stumbled over his words, but she let him take his time, giving him the space he needed to express what he was feeling. It had been a long time since they had actually sat down like they were doing now and talked, really talked, telling each other what was on their minds. And so, she watched him struggling with his emotions and thinking how much she loved him. Unquestionably. Now it was her turn to feel ashamed. Ashamed of how she had re-acted when she heard about her father's plans to re-marry, especially being so eager to agree to Colin's suggestion to make him draw up a pre-nuptial agreement. She inwardly cringed at the memory; the way she had insisted to Colin about their inheritance and in particular, the collection. The possibility of inheriting anything was rapidly fading into insignificance, lost in importance. None of it mattered now. What did concern her, what reached to the very core of her being, was her husband, her marriage and the children and she was prepared to do anything to hold on to that.

'I feel I've let you down, Nanette.'

'Please,' she smiled at him, 'don't. Don't torture yourself like this. You haven't let me down at all. What's done is done and between us we'll get everything back on an even keel.'

'Thank you for that, my love.'

'I'm not pressing you,' she said slowly, 'but don't you think the best thing to do is to put an immediate stop to these payments and ignore any future demands. Where will it end otherwise, Alan?'

'You're right; I'll cancel the standing order tomorrow. It's not due to come out of our account for a couple of weeks.'

'Good, that will be a start. We can always get legal advice, you know.'

'Can we?'

'Of course we can. There's dad's lawyer, Mr Brutton. I've known him since I was a child; he was dad's friend as well; he'll advise us and we can trust him, Alan. I know we can.'

'That could be a good idea, meanwhile, sweetheart,' he said, 'the funeral. Has Colin phoned again?'

'No, although I did call him this morning. I had to tell him we hadn't had the chance to talk yet, but I'll have to ring him tomorrow. I don't feel up to talking to him this evening. He was going to get in touch with Wendy, so I expect she'll be coming over. Oh, Alan, there is so much to think about.'

'I know. I know.' he said, pulling her to her feet and putting both arms around her, holding her tight against his chest, 'I feel stronger now. You've made me see things in a different light.'

'I'm glad.'

'Come on,' he said, taking her hand, 'let's join the boys and watch the tail end of 'Casino Royale'. A good dose of James Bond at his brilliant best should do us both good. We can eat later.'

*

'Eliza, darling! What a relief to hear your voice. Your father and I only got back home this afternoon; we've been to the cottage for a few days and you know what it's like there: no radio, no newspapers and, as far as I know, there are no more than half a dozen television sets on the island. So, darling,' she continued breathlessly, the way she had as far back as Eliza could remember, the words running and skipping ahead of her until she was forced to pause to catch her breath, 'these murders!

Two of them no less and practically on your doorstep! How absolutely dreadful for you, Eliza! You must have been terrified!'

'It hasn't been too bad, mother,' Eliza managed to break in between the exclamations, 'of course it was a shock, especially having only arrived here on Saturday, but at least now the police have gone and everything appears to have quietened down.'

'But, Eliza, aren't you nervous living there on your own? It isn't as if you are actually in Meadowbank, is it? And what about neighbours? How close is your nearest neighbour, darling?'

'I'm alright mother, honestly,' she said, 'you mustn't worry about me.'

'But I do, Eliza. We both do. You simply cannot imagine how we felt when we read about what had happened. It was literally splashed all over our local paper.'

'Oh, dear, I hadn't realised. I'm sorry; it just didn't occur to call you. I should have done, of course.'

'Well, if you had, darling, we wouldn't have been here!'

'You still haven't invested in a mobile phone then?'

'No, we haven't. You know what your father is like. He is totally opposed to them. Besides, there is nothing wrong with the ordinary telephone, also hardly anyone around here have mobiles.'

'They have their uses though.'

'I'm sure they do, but quite honestly, we have managed to exist without one and no doubt we will continue to do so.'

'They can be a bit of a pain.' Eliza said, smiling to herself. Her mother was really and truly an enigma. Most of the time she was extremely modern in her thinking, verging at times on the avant-garde, then there was another side to her, not wanting to move ahead, quite content with the ways things were and having absolutely no wish to change something which had always worked. In many ways she was right, Eliza concluded. Perhaps in some respects she wasn't too dissimilar.

'You haven't answered my question, Eliza?'

'Which one was that, mother?' there had been so many; she really was difficult to follow at times.

'Your neighbour or neighbours!' exasperation creeping in to her voice, 'in other words, are you completely isolated living on the estate?'

'I have one neighbour.' Eliza began slowly, selecting her words with care. Her mother had an extremely well-developed antennae.

'Yes?'

'He owns the old watermill up the road from here.'

'And you've met him.'

'Yes, I have.'

'Is he married?'

'Mother! Please!'

'Sorry, darling, I'm overstepping the mark, but I do hate to think of you on your own, especially now, when you're no longer in London. Don't you miss the life there and what about all your friends?'

'Well,' Eliza said, stifling a sigh, 'I've only been here for four days and so far I don't miss anything and as for friends, I didn't have all that many, you know, but I won't lose touch with them.'

'Good, I'm glad to hear it. I don't want you to turn yourself into a hermit!'

'I won't.'

'Your father met him once, you know?'

'Who?'

'Major Tilsly, of course, Eliza. Who else?'

'When was this?'

'Oh, years ago. In Nairobi; Major Tilsly had taken his regiment out there on training exercises and was invited to Government House for a meal, rather a grand affair it was. He was quite young, no more than forty, very handsome, reminded me of that actor in 'Jewel in the Crown'. He was quite debonair, an eye for the ladies; I don't think your father thought too much of him. Jealous, I expect!'

'Oh, mother,' Eliza laughed, 'you are impossible!'

'I suppose I am, darling,' she chuckled, 'anyway, I hope you have a spare room because we have to be in London on Saturday; some boring reunion function, ex-diplomats, that sort of thing, but your father is very keen to go and of course I will be able to do some much-needed shopping; I'm beginning to look quite shabby!'

Chapter Fourteen

The inquest was scheduled for eleven o'clock. Simon, after having considerable difficulty in finding a parking place as near to the court as possible, walked along the pavement, arriving there shortly before eleven. The first person he saw was Colin, sitting on one of the bench seats, cradling a plastic cup of coffee. Next to him was a man he hadn't seen for years: Arnold Brutton, looking, naturally enough, considerably older. The last time he had been in his company was shortly before his parents moved to France, ten years ago. Arnold had been an old friend of his father, that friendship going back to their university days. He had been a frequent visitor to the mill, their evenings spent playing chess, sometimes well on into the early hours.

'Simon,' he said, standing up and walking up to him, holding out his hand, 'it has been a long time.'

'It certainly has,' Simon said, 'and this business isn't good, is it?'

'Tragic, Simon. Tragic. I'd known Reginald for years, almost as long as I've known your father. Tell me, how are your parents? Still enjoying life in France?'

'They love it.'

'I'm glad.' Arnold Brutton said, looking at his watch and nodding over to Colin.

How tired Colin looks, Simon thought, watching as his friend slowly got to his feet; much older than his forty-six years. Losing his father must be affecting him badly, but only understandable, especially how he had died.

'Hello, Simon,' he said, 'I didn't expect to see you here.'

'I felt it was the least I could do; thought you might appreciate some support at a time like this.'

'That was thoughtful of you.' he said, attempting to smile, but failing, 'And you're right, that is exactly what I do need. So thank you, Simon.'

'We can go in now,' the lawyer said quietly, placing a hand lightly on Colin's arm, 'I know this is an ordeal for you, Colin,' he went on, 'but I think you will find the proceedings to be a formality only. We'll hear the police and the pathologist's report, a run-through of the facts, followed finally by the verdict of which we are already aware.'

The verdict was as Arnold Brutton had said: 'Murder by person or persons unknown' and in less than forty minutes they were filing out of the courtroom, the lawyer shaking hands with them both before leaving them; his tall thin frame as erect as Simon remembered with only a slight stiffness as he walked down the steps on to the pavement, suggesting perhaps the onset of arthritis. Seeing him again after so long had reminded him of how quickly those years had passed. He didn't often dwell on such negative thoughts, but sitting through the proceedings of the untimely death of a man he had known since he had been a child had depressed him. He had noticed Brenda Masters in there and her presence had merely added to his mood. He would call Eliza later he decided; certain that time spent with her would go a long way to lifting his spirits.

'Have you time for a coffee, Colin?'

'Good idea,' he agreed, 'although I must admit I'd rather have something stronger.'

'We can if you like.'

'Tempting, Simon, but I'd better not. I have to get back to the office but it will give me something to look forward to this evening.

They chose a small cafe quaintly called 'The Boiling Kettle'; low beams, sloping wooden floors and chintzy curtains at the pebble-glass windows, reminiscent of Dickens' 'Old Curiosity Shop'.

'I know,' Colin said giving him a quick lop-sided grin, reminding him for a brief moment of the schoolboy he had once been, 'a bit twee, but they make excellent coffee. Real coffee beans.' he added.

'I honestly didn't think there were any of these places left.'

'Don't you believe it, Simon; this town has an abundance of them. For the tourists of course, to convey to them that Winchester, although in many respects ultra-modern with its shopping malls, is still very much an ancient historical town positively steeped in history going as far back as King Alfred the Great, but still holding on to its past with tea rooms such as this one.'

'With little old ladies you mean, carrying their Miss Marples' shopping baskets!'

'Don't mock it, Simon.'

'I'm not. It so happens I agree with you.'

'There are times like this, you know,' Colin went on, 'when I would give anything to turn the clock back.'

'It's pretty grim for you, I realise that,' Simon sympathised, 'and for Nanette and Wendy too, of course.'

'You're right. Naturally it was a shock for Nanette when I phoned her on Sunday, but you know Nanette. She's tough. Quick to bounce back and face facts.'

'And Wendy?'

'Well, I did try to get through to her, but she must have been away. Anyway, Arnold Brutton has done the job for me. I am only too well aware I was being a bit of a coward there and I'm not too proud about that, but I dreaded breaking the news to her. Hong Kong is so bloody far away! She could never see any wrong in dad.'

'And you could?' he asked him, trying to understand this new Colin. He seemed to him to be brimming over with bitterness. A totally different guy from the one he used to know. There was also a jaundiced despair about him and he couldn't help feeling this wasn't totally to do with what had happened. Simon recalled the last conversation he had with Reginald Tilsly, only four days ago. Incredible, he thought. Little had he realised that his old friend had only a matter of hours until he would reach the end of his life. And so violently, too. If it was taking him time to come to terms with his death, what he wondered, must it be like for Colin and his sisters.

'The funeral is on Friday, Simon.'

'I was going to ask you about that. I'll be there of course. That should go without saying.'

'For the second time today,' Colin said, 'thank you, my old friend.'

'I suppose it's too early to know yet,' Simon said slowly, not wanting to appear presumptuous, but he had an ulterior motive for asking the question, 'the manor? What will happen to it?'

'Absolutely nothing.' he answered abruptly, draining off the last of his coffee, 'Arnold Brutton spelt it out to me in no uncertain terms. The manor is not for sale; the whole estate has been left in trust for the family. The only way round this would be if the three of us were to agree unanimously to sell. Dad knew what he was doing, you know, Simon. He knew damn well I would have no sentimental regrets about getting rid of it, Nanette feels the same, but Wendy, although she chooses to live several thousand miles away and has so far not shown any signs of returning, thinks quite differently. So, no selling the place, no developing the land –'

'- it is a green belt area.' Simon reminded him.

'And don't I know it. Anyway, it looks as if the three of us are lumbered with it until goodness knows when!'

'It can't be that bad though, can it?' Simon commented, 'you could always move in there. Easy enough to travel into Winchester each day.'

'That's true, but whether Rachel would agree is another question entirely and, quite frankly, I doubt if she would, but then as you've said, it's early days yet.'

'I'm sure you'll get it all sorted out in the end. Mind you, it must take a fair bit to run the estate, maintenance of the building and all that.'

'Apparently,' and this time Colin was making no attempt to hide his frustration, 'this famous trust has adequate funds for that and there is the rental income from the water meadows and now from the leasing of the lodge.'

That was what he wanted to hear, albeit in a roundabout kind of way, but at least Eliza's tenure would be secure. He knew he was being selfish, but having only met her he didn't want to lose her and if she was forced to give up the lease that was possible. Their friendship was too new, too fragile, for that to happen.

'I'm sorry, Simon,' Colin said, glancing at his watch, 'I'm lousy company at the moment. In fact,' he added, rising to his feet, 'I'm not fit company for anyone. I'll see you on Friday;' beckoning over to their waitress for the bill, 'the service is at two o'clock by the way.'

'I'll be there, Colin.'

There was a message waiting for him when he got back to the mill. Eliza, sounding more Scottish on the phone and inviting him for supper. Hearing her voice acted as an instant fillip, giving him the impetus he needed to get on with some work. He had already lost a morning and there were a lot of things he needed to do before the weekend and especially as a good part of Friday was going to be taken up with the funeral. He had a meeting in London the following Tuesday with the National Geographical Society and he still hadn't sorted out all those negatives and slides. This week was turning out to be made up of stops and starts, with far too many of the former, when he would break for a coffee, taking it outside with him to enjoy the warmth of what promised to be a good summer. Now, putting Colin Tilsly to the back of his mind; it was obvious he had problems and quite serious ones at that to explain his edginess, but Simon didn't think he could be much help to him. He pulled off his shirt, tossing it into the linen basket, followed in quick succession by the remainder of his clothes and stepping under the shower, turned the spray on to full.

Five minutes later, a towel wrapped around his waist and feeling much better; it was as though the jets of water cascading over him had done more than merely refresh his body, but his head felt clearer. He still felt a weary sadness over losing his old friend, but he could live with that and now he was looking forward to the evening and to seeing Eliza again. It had only been the day before yesterday he reminded himself; love-sick guy that he was! But, like the song went: '.... you get under my skin....' corny though it sounded, he knew what 'Old Blue Eyes' had meant.

*

'How did it go this morning?' Eliza asked him. She had been standing outside the lodge waiting for him, looking truly exquisite and even more like Isadora Duncan. A floaty froth of pale lemon muslin falling in a straight line from a deeply cut neckline, her hair this evening brushed free and framing her face which, after only a few days, was already lightly sun-tanned. She wore little make-up he noticed, only a shimmer of pale pink lipstick and the smile with which she greeted him made him feel ridiculously light-headed.

'So-so, I reckon.' he said, resisting the impulse to kiss her, but the last thing he wanted was to do anything which may offend her. It was too soon. Also, since he came back from Winchester he had a reluctance to discuss, not just the inquest, nor the unsettling conversation with Colin, but to be reminded of what had happened. To Simon, as he followed her inside, the major, strong character as he had been, still remained in his mind.

'You don't really want to talk about it.' A statement; not a question. She understood and he was grateful. 'I believe I know how you feel, Simon,' she said softly, 'it must all seem quite unreal to you.'

'It does, yes.' he admitted, 'I think the worse was having to sit there in that court room and hear his death being discussed in such a clinical and detached way. The man they were talking about didn't even sound like someone I had known for most of my life. Sorry, Eliza,' he added, 'I don't mean to be like this; filled with such gloom and despondency, but quite frankly, his murder is just so shocking.'

'I know.' she smiled, gently putting an arm around him and for a fraction of a second he allowed himself the luxury of being close to her, to enjoy the softness and warmth of her and to inhale the elusively sweet summery fragrance of her perfume. Reluctantly, he pulled away and this time he did kiss her, lightly and, only the once, on her cheek.

'A drink?'

'Please.'

'Beer or a wine?' she asked.

He asked for a wine and watched her as she went through to the kitchen. For the first time he noticed she had made a number of changes since he was there on Sunday. Not many, but some velvet cushions and a fringed cotton throw across the back of the old sofa; leather-bound books on the top shelf of the book-case he didn't remember seeing before and a few ornaments, mainly porcelain figurines, delicate pieces, all of which instantly made the room uniquely hers. But it was the picture above the fireplace which caught and totally captured him. An African sunset: dusk about to fall and the orange flaming ball of sun tilting drunkenly on the horizon, appearing to almost touch the tips of the trees, the last long rays spreading outwards and beyond and reaching the edges of the impenetrable density of the bush. Mesmerised, he went up to the painting, knowing even before reading the name of the artist that this was one of Leonora Farthing's. He had admired her work for years, having discovered it during one of his trips to Kenya – over fifteen years ago it must have been. A small gallery in Nairobi he recalled and remembering how he had stood, as now, totally entranced. Of course he should have bought one and often he had asked himself why he hadn't done so. He reckoned it was one of those much-regretted moments in life when you always thought there would be another opportunity, but regrettably he never came across anymore of her paintings and he had always regretted the lost opportunity. He had immediately fallen in love with her style, the magical way she managed to capture the intense pervading essence of the African continent.

'I can't believe you actually have a Leonora Farthing!' he said, hearing Eliza come back into the room, but unable to take his eyes away from the painting. 'I've been a great admirer of her work for a long time, but unfortunately I've never been able to find out where she exhibited. And it hasn't been for the lack of trying,' he added, 'all I did learn was that she had returned to England and then I came up against a brick wall.'

'To Scotland, actually.' Eliza said quietly, a tiny smile flickering on her lips, as she handed him his wine.

'You obviously know more than I've ever been able to find out,' he said, raising the glass to her, 'so, that's where she went. I often wondered. And does she exhibit there?'

'She tries to avoid it. In fact, she doesn't seem in the least bit interested.'

'You know her, don't you?' Simon asked.

'She's my mother.'

'No! Really!'

'Yes, really.' Eliza, unable to stop laughing. No doubt thought he was behaving like a complete naive idiot. 'I'm sorry, Simon, I shouldn't tease you like this, but you see, I suppose you could call it familiarity; my mother has been an artist practically all her life, and certainly all my life. I am used to her. That doesn't mean to say I don't recognise and admire her talent.'

'But, the name,' he was still trying to take in that this woman he had just met was the daughter of an artist he had so long admired. Unreal. 'Not Brent?'

'Farthing was her maiden name;' she told him, 'already, before she married, she had become quite famous.'

'Of course. And you, too, are artistic, Eliza. I've often wondered what she was like.'

'Well,' the smile was back again, 'you'll be able to see for yourself tomorrow. They will be spending the night here and rather than cook a meal I thought I would take them to the 'Salmon's Rest'. Would you like to join us?'

'There's nothing I'd like better.'

Chapter Fifteen

The Cathay Pacific flight from Hong Kong arrived exactly on time at Heathrow airport. Wendy Tilsly, checking her bag for her travel documents, shaking hands with the man who had been her travelling companion for the duration of the flight, followed the rest of the passengers, nodding automatically her thanks to the cabin crew as she passed them at the open door. London. England. Back to the grim reality of what lay ahead. Less than forty-eight hours since she had heard and listened with a growing dread to every single word he had to tell her about her father. Mr Brutton, not only their lawyer, but a close friend of the family and someone she had known since she had been old enough to remember anyone. Poor man, he had done his best to break the news to her as gently as he could, but even as shocked as she had been, she realised nothing could neither disguise nor soften the fact of what had happened in the home she had been brought up in. Her father had been murdered. Brutally and from what Mr Brutton had said to her, totally unpremeditated.

Wendy had only the evening before returned to Hong Kong from Beijing, tired but elated from what had turned out to be a successful marketing trip and bringing back with her two substantial corporate sales, also strong possibilities for future business in China which would be a new and exciting venture for her publishing house. She had been looking forward to meeting with her directors the following morning, a board meeting already arranged for ten-thirty, placing her report in front of them and becoming involved in what promised to be an exciting expansion to their business. Instead, she had had to e-mail her report into the office; there was no way she could have concentrated. Both her directors had been understanding although she couldn't help sensing their impatience. She had worked for them too long not to notice. Now, one of her colleagues would be taking her place and following up on the leads she had spent months working on, but none of this seemed to matter to her all that much. From the moment she had heard about her father the world she had lived in for ten years had rapidly disintegrated and lost its edge. All Wendy wanted to do was to get back home and to stay there for as long as it took to come to terms with his death and try to decide where her own life was going. Dan had not offered to come back with her, but then why should he? Theirs was a roller-coaster sort of relationship. They had met not long after she had arrived in Hong Kong: she had been instantly attracted by his easy charm, his confident sophistication. He had told her right at the beginning about being married, how his wife preferred to stay in America; California having more appeal to her than what she had described to him as the harsh brashness of Hong Kong. Wendy had accepted this, reluctantly at first, but as the years went by had become accustomed to his short absences, and each time he returned to her in Hong Kong, being with him again seemed perfectly natural. But recently, she had begun to question her passive acceptance of the arrangement. Perhaps it was time to reassess a situation which was not going anywhere. With their roles reversed, with her leaving Hong Kong now, instead of him, she had expected to feel upset, but there was no room in her mind for anything else but her father. She scarcely remembered her mother; it had been her father who had been the key figure in her young life. Although he spent time away from home, somehow it hadn't made any difference. He had been the person she had turned to, knowing even at a very young age he had always treated her differently than the other two. As they had said to her often enough; in his eyes she could do no wrong and knowing how this used to irritate them. Even when she moved to London and by that time he had retired from the army, he hadn't made any attempt to keep her at home, making it much easier when she told him later she was going to live in Hong Kong. She should have returned more often than she had done. Too late now, of course, she thought, turning her face towards the window and making an attempt to blink back tears which had been threatening ever since she had boarded the plane and for the first time having nothing more to do but think. Not good she concluded, taking a deep breath.

'Here you are,' a quiet voice said next to her, 'have this.' passing a large white handkerchief to her.

'Thank you.' Wendy said, taking it from him. 'Sorry, but I couldn't help it.'

'You don't need to be,' he said and she looked at him for the first time: a kind face; rugged, cornflower blue eyes, dark lashes and a thick mop of brown hair, 'I'm a good listener, that is, if you think it would help.'

And she had told him everything and he had been right. He listened to her, saying little, his expression becoming more solemn as she came to the end.

'I'm sorry.' was all he said.

'Thank you.' she said, making to give him back the handkerchief, but he told her to keep it, adding that he hoped she would not really need it, but just in case.

'As an insurance.' he smiled.

'Do you work in Hong Kong?' she asked, considering it was time she stopped talking about herself.

'No, London; this was a very brief business trip.'

'What are you in?'

'Publishing.'

'That's a coincidence,' she smiled, 'so am I.'

'Really! In Hong Kong?'

'Yes, the sales and marketing side.'

'And you enjoy it; living and working in Hong Kong, I mean.'

'Well,' she hesitated for a fraction of a second, wondering as she did so, why she was confiding in this man; it was not something she did very often, preferring to keep her thoughts, at least the negative ones, to herself, 'I did up to now, but I believe I've reached a kind of watershed in my life, perhaps being back in England I'll be able to get things back into perspective.'

'That's understandable. I would imagine you'll have quite a lot to sort out in your mind. I've always found it helps to break away from what you've been doing and try to rationalise without the day-to-day interruptions.'

They had spent a good part of the journey talking, exchanging publishing experiences; books they had read and, like her, he had read many of them more than once. He was utterly different from Dan who would often dismissively say he couldn't remember when he had last read a book. As they began their descent he gave her one of his cards, saying if she ever considered returning to London to get in touch with him. His name was Mark Wood and told her he'd only had his publishing firm for five years and recently he and his partner had been talking about expanding their marketing section. She promised to seriously think about it and put the card in her wallet. Later. She would think about it all later and now, here she was, walking towards the baggage reclaim and, for once, not having long to wait until her much-travelled case appeared on the carousel. Dragging it on to a trolley, she headed towards the car hire desk.

Joining the M3 motorway, once clear of Heathrow, the Peugeot responding well, Wendy, as she had done countless times before when going back home, settled down to the tedium of the drive. By the time she had reached the Basingstoke Service Station she felt the need of a coffee to stimulate her for the last lap. Taking the slip road, she pulled into the car park and walked the short distance to the restaurant area. People were milling around in the vestibule, a queue she noticed at the toilets. England doesn't change, she thought wryly, pushing open the swing door to the coffee shop. Simultaneously, the door was opened from the other side, the man striding towards her bumping into her and for a moment making her lose her balance. He didn't stop and she wondered if he had even noticed her. Frowning, she walked inside and, taking a tray from the rack at the end of the counter, ordered a mug of black coffee. She was at the cash desk when the screaming began; a long drawn out scream which made her gasp, the tray shaking unsteadily in her hands. At the far end of the room a handful of people had gathered; one of them had an arm around the waitress who, by this time, was sobbing uncontrollably, while someone else, ashen-faced stood transfixed and staring at the figure slumped across one of the tables. Even from where she was standing Wendy could see the blood; a large patch, scarlet and matting the blond hair of the man's head.

Two hours later Wendy reached the manor, by now not only exhausted but still shaken. The police had been quick to arrive, in fact within minutes, or so it seemed, and it was some time before everyone who had been in the coffee shop had given them their names and addresses. A formality and, while everyone agreed necessary, Wendy had heard many mutterings of protest. As far as she was concerned, a delay of another thirty minutes made little difference. All she wanted at that moment as she drove slowly past the lodge, noticing signs of occupancy, also a car parked outside the front door, was to have a shower and a change of clothes. She had telephoned Mrs Plenderneath before she had left Hong Kong to tell her she would be arriving. Not that she expected, or indeed wanted, much of a welcome, but she had always been fond of her father's housekeeper and it would be comforting to speak to someone she actually knew. She felt she had quite literally been on the move for days which was in fact the case.

'Wendy.' Mrs Plenderneath called out to her from the open front door, 'You're here at last. Come along in, dear,' she added, 'and don't worry about your luggage, I'll do that for you. But, first things first, some coffee and I've got your favourite biscuits.'

'You spoil me, Mrs Plenderneath.' Wendy said, following her into the kitchen which looked exactly as it had always done: gleaming white Formica work tops; the row of copper pans on the wall above them and in the centre of the stone-flagged floor the sturdy old wooden table.

'It's the least I can do, Wendy,' she smiled at her sadly, pouring out coffee and placing the plate of Abernethy biscuits on the table, 'you look a trifle pale, but then you've been on a long journey.'

'Just tired.' Wendy explained, helping herself to a biscuit, enjoying again their special buttery crunchiness. She wouldn't tell her what had happened at the service station. It would be unkind to unburden her feelings on to the poor woman. She had been through enough. Mr Brutton had already told her that she had been the one to find her father.

'This must be terrible for you, dear, having to return at such a sad time. I miss working for your father; he always treated me fairly. A good man.'

'But you will still be here at the manor, won't you?'

'I don't know yet what is going to happen, Wendy,' she said, 'but of course if I'm asked I will be only too happy to stay.'

As if on cue, the telephone in the hall rang. 'That will be Colin, I expect,' Mrs Plenderneath said quickly, 'he said he would call to find out if you had arrived safely.'

She was right. It was Colin and as she spoke to him, she experienced again the mixed feelings she had towards him. Her big brother, her protector when she used to tag along behind him and Nanette, refusing to allow anyone to boss her around as her sister had been in the habit of doing, but there was another side to him which had steadily developed over the years and one she was not too keen on. He had become calculating, giving her the impression he was solely motivated by money, this becoming unpleasantly apparent the last time she spoke to him when he raised the ghastly idea of a pre-nuptial agreement.

'Wendy,' he was saying, 'I have been trying to call you since Sunday.'

'I know,' she explained, 'Mr Brutton told me. I had been in Beijing for a couple of weeks'

'And how are you?'

'Apart from feeling pretty tired, I'm fine.'

'This has all been a terrible shock.'

'I know. Have they any idea who did it, Colin?'

'I don't think so. At the moment Brenda Masters seems to be going around the place suspecting practically everyone she sees!'

'I suppose she has to.'

'Perhaps, but it isn't very pleasant to be one of them.'

'You mean, you? But why?'

'Because someone kindly told her I had an argument with dad that evening.'

'And did you?'

'As it happens I did.'

'I won't ask you what you were arguing about, but I can guess.'

'I don't want to discuss it, Wendy.'

'Neither do I. Let's just get through tomorrow.'

'You're right. What about this evening? Do you want me to come over to Meadowbank?'

'No, Colin, thanks, but I don't feel all that sociable. I'll make myself something light to eat and have an early night. I have a lot of sleep to catch up on.'

Chapter Sixteen

Eliza was standing at the kitchen window waiting for her parents to arrive when a cream Peugeot turned into the estate. She noticed in particular how pale the young woman behind the wheel looked: short blonde hair, high cheekbones, small, slender hands on the steering wheel. A member of the Tilsly family she wondered. The daughter, the younger one who lives in Hong Kong, perhaps, immediately feeling sorry for her. Not a pleasant homecoming. Then, following almost immediately behind the Peugeot, the familiar sight of her father's old Rover made its appearance, her mother's sun-tanned arm waving from the open window. How good it was to see them after such a long time she thought guiltily. She always felt like this after long absences even although she knew it wasn't entirely her fault. Both her parents understood how pre-occupied she had been in recent months, finding a buyer for the flat; completing the sale and all that that had involved; severing ties with her company; following up leads and contacts for the new business and then, settling into the lodge, but it did not make any difference to the way she felt. She should have made the effort; there had been time between leaving London and coming down to Hampshire. And now, with everything which had been happening these past few days there really was not much room in her mind for anything else.

'Darling!' Leonora called out to her even before the car had come to a complete standstill; her father continuing to negotiate into the space alongside her Fiesta. 'We thought we would never get here!' she added, opening the door wide and stepping daintily on to the drive.

'You'll be glad of something cold to drink, then.' Eliza smiled, putting both arms around her, inhaling the familiar fragrance of her perfume: light and summery, instantly epitomising her personality.

'How right you are, darling. You know what your father's like! Once he gets behind that wheel he is most reluctant to break the journey and then, would you believe it, when I finally managed to persuade him to stop at one of the service stations they had actually closed the coffee shop!'

'Why?'

'We're not quite sure, Eliza,' James Brent said, kissing his daughter on the cheek, 'There was something going on, that's for sure. They had one of those taped police barriers across the entrance. You know the kind I mean; we've seen them many times in television dramas?'

'And, quite honestly,' Leonora put in, linking arms with her, 'I never expected to see in this country.'

'It must have been serious though.'

'I'm sure it was, darling.' she said, 'Do you know, Eliza, I am beginning to wonder whether it was such a good idea of yours to come and live in this part of England. Two murders, for goodness sake! And now, only about thirty miles or so away, another –'

'– Really, Leonora,' James Brent interrupted, 'we don't know what it was all about. Might be all or nothing.'

'Don't you believe it, James,' she said, 'I heard someone say; you didn't hear, you were striding back to the car, there had been a shooting. I ask you! What *is* going on around here?'

'Come on, let's go inside.' Eliza coaxed, trying to distract her. Once Leonora was into her stride there was no stopping her and her father may have been right; whatever had happened at the service station may not have been as dire as it had appeared.

'A beer, dad?' she asked, taking them straight through the lounge and outside on to the terrace, 'and I've already opened a bottle of wine. Unless you would prefer a soft drink, Leonora?'

'What do you think, Eliza?' Leonora said, the smile immediately radiating her face. How lovely she is, Eliza thought. She really did not appear to age at all. Her skin; smoother than her own, but with the same sprinkling of freckles across the bridge of her nose. As she went into the kitchen to fetch the drinks she wondered what Simon would think when he met her. Eliza knew the immediate impact her mother had on any new people she met: they were instantly attracted and captivated by her. There was no other way to describe the reaction and it was not as if her mother was in any way coquettish; far from it, she just was not aware of the affect she created.

'This is wonderful,' Leonora said when she rejoined them, 'such a pretty house and a lovely terrace like this. You *are* happy you've made the move, darling, aren't you?'

'Yes, I am.'

'I'm sorry,' she put in quickly, 'that was crass of me! For the moment I had completely forgotten about the murders!'

'Leonora!'

'It's alright, James,' she looked at him, patting him lightly on the knee, 'nobody can hear me. But, seriously, Eliza,' she went on, taking the glass of wine from her and lowering her voice dramatically, 'aren't you in the tiniest bit nervous? Only literally yards away from where IT HAPPENED.'

'Strangely,' Eliza said, sitting down between them, 'I'm not. Perhaps I should be, but then, I had only just arrived that afternoon and it isn't as if I saw anything that night.' Not exactly the truth, but she had no intention of telling them anything more, especially about Steve's visit. They were concerned enough about her.

'You don't convince me, you know,' Leonora persisted, 'no, Eliza, let me finish. I can tell by that dogged expression on your face, you don't want to discuss this, but think about your safety, darling. I've just had an idea; why don't you come back home with us on Sunday. Until it has all blown over, I mean?'

'I'm okay, mother. Honestly.'

'If you're sure,' Leonora said, leaning forward to slip off her sandals, wriggling her toes, just as she had always done, 'but then,' she continued, looking at her above the rim of her glass, 'you have your neighbour. And,' she added, a tiny enigmatic smile hovering on her lips, 'you still haven't given us his name.'

'Simon Grant,' Eliza said, not fooled by her mother's pretence of casual interest, 'and, as I said on the phone, he owns the old watermill next door.'

'And he isn't married?'

'Mother!'

'Ignore her, Eliza,' James Brent smiled, pouring the remainder of the beer into his glass, 'she's only trying to find out more than you've told her so far.'

'There's not much more to tell,' Eliza said returning his smile; they both knew Leonora so well, recognised her thinly veiled tactics and neither of them were fazed by them, nor remotely irritated. To have been would have been a total lack of energy. 'he's a photographer,' she went on, 'and has a brilliant display of his work at the mill. Also,' she paused for a second, anticipating her mother's reaction, 'he's been one of your admirers for ages.'

'Has he indeed? Now, I *am* interested, Eliza.'

'I thought you might be,' Eliza smiled at her, 'anyway you'll have the chance to talk to him this evening. I've booked us all a table at what must be one of Hampshire's best restaurants.

'An excellent idea, Eliza,' James Brent said, 'in fact, I was going to suggest we eat out. Far too hot for you to be spending any time in the kitchen.'

Simon was already at the 'Salmon's Rest' when they arrived, sitting at the same table she had shared with him on Sunday. He rose to his feet as soon as he saw them, smiling first at her and as she introduced his parents she saw the way his whole attention was focused on Leonora.

'You have no idea,' he said, once they were all seated, 'how much I have wanted to meet you Mrs Brent —'

'- oh, please, Simon,' Leonora interrupted quickly, 'call me Leonora. Most of my friends do, it makes me feel a little bit younger. There was no trace of any vanity about her mother: what she said and how she said it was never contrived, but as so many times in the past Eliza could recognise and interpret first the surprise, followed by disbelief and finally realisation that here was a woman who was quite lacking in any feminine guile. She meant exactly what she said. She had no interest whether by saying what she did made her actually appear younger; in fact, she had no illusions about herself. Now in her late sixties and Eliza secretly thought her mother was rather proud of the fact and was probably looking forward to celebrating her seventieth birthday at the end of the year. And Simon's reaction was no different. She could see how relaxed he was with her, as if he had known her for years and with her father also. She could tell he liked Simon. James, a quiet man, although having spent most of his career overseas, mixing in diplomatic circles, attending and hosting formal dinners, liked nothing better than to relax. Be himself and talk to someone on the same level with similar interests as himself. He had little time for small talk, adroitly leaving that to Leonora. Eliza had noticed since his retirement and returning to his beloved Scotland he had come into his own and probably for the first time since leaving university back in the fifties, he was able to choose his friends, rather than having to, as he had often described it to her, put on an act, when all he really wanted to do was have a peaceful evening at home, eat a meal of his choice and round it off with a fine glass of port.

They were early and the restaurant was only half full. No sign of Danielle yet and Eliza wondered if the man standing behind the bar in the centre of the room was her husband, the owner of the voice she had overheard the last time she was there. They were sitting a short distance away and for a second she was sure he was going to come over to their table, but instead, as though changing his mind at the last minute, remained where he was, continuing to polish the already shining optics on the glass shelf at the back of the bar.

'Is that Danielle's husband?' she managed to ask Simon before the waitress reached their table with the menus.

'Yes,' he nodded, 'not exactly front of house material but, as I'm sure you'll agree, Danielle more than makes up for that, even if she is a trifle waspish at times!'

'Would you like to see the wine list, sir?' the waitress was asking James.

'Ah, yes, the wine list. Excellent.' he smiled at the girl. He had been miles away Eliza thought. Wherever his mind was it certainly wasn't there with them in the 'Salmon's Rest', but her father could be like that at times. Always had been. Even as a young child she remembered often being in the middle of telling him something, which to her had been of the utmost importance, only to find he wasn't really listening to her. She was used to it, but to others she realised it could be a little off-putting, even rude, although that was something he never intended and since his retirement he had become more and more like the proverbial absent-minded professor. Amused, she watched him make a physical effort to concentrate on selecting the wine.

Danielle Taylor brought the wine to their table, expertly opening the bottle and passing the glass for her father to taste.

'Perfect,' he smiled up at her, 'but only what I would expect from a bottle of Merlot.'

'Thank you,' Danielle said, leaning over to fill the other glasses, 'and, Eliza,' she said, 'you don't have to tell me that this lady is your mother. You look remarkably alike.'

'Sorry, Danielle,' Simon said quickly, 'I was about to introduce Eliza's parents to you.'

'I expect you've come to Meadowbank which is, incidentally, rapidly turning into a police state,' Danielle said, once the introductions had been made and subjecting Leonora to one of her close appraisals, 'to see how Eliza is coping?'

'Well,' Leonora said slowly, 'raising her glass to her lips, at the same time looking across at Eliza, 'we were concerned when we heard the news, it's true, but –' she paused and Eliza could tell what she was thinking. Leonora was having difficulty in understanding Danielle, ' - but,' she repeated, 'Eliza has assured us we have nothing to worry about. Whatever has happened, and I'm not discounting the seriousness of it for a minute, I'm sure the police will continue to keep an eye on the place.'

'The police!' the scathing words exploding from Danielle.

'Come on, Danielle,' Simon said, 'they are doing their best to get to the bottom of things. It can't be easy.'

'You say that, Simon,' Danielle threw back her head impatiently, 'the town this week has been crawling with them. They have been absolutely everywhere and in my opinion seem to be conducting their investigation in a most *bizarre* manner.'

'In what way?' Eliza asked her, intrigued in spite of not wanting to talk about it. Too much she felt had been said already.

'Well, Eliza,' Danielle turned round to face her, the dark eyes flashing, 'that chief inspector woman actually came here to question *me* today! *Moi!* Would you believe it!'

'Not as a suspect of course?'

'Please, Simon, do not make light of this. If you must know, I took it as a personal insult that she should call. It would seem that busybody of a housekeeper had told the police I had telephoned Major Tilsly and for that reason they decided in their so-called wisdom to ask me, Danielle le Breton, which was my name before I married Peter, why!'

Very much wanting to know why she had phoned the major, but not wanting to ask, Eliza was spared this when Simon, with the same barely suppressed smile he'd worn on Sunday, did it for her.

'You are being intriguing, Danielle,' he said, 'do tell us. I wasn't aware you even knew Reginald Tilsly.'

'I didn't, of course, but I had heard about his art collection and seen photographs of many of the paintings, one in particular, a Monet. I wanted him to sell it to me, that's why I called him. And how I wish I had not done so. Do you know, he wouldn't even discuss the matter with me; in fact, he put the phone down on me! Such a rude man!'

'He could be a little abrupt.' Simon admitted and Eliza could tell he was trying to pacify her. The visit from the chief inspector had obviously upset her, not that it would have taken too much to do that. Danielle Taylor was on a very short fuse indeed.

'What an angry young woman.' Leonora remarked after Danielle had gone.

'I would say, also,' James put in quietly, watching Danielle flounce back into the kitchen, 'also, a desperately unhappy one.'

*

Friday morning, the day of the funeral, was overcast and, in the distance, the faint rumbling of thunder. We are in for a storm, Brenda Masters thought, switching on her desk lamp. She already knew there would be a large turnout at the church, whether the late major had been a popular or even likeable resident of the community or not. The Tilsly family went back more than a hundred years and to many, especially the older generation, that was all that mattered. The fact he had been murdered would no doubt attract many inquisitive outsiders, not to mention the press who seemed to have taken up permanent residence in the town. Less than a week since his death and already she was getting pressure from her superintendent to come up with a solution, and a rapid one at that. The fact she was no further forward since they had been called to the manor on Sunday, only increased her frustration. What few leads they had followed up on had taken them no further. Suspicions alone were not enough and would only act to further enrage her superintendent's chronic state of intolerance. So, what did they have? Colin Tilsly's argument with his father earlier in the evening. Did he return later or didn't he? They only had his wife's word they had spent the remainder of the evening together. Then there was Steven Blackwood, a man with a prison record and who happened to be in the area telling them he'd taken the opportunity to visit his ex-wife. As unlikely as that sounded they were stuck with it, at least for the present. And, what about this man who had been booked into 'The Market Inn' and had actually spent time on his own in the gallery. From Singapore on a business trip, according to what he told Melissa. How vague can one get, Brenda thought. It was pathetic. Also, they were still waiting for some feedback from the car hire firm. It may turn out that Anthony Appleyard wasn't the man's real name, but surely the firm would have asked to see some form of identity from him. The phone ringing at that moment only added to the way she was feeling and fully expecting to hear the deep gravelly voice of her superior demanding an immediate meeting, she was relieved to hear her opposite number, Graham Ford, from Winchester Police Headquarters, on the other end of the line.

'Good morning, Graham. What can we do for you?'

'It's more what we might be able to do for you, Brenda. We could be barking up the wrong tree mind you, but I believe we may have found a link, although a tenuous one, with the Tilsly case.'

'Really?'

'Yes, you heard about the shooting here yesterday? At the Basingstoke service station to be more exact.' he added.

'I did, yes.' she said slowly, feeling the first quickening of excitement, her hand gripping the receiver. She had known Graham for years, since they had both joined the force. Like her, he never jumped to conclusions; perhaps, she thought, this was going to be the breakthrough they needed, waiting for him to elaborate.

'You won't know the name of the man who was shot though.'

'No, they said they were withholding it until his next of kin had been informed. I didn't hear about it officially, Graham, only from the nine o'clock news last night. Who was it, then?'

'Steven Blackwood.'

'What!'

'Thought that would surprise you,' Graham gave a dry chuckle, 'I already knew from the up-dates we get at the station that the metropolitan police had questioned him in connection with the Tilsly case.'

'They did, yes, once they managed to catch up with him when he got back to his flat in London, but this is the last I expected to happen to him, Graham. Also, I might add, he was one of my main suspects.'

'He certainly had a long police record as far back as his spell in Borstal. It's interesting, wouldn't you say?'

'I should say so. What else have you got?' greedy now for even the tiniest snippet of information, anything which might strengthen the link between the murders.

'Well, not much, Brenda, but a different type of gun was used from the one which shot Major Tilsly.'

'So,' Brenda said, 'we either have two killers or one killer with two guns which, quite frankly, I find difficult to believe.'

'I know.'

'And,' Brenda went on, 'not forgetting what happened to the poacher, it does seem more likely he was killed by murderer number one, although, again, we've no proof.'

'A lot of loose ends, eh?'

'Far too many.'

'Here's another one for you then, Brenda. We made a list of everyone in and around the vicinity yesterday, also their addresses, of course, and one name in particular jumped out at us.'

'Go on.'

'The major's daughter was there, Wendy Tilsly. She'd arrived a couple of hours earlier from Hong Kong – we've checked it out and she was on the flight alright – she told my officer she had stopped off for a coffee before driving the rest of the way to Meadowbank.'

'I hate to say it, Graham, but this could be a coincidence.'

'It's probable, but we need to be sure.'

'I know. Did she see what happened?'

'No such luck, I'm afraid. She had been waiting to pay at the cash desk when one of the waitresses noticed him. At first the girl thought he had fallen asleep and then she saw the blood, so you can no doubt imagine what happened next.'

'Pandemonium, I bet.' Brenda said, 'and no-one saw anything suspicious?'

'Apparently not.'

'What about when the shot was fired. Didn't anyone hear that?'

'Believe it or not, Brenda, no.' Graham explained and she recognised exasperation in his voice, 'he had used a silencer and there was already a great deal of noise; you know yourself what it's like at these service stations. A continual clatter, kids yelling and everyone talking at once.

'I still find it incredible,' she said, 'that not one person noticed anything.'

'It appears not. He would, of course, have had the weapon concealed in something; we found shreds of charred newspaper print around the wound.'

'I see. And how many people I wonder, especially if they are travelling on their own, stop first to buy a newspaper before going into the cafe.'

'Quite. So, there we are, Brenda. I'll leave you to it; if I have anything more I'll be in touch.'

Brenda had no sooner put the receiver down when the phone rang again. This had to be the big boss she thought with a sinking feeling. It had to be. And now, with the latest development, there were things she could be doing: as a start, pay another visit to Eliza Brent. She was not entirely convinced that Steven Blackwood had severed all ties with her. She had no rational explanation for thinking this. It could not even be described as a hunch. Brenda Masters did not have hunches. Her way was sifting through plain facts, methodically and systematically, until a credible conclusion was reached. Each time she was working on a case which appeared to be unsolvable she was reminded of a game she used to play as a child. She had forgotten the name of it, 'pick-up-sticks' it might have been, not that it mattered, only that the long thin coloured sticks had to be dropped on to the table, the position they fell each time forming a different pattern but the real skill had been to remove each stick without shifting any of the others. This was exactly how this case felt to her, mentally shuffling and re-arranging each section of the shreds of information she had so far. Somewhere there must be a pattern and somehow she must painstakingly find it, removing each single extraneous scrap of worthless dross until she revealed the truth. These thoughts, not new ones, threaded their way rapidly through her brain as with a sigh she picked up the receiver.

'Brenda,' Graham Ford said, 'sorry to bother you, but something has just come in.'

'Yes, Graham?' another reprieve she thought with relief.

'We've just got the results from Steven Blackwood's mobile; he didn't have a phone in his flat, so presumably most of the calls he made would have been made from the mobile.'

'And?' she prompted.

'And,' another of his dry chuckles, 'he hadn't made many in the last seven days or so, but those he did make may be of some help to us. There was only one we haven't been able to locate,' he went on, 'it was to another mobile number, on Monday morning, ten-thirty-five to be exact.'

'And the others?'

'One to Lloyds Bank, the Oxford Street branch, on Tuesday midday to close his current account; he didn't have a deposit one and one on Wednesday morning at ten-fifteen to Thomas Cook, once again in Oxford Street, to confirm his travel arrangements.'

'He did have a busy week, didn't he?'

'You could say that.'

'So where was he planning to go then?'

'Brazil.'

'Brazil! This is beginning to sound all too familiar.'

'I know, he had the Friday morning flight booked to Rio de Janeiro and told them he would call in before they closed on Thursday to collect the tickets.'

'You did say tickets?'

'I did, yes,' he answered, 'the girl I spoke to at Thomas Cook's said they were for Mr and Mrs Steven Blackwood.'

'Odd'

'In what way?'

'Well,' she said slowly, trying to make some order of what she was beginning to suspect, unlikely though it may appear, 'you probably didn't know, but Steve Blackwood's *ex*-wife is living in Meadowbank; she moved into the lodge on the Tilsly estate last Saturday. Also, he called to see her the same afternoon.'

'Interesting.'

'Very.'

'Had she been expecting him to turn up do you think?'

'She says no.'

'And what do you think, Brenda. Did you believe her?'

'She *appears* genuine enough,' Brenda emphasised, 'but she could be lying. Hard to tell. She told us she hadn't seen him since their divorce, a year ago. She may or may not have been aware he had re-married, if indeed he had. Let's say, Graham,' she went on, 'I'm more than a little puzzled by those two air tickets, but, I know one thing, I'm going to have a few more words with her. In particular, I would like to see her reaction when she hears the latest, unless she knows already.'

'He made three more calls this week, Brenda, which I'm sure you will want to follow up on.'

'Yes?'

'They were all to the same number,' he continued and if she didn't know him better she would have thought he was deliberately keeping her in suspense, 'one, on Monday morning at eleven-ten; the second, the following morning at the same time and the third, an hour later exactly.'

'And you know who it was?'

'We don't know who he spoke to, only that they were made to a Meadowbank number, the 'Salmon's Rest' restaurant.'

'Well, well, this certainly opens things up somewhat.'

'You know the restaurant?'

'Quite well, the couple who have it have only been there since the end of last year. Peter and Danielle Taylor. She's French, from Paris originally, but moved to London about six years ago and bought her own restaurant in the West End. We haven't much background on him though, only that he worked with her in London for the last twelve months, before then we would have to make some enquiries. Interestingly enough though, Graham, Danielle Taylor had been trying to persuade Major Tilsly to sell her one of his paintings, but according to her he refused point blank.'

'There's certainly a great deal of mud about, Brenda. Look, I'll leave the Meadowbank end to you, and we'll check out the background on this guy Peter Taylor if you like.'

'Sounds alright to me, Graham. Speak to you later.'

*

The rain held off until after the funeral, sparing the mourners those last few moments at the graveside, which would have only added to the melancholic atmosphere of the occasion, although when it did arrive it was with a vengeance, relentlessly hitting the library windows, white sheets of it sliding down the glass making it impossible to see out. Mrs Plenderneath had lit the log fire, but in spite of the warmth, there was a chill in the air. Maureen Summers looked around the room for the first time, appreciating the comfort, although decidedly masculine, in particular, the old-fashioned dark teak desk and the high-backed wing chair which Colin Tilsly had suggested the lawyer take, while the rest of them arranged themselves in what reminded her of the final scenes of an Agatha Christie film. It was true, she thought, in many ways this was an ending: the ending for her at least, as for the others from what Reginald had told her, his demise would not make a great deal of difference, except for their inheritance. At the very thought of the word, she inwardly cringed; how she disliked this impression she had of anticipation and how appalled she had been when Mr Brutton had told her earlier in the week she would be expected to be here also. These people, apart from Colin whom she had only met a couple of times, were complete strangers to her and she was not imagining their hostility, except for Reginald's younger daughter. Wendy had gone out of her way at the church to talk to her, even suggesting she sit with the family. Although she had declined she had appreciated the gesture. The other daughter had barely looked at her when they had been introduced, although now and again throughout the service she caught the sideways glance Nanette Tilsly threw in her direction. As for Colin's wife; Rachel she was called, although polite, making light conversation, talking about everything except what was in all of their minds. Each of them, she was sure, had seen a different side to Reginald, while she, although she had known him for a number of years, had seen him as a loving and kind man. He had often told her he didn't understand his family, except for Wendy. She's like her mother, he had once said, a dreamer, but with a good head on her, and totally lacking in ambition. And yet, Maureen thought, as she looked at the younger woman, although the grey-blue eyes, so like Reginald's, were downcast as she waited for the lawyer to sit down and sort out his papers, there was definitely what she could only describe as a no-nonsense look about her. She was thirty-eight, the youngest of the family, and in colouring and build, nothing like either her brother or sister.

'This will not take long,' Arnold Brutton was saying, changing into his reading glasses, 'always a distressing part of the proceedings I always think, but I'm sure you will agree made very much worse by the circumstances.'

A slow nodding of heads was the only answer he was going to get it would seem, although Maureen noticed the impatient way Colin shifted in his chair. No doubt wants him to get on with it, she thought wryly. He would have to curb his impatience; Maureen had worked for the senior partner almost from the first months when she had joined the firm and she knew him well. He was thorough, deliberate in his speech at times, but he would never permit himself to be rushed, although when he had said the meeting wouldn't last long he had meant it, but if anyone tried to speed up what he had to say, it would only result in prolonging things.

'First, the estate,' the lawyer said, 'as I believe you are already aware, this has to remain in the family and that includes the manor house, there is adequate income from the company who have the ongoing lease of the water meadows at the rear of the property. This money is allocated for the upkeep of the building and the remaining grounds, including the wages of the housekeeper, Mrs Plenderneath. It was your father's wish that she be retained until such time as she is ready to retire, and from that date she will receive a small pension for life. It was also your father's wish, although understandably cannot be enforced, that a member of the family should live in the manor. You probably haven't had time to discuss this among yourselves, but when you have decided I will be pleased to be of assistance with the necessary formalities.'

'Mr Brutton,' Colin said quickly, his voice harsh to Maureen's ears, 'you say the estate has to remain in the family, surely that isn't entirely correct.'

'That was your father's wish, Colin and I would add it was also your mother's. The Old Manor House has been in the family for over two hundred years, they both dearly wished it to remain so. However,' he went on, 'you are technically correct in what you say, but I did not consider this the appropriate moment to elaborate on the proviso.'

'It's still part of the will though, isn't it?'

'Oh, yes.'

'So,' Colin insisted, 'if the three of us were to agree to sell, there would be no objection legally?'

'None at all, Colin.'

'Thank you,' calmer now, Colin leaned back in his chair, his hands clasped on the table in front of him, 'that's all I wanted to hear.'

And so Mr Brutton went on. No more was discussed about the estate, much to Maureen's relief. The atmosphere, almost tangible, had become not only embarrassing to her, but unpleasant, making her wish she was anywhere than in this room surrounded by members of Reginald's family, who in the main were probably feeling the same way. Most of the details of Reginald's will, although not known to her, were predictable and absolutely fair. Maureen had no idea, in fact had never expected to benefit, although having been invited to attend this meeting had already come to the conclusion there had to be something in the will which concerned her, but she was not prepared for the generosity.

'As I have said,' Arnold Brutton continued, removing his glasses and looking at each of them in turn, 'although your father could not have been described as a wealthy man, he had acquired substantial sums of money over the years, all of which he had re-invested wisely, enabling the three of you, Colin, Nanette and Wendy, to benefit quite handsomely. The yield in many of these investments has in fact been considerably higher than your father had anticipated, making this possible. 'Maureen,' he said, looking at her, 'as I am sure you know, Reginald was not a man who shared confidences easily, and I believe, as one of his oldest friends, I was one of those few and this, my dear, was a privilege. It was his wish and something he had intended doing even if he had not met such an untimely end, which was to provide sufficient funds for your daughter's education.'

Apart from a quick gasp from Nanette which she made an attempt to stifle by putting a hand over her mouth, there was absolute silence in the room, except for the rain continuing unremittingly to thrash against the windows. But not for long. Predictably perhaps, it was Colin jumping to his feet and pushing his chair back, who was the first to speak: '*Her* daughter! I have *three* daughters! What about them?'

'Colin, this is unseemly. I have already told you that all the children, including any Wendy may have in the future, are being provided for; in trust until they reach the age of twenty-five.'

'Colin's right,' now Nanette's turn, 'it doesn't seem fair!'

'What doesn't seem fair, Nanette?' words quietly spoken, but Maureen, already disliking intensely the way the conversation was going, recognised that look on Arnold Brutton's face. She had seen it often when he had been coping with recalcitrant and belligerent clients and inevitably they always came off worse. That mild, even benign expression could very quickly be replaced by one of steel-like inflexibility, one of the attributes which made him an excellent lawyer.

'Well,' Nanette went on, imperviously, 'this girl isn't family, is she?'

'I think it is time we brought these proceedings to a close, Nanette,' he said coldly, 'and this girl as you impolitely describe her, is the young daughter of the lady your father had hoped to marry and she would, as you must realise, have then become part of the family. Unfortunately, that was not to be. Major Tilsly was, in drawing up his final will, attempting to cover the eventuality of dying before that marriage could take place. Now,' he paused, taking his eyes away from Nanette's flushed face, and once again surveying each of them, 'Wendy, have you any comment you would like to make?'

'Only,' Wendy Tilsly spoke for the first time since they had come into the library and giving Maureen a sad apologetic smile, 'I think it's only right and proper. A fine gesture.'

'It's all very well for you to talk, Wendy,' Nanette turned round angrily in her chair to glare at her sister, 'you're not married and you don't have any family. Have you the remotest idea of how much that costs!'

'I honestly don't think that's either here or there. Surely you didn't expect dad to provide for your increasing cost of living?' followed by another gasp from Nanette.

'Ssh, Nanette,' her husband nudged her on the arm, 'you've said enough.'

'And what about the collection,' Nanette demanded, her voice rising angrily and pushing his arm away, 'you didn't show the slightest interest in it, were in fact completely unsupportive with what Colin and I wanted to do! I firmly believe we have a right to that!'

'I explained the position to Colin earlier this week,' Arnold Brutton smoothly put in, 'also I have read out, in full, the terms of your father's will. As he wished, the whole art collection will be bequeathed to the Tate Gallery and that, I would add, is final, also incontestable.'

Chapter Seventeen

James said little for most of the way and it was only when they were approaching the end of the motorway he broke the silence. Leonora had learned not to interrupt him when he was like this and she knew it was not only his need to concentrate on the steady flow of traffic heading towards London; he had been more than usually distracted since they had left Meadowbank. There was something bothering him and with her practised ability to give him the time he needed to sort out what it was, she was content to wait, patiently sitting next to him, drowsing off now and again which was her normal reaction to the sheer tedium of motorway driving. How anyone could actually enjoy this every working day of their lives was a complete mystery to her and suddenly she wished instead they were heading back up north to the sanctuary of their quiet and predictable lives in their wonderful house perched on the hill overlooking the ocean, instead of the clamour and discomfort of London and the excessive grandeur of the following evening's banquet. But, although James shared her views, she knew he looked forward to this occasion each year: the reunion, albeit a formal one, but more importantly for him, meeting up with old friends and ex-colleagues, most of them, like him, now retired and living a quite different life. Stifling a sigh, she looked at him and, as though sensing her eyes on him, he smiled.

'It's just come to me, Leonora,' he said at last, 'that chap in the restaurant last night. The one behind the bar; did you notice him?'

'Not really,' she admitted slowly, trying to remember, 'I had my back to the bar, of course, although I did catch a glimpse of him.'

'Did he look familiar to you?'

'I can't say he did, darling.' sorry to disappoint him, but it was the truth. She had paid him little attention, far more interested in listening to Simon telling her about his various assignments and how much he had enjoyed photographing in the more obscure parts of Africa. 'Except his height, I suppose; quite tall, almost six foot and he had light brown hair, cut rather fashionably, if anything a little effeminate, but it was only a fleeting impression. I don't believe I would recognise him again.'

'Pity.'

'Why?'

'Because I did recognise him, at least I am ninety-nine per cent certain, although it has taken me until now to decide it must be him. In actual fact, Leonora, he hasn't changed all that much in the last ten, eleven years. I suppose it was seeing him out of context which threw me at first.'

'And you think I should have recognised him?'

'I'm surprised you didn't, but then as you say you were sitting with your back to him.'

'Aren't you going to tell me who you think he was then?'

'Paul Thomson.'

'Paul Thomson? Oh, I know who you mean! He had something to do with that dreadful affair in Mombasa. We never actually met him though, did we?'

'No,' James admitted, 'in fact we only saw him a couple of times when we were in Mombasa; at the club. He didn't mix with the same crowd as we did, but I remember him being pointed out to me when the rumours started about him having something to do with the break-up of Sally and Eric's marriage and then later, after Eric's death, he did a rapid disappearing act. They never did find him you know, Leonora. It was as if he had just vanished into thin air.'

'James, darling,' she said carefully. It was not as if she mistrusted his judgement in any way; far from it. No longer young, he had not lost his ability for total recall, even with people he had only met briefly. James never forgot a face and she had never known him to be wrong. 'don't you think,' she went on, remembering back to what had been a shocking scandal causing such a stir among the expatriate community of Mombasa, even reaching as far away as Nairobi and giving the gossipmongers plenty of scope, 'if this was Paul Thomson, he would have done something to change his appearance?'

'You would think so, yes,' he agreed, 'but then he was clever. Nobody ever doubted that for a minute. Take for example the ongoing mystery of Lord Lucan. How many sitings do you think there must have been? Hundreds, I would say. And when you think about it, Leonora, that in itself is quite smart.'

'You mean Lord Lucan realising there were several men who looked exactly like him, there would be no point in disguising himself? A bit like Russian roulette! Or, and I know this would be described today as being politically incorrect, but like the child's rhyme; Eeny, meeny, miny mo –'

'– Quite.' James said.

'I could be right, though.' Leonora smiled at his disapproving profile, 'Better to look like everyone else in a crowd and I did say a few minutes ago I doubted whether I would have recognised him.'

'The evidence against him was pretty damning, you know. Apart from it being common knowledge of what was going on between him and Sally, he was the last person apparently to see Eric.'

'Was he? I didn't know that.'

'I'm sure you didn't, my dear. How blessed I am to be married to a woman totally lacking in curiosity.'

'Living in a world of her own, you should be saying!'

'At times it does seem like that, but it doesn't bother me. In fact, I've always found it quite refreshing. But, seriously, Leonora, it was a very bad business. And, naturally, when he made himself scarce the way he did it looked even more likely he had something to do with it.'

'What are you going to do about it, James?'

'There's nothing I can do personally, of course; not that I would want to get involved, but I think I'll have a word with my old friend Raymond Hill in the foreign office; he'll know the right people to contact and then they can suss the chap out.'

'I can't help wondering why Danielle and he would choose a small town like Meadowbank. It was quite obvious to me she doesn't like it there. Eliza mentioned they weren't terribly popular in the town, not into socialising, although she did say she rather liked her.'

'Well, all I can say is, I hope Eliza doesn't get too friendly with the pair of them. The man is bad news, Leonora.'

'You really do believe he's Paul Thomson, don't you?'

'Yes, I do.'

'It's just occurred to me,' Leonora said quickly, 'if you recognised him, don't you think he may have recognised you, darling?'

'I hope not, but I suppose it's possible, but now you come to mention it, there was something which struck me at the time.'

'What?'

'Nothing much and I could have been mistaken, but I had the impression he was about to come over to our table, but then changed his mind.'

'That's fairly conclusive, don't you think?'

'Not necessarily,' he said slowly, but she could tell by his expression; the way his jaw had tightened as it always did when he was worried, 'he could have had a change of mind.'

They had now left the motorway and were approaching Tower Bridge which meant James needed all of his concentration. It was not as if he wasn't used to driving in London, but it had been some months since they had been there and as they always said each time they returned, the traffic with the resulting congestion seemed worse than ever. They should be reaching their hotel within ten or fifteen minutes Leonora thought and then she would give Eliza a ring. She had not wanted to say anything to James; he had enough on his mind, but she could not help worrying about her. Far too much had happened there recently and the fact that someone like Paul Thomson was actually in Meadowbank unnerved her. She tried to rationalise. Eliza was a mature woman, she wasn't gullible. She was shrewd and would never do anything impetuously. All the same she desperately wished that just this once James was wrong.

*

Steve was dead. Not a natural death. Nor an accident. He had been killed, murdered. Shot in the coffee shop at a motorway service station. Although unfamiliar with the M3 motorway, Eliza knew where the Basingstoke one was. The same one her parents had stopped at the day before. And she remembered how annoyed Leonora had been at finding the place closed and how she had overheard someone say there had been a shooting. And how her father had made light of it, not really believing her. How wrong he had been Eliza thought. She knew how irrational she was being, but after Chief Inspector Masters had left, her brain was incapable of assimilating the facts of what she had told her in such a cold unemotional way. It was too soon to ask herself how she felt about such a violent end to Steve's life. She had not loved him for a long time, but she had been married to him and although most of those years had been unhappy, he had played a large part in her life. She had never expected to hear from him again and seeing him last Saturday still had a disturbing affect on her. But, why had he been at that service station in the first place? Had he been coming back to Meadowbank? To see her again, or could there be a more simple explanation; one more in keeping with his secretive nature? Had he arranged to meet someone there? He may have. Or, and this was something she really did not believe, had he merely been in the wrong place at the wrong time. No, that couldn't be right. He must have had a reason. A neutral meeting place. Brenda Masters had implied as much, also, although she hadn't actually said so, that *she* was the person Steve had arranged to meet there! Eliza had the distinct impression that as far as the chief inspector was concerned she had not yet been eliminated from her original enquiries even although it now transpires Steve had re-married. And where was she, Eliza wondered. Had there been any sign of her when the police went to his flat, which presumably they must have done last Sunday. Brenda Masters had been very sparing with anything further she may have found out about him. Danielle had been right she thought wryly; the police did seem to be working at random, there didn't seem to be any rational method to their investigation. Was this the way they always worked she wondered as she watched the rain streaming down the kitchen window practically obscuring her view of the drive. And now, just because she had been married to Steve, once again she was being considered as guilty. She regretted now not telling her parents more. She needed their support, especially that of her level-headed father. But for too long she had coped on her own, building up a barrier of independence. Why should she waver now? It would not be fair to either of them. Her father had worked hard for his retirement; just because she felt threatened by the treatment she was getting from Brenda Masters was no reason to weaken. What could he do anyway? Sympathise. Of course she would receive plenty of that, but it would not be enough. Sighing, she turned away from the window, and went upstairs to the studio. She needed to do something active. Something positive; like work. That was the answer she decided, switching on the table lamp. Although she preferred natural light this would have to do. There was a pile of correspondence still waiting to be answered, but she was not in the mood. That could wait. For now, she would make a start on the initial sketches of a new set of summer designs she had promised her manufacturers. And then, provided there were no more interruptions, she may have them ready to take with her when she went up to London the following week.

*

'Peter,' Danielle muttered under breath, 'I just do not believe this! They are coming back!'

'Who?'

'Her! The chief inspector! This is really too much! What on earth are our customers going to think?'

'Don't worry, Danielle,' he said, 'you carry on; I'll tell her it isn't convenient. They'll have to come back later when we're closed.'

'Hmmh!' Danielle stifled the explosion and turning her back on her husband walked quickly into the kitchen. Even from where he was standing at the other end of the restaurant he could hear her. Giving the staff the benefit of her wrath no doubt he thought.

'Good morning, Mr Taylor.' Not bad looking Peter thought. It wasn't as if she was in uniform anyway, he didn't know why Danielle was so concerned. Most of the customers were visitors to Meadowbank in any case, he thought, his admiring glance taking in the slim figure of the woman walking towards him. The man following closely behind her could hardly be described as the memorable type, although Peter remembered seeing him a couple of times in the pub. Someone had mentioned he was with the police. Ian Ash he thought he was called.

'Good morning,' Peter said, 'I'm afraid you've come at a rather busy time, Chief Inspector, my wife really can't –'

'– it isn't your wife we've come to speak to, Mr Taylor.'

'Oh?'

'Is there somewhere more private we could talk?'

'Yes, of course,' he said quickly, 'my office, but I don't see how I can be of any help to you. I take it you're here about the late Major Tilsly?' he added, leading them up the short flight of stairs.

'There are a few questions I would like to ask you,' the way she adroitly evaded his question did not escape him, also how she waited until they were in his office, the door firmly closed behind them, 'there has been another murder and I'm hoping you will be able to clear up a few points for us. It won't take long. We realise you have a restaurant to run, but I'm afraid our enquiries must take precedent.'

'You say there's been another murder? I hadn't heard. In Meadowbank?

'No, not in Meadowbank, but we believe there could be a connection with the deaths of Major Tilsly and Len Roberts. Mr Taylor,' she continued and he watched Ian Ash take his notebook out, opening it at a fresh page, 'does the name Steven Blackwood mean anything to you?'

'No,' he answered, 'should it?'

'Steven Blackwood made three telephone calls to this restaurant. One on Monday and the other two on Tuesday and then two days later he was shot. This happened at the Basingstoke service station; you may have heard about it. It was on the nine o'clock news last night.'

'There's no way we can ever have the time to watch television.'

'Well,' she said slowly, 'the fact remains he did make those calls here.'

'He may very well have done,' he said, 'we receive several calls each day. They don't all give their names, except when they make reservations, of course. My wife may know, but –'

'– we will speak to her later, but for now I want you first to think about those calls you took on Tuesday. You say you get several, I don't expect you to remember them all naturally, but if a person were to telephone three times, I would expect that to remain in your mind.'

'Well, I'm sorry not to be of any help, although I remember my wife mentioning to me that a man had phoned a few times and for some reason wouldn't give his name. I think she assumed he was cold selling. We get a number of them as you can imagine.'

'How many times did she say he rang?'

'I believe she said twice.'

'And would this have been on Tuesday? I can give you the times. Sergeant Ash?'

Ian Ash, without looking up, turned back a couple of pages, stopping when he came to what he was looking for: 'Eleven-ten on the Monday,' he read out, 'eleven-ten the following morning and the other call one hour later.'

'Do you remember answering the phone at any of those times?' Brenda Masters asked him.

'Can't say I do,' he said, 'certainly not on the Monday morning; I would have been at the Cash & Carry in Winchester. As for the Tuesday, although I must have been around, the only calls I had were from suppliers.'

'And when you aren't here, Mr Taylor,' she persisted, 'your wife would have answered the phone.'

'Of course.'

'No-one else. Any of your employees, perhaps?'

'It's very rare we are both out at the same time, Chief Inspector.'

'But you do have an extension from your office here down to the restaurant?'

'Yes, also to the kitchen.'

'I see. Yesterday afternoon, Mr Taylor,' she said, her eyes unblinking as she looked directly at him, 'were you in the restaurant.'

'Yes, as I am every afternoon.'

'All afternoon?'

'What are you suggesting?'

'I'm not suggesting anything, all I'm trying to do is eliminate as many people as I can; that way, I can leave you alone. You were busy yesterday lunchtime?'

'Very. We have been every day this week. In fact, suddenly Meadowbank and including, somewhat fortuitously for us, the 'Salmon's Rest', have become extremely popular.'

'What time do you usually close?'

'The last orders are taken at two o'clock, but by the time we've finished clearing up around three and then we're back at six to prepare for the evening.'

'And yesterday, after you had closed the restaurant, did you or your wife go out?'

'Danielle, as far as I know, didn't go anywhere.'

'As far as you know? Were you not here then?'

'I had an appointment in Winchester at a quarter to three and I got back here about a couple of hours later.'

'I see,' Brenda Masters said, 'and your appointment was with whom?'

'With my dentist, Chief Inspector,' he said, 'for my six-monthly check-up.'

'Would you mind giving me the name of your dentist?'

'Not at all,' he said, 'Nigel Prescott, in Jewry Street.' watching as the sergeant slowly wrote down the name. What next he wondered. She was like a bloody terrier, tenacious and systematic, never letting go for one single second and he waited for her next move.

'You say you were away for a couple of hours; that means you would have been back by five. Do you think you could be more precise?'

'Not really, I wasn't in any particular hurry and I knew I didn't need to be here until six in any case. Actually, I called in at the Royal Oak for a drink first.'

'And your wife was in when you got back?'

'Yes.'

'Anyone else?'

'No, it was too early for any of the staff. Look, Chief Inspector,' he said quickly, sensing it was time for him to show some kind of indignation for the way her questioning was going, 'you don't honestly believe I killed this man, someone I didn't even know? How could I possibly have had the time?'

'Mr Taylor,' moving slightly in the chair, but without taking her eyes away from him, 'that is something we will have to establish; the time factor I mean. As you hadn't heard about the shooting how do you know what time it took place?'

'I don't of course, but I was only away for a couple of hours!'

'Your dental appointment was at two forty-five you say?'

'That's right.'

'And did you have to wait?'

'No, I was seen straight away.'

'Your check-up; would have lasted how long?'

'No more than fifteen minutes, less even.'

'And afterwards, you drove straight back to Meadowbank?'

'Stopping off at the 'Royal Oak''

'How long did you stay there, Mr Taylor?'

'I can't remember.' he answered, the intensity of her gaze beginning to get on his nerves. It was as if she could see right into his mind, anticipating his every reaction. He found himself holding his breath unless she detected the slightest change in his manner, no matter how slight and under normal conditions would be quite normal, but this was no normal situation. The rapidity of her questioning did not give him enough time to think through what his responses should be.

'Did you talk to anyone there, except presumably the barman?'

'No, I didn't. The place was packed, there had been a seminar and a whole crowd of them had finished for the day I think. They all wanted to be served at once.'

'Do you go there quite regularly?'

'I wouldn't say regularly,' he answered, trying to slow her down, 'now and again. Why do you ask?'

'I'm just wondering whether the barman or any of the staff would have recognised you.'

'I suppose they could have done; you'll have to ask them.'

'We intend to, Mr Taylor. Now, before we leave, I would like to go over the times again.'

'Yes?'

'You would have left the surgery at three o'clock. Am I right?'

'Around then, yes.'

'Your car, Mr Taylor, how far away were you parked?'

'Not far, one of the streets off Jewry Street; a five minute walk.'

'And the drive back to Meadowbank; forty minutes, forty-five minutes at the most.'

'The traffic was heavy that afternoon.'

'It normally is,' the caustic tone not lost on him, 'however,' she went on relentlessly, 'you would have arrived at the hotel about four. Would you agree?'

'Sounds about right.'

'One final question, Mr Taylor,' pausing, whether for affect which he doubted; more likely to gauge his reaction, 'do you possess a firearm?'

'No, I don't.'

Danielle was at the reception desk when they went back downstairs. The restaurant was filling up, it was not even midday and already more than half the tables were occupied and then he remembered this was the morning of the major's funeral. At the far end of the room he recognised a group of press reporters who had been in several times since the beginning of the week. Business was certainly good Peter thought as he walked over to her. Even Danielle could not complain about that, although judging by the frown on her face as she looked up at them, she was not in a good mood. They were in for a difficult day he thought stifling a sigh.

'It's obvious, Mrs Taylor,' Brenda Masters said to her before Danielle had time to make any sort of protest, 'you are extremely busy and I promise you this will only take a matter of minutes.'

'I hope so, Chief Inspector,' the frown remaining, 'I have already been subjected to a barrage of questions about Major Tilsly.'

'This is not about the major, Mrs Taylor. Another matter entirely.'

'Really?' even Danielle's sarcasm didn't penetrate. His wife was certainly a match for the indomitable woman standing squarely in front of the desk. Now it was Danielle's turn to be subjected to the stare.

'It's about phone calls which were made to this restaurant, three in all, and the caller I understand wouldn't give his name. Your husband doesn't remember receiving any, but he has told us you did.'

'I did, yes, but why the interest. It was probably someone trying to sell us something.'

'Perhaps, but can you remember anything about them.'

'Not really, no, just that he asked to speak to my husband.'

'How many times did he call?'

'Twice; once on Monday morning and the next time the following morning. I didn't mention the first one to Peter, I suppose I forgot to, but when he phoned the next day, I realised it was the same man.'

'Only the two calls? Are you sure?'

'Of course I'm sure. What on earth is so important about someone phoning the restaurant and refusing to give his name?'

'You use the word refuse. Did you actually ask him for his name?'

'I did, yes, and each time he put the phone down.'

'I see,' the Chief Inspector persisted, 'you say he asked to speak to your husband, Mrs Taylor. Was this by his surname –'

'– no, his Christian name. He said "could I speak to Pete"; that was all.'

'And yet,' here it comes he thought and right on cue, without the slightest hesitation, 'you refer to your husband as Peter?'

'Everyone does, Chief Inspector.'

'Everyone?'

'As far as I know. I've never heard anyone call him Pete before.'

'Mr Taylor,' Brenda Masters swivelling on her heels to face him, 'you have nothing further you would like to add to what you have already told us?'

'Absolutely nothing, Chief Inspector.'

Chapter Eighteen

She looked much prettier close-up, although black did not suit her, draining her of any natural colour and making her look even paler than the day before, but then nobody ever looked their best at funerals, especially family funerals and from what Simon had told her Wendy had been very fond of her father. It was late afternoon when Wendy made a surprise visit to the lodge. The rain had stopped at last and for the first time that day the sun was shining, promising a warm evening without the stifling clamminess before the storm. Eliza had been on the point of clearing away her drawing materials, feeling reasonably satisfied with what she had managed to achieve. She only needed a few more hours and the sketches would be finished: a brand new collection; this one she hoped symbolising summer, the fragile soft hues of a dragonfly intertwined with shreds of honeysuckle. Unusual, she knew, but she believed it would work well, for the drop earrings and as a buckle on a pale cream satin belt.

'Hello,' she said, standing in the open doorway, a soft leather bag on a gilt chain swinging from her shoulder, giving the only relief from the sombre and unflattering black, 'I'm Wendy Tilsly. I thought it was time I introduced myself, but – ' she faltered, '- but, perhaps I've called at a bad time; you're busy aren't you?'

'No, I have been, but I've finished for the day,' Eliza smiled at her, 'come in, won't you. I was just about to make some coffee, would you like some? Or a glass of wine, perhaps?'

'Wine would be lovely.'

'I was so sorry to hear about your father,' Eliza began, not knowing what to say, or even how to commiserate. Also, Steve kept creeping into her mind, and, as always, unbidden and unwanted and she hoped he'd had nothing to do with what had happened to the major. That would be extremely difficult to live with; how on earth would she be able to face someone like Wendy Tilsly? Although the whole business had nothing to do with her, the shame of what she already knew about him remained. 'I never met Major Tilsly,' she went on, 'but Simon has told me how much he liked him and of the time when you were all children.'

'Thank you,' a smile which immediately transformed her features, making her seem a lot younger than her thirty-eight years, 'those were happy times,' she sighed, 'but you can't stay young forever, can you?'

'It would certainly be a funny old world if we could!'

'True, but ever since I heard about his death I've found it so difficult to think of the present. My mind keeps going back to when I still lived at home; it's as if I am living in a time warp. Do you know what I mean?'

'I think so, yes,' Eliza said gently, opening the fridge door and taking out a bottle of wine, 'how long do you plan to stay?'

'I haven't really made up my mind yet. Of course I'll have to go back to Hong Kong sooner or later.'

'You're in publishing aren't you?'

'Simon again?'

'Yes.' Eliza admitted.

'He told me about you as well when I was talking to him earlier today; of how you wanted to get away from London to start up your own jewellery design business. Sometimes I wish I had the courage to break away, step off the treadmill.'

'Away from publishing?'

'Oh, no, never that. I suppose I mean people really, or should I say one particular person.'

'A man?'

'How did you guess?' Wendy laughed for the first time; a soft tinkling laugh which lingered even after her expression grew serious once more.

'Because it usually is,' Eliza said, pouring out two glasses and handing one to her, 'I suppose at one time or another we all go through it.'

'I know my situation is not unique,' Wendy said, taking a sip of her wine, 'but I guess I've reached what you could describe as a crossroads in my relationship with Dan. I'm in a quandary as to which road I should take. With dad going it's made me take another look at my life, the way it just isn't moving. It has become static, going absolutely nowhere and quite frankly I'm beginning to realise it never will if I don't break away from Dan. I expect you've guessed he's married?'

'It did cross my mind,' Eliza sympathised, 'perhaps being away from him for a time you'll be able to get your thoughts into perspective.'

'I hope so. I really do.'

'Tell me about Hong Kong. It's always struck me as a very vibrant place, the exotic east.' doing her best to lighten her mood; to make her smile again. Eliza was not too surprised that a virtual stranger should so readily want to take her into her confidence. It wasn't the first time; for some reason which she had never been able to work out, people did confide in her. Paradoxically, she always found it easier to view other people's problems, free as they were, from her own emotional clutter.

'That's how I used to see it when I first arrived there but now, well,' she paused for a couple of seconds, 'I guess work has got in the way and I've allowed myself to drift along not giving much serious thought to the future. I just never seem to get the time to just sit back or perhaps haven't wanted to, shying away from facing facts perhaps.'

'Sounds exhausting.'

'Oh, believe me, Eliza, it is!'

'Would you say more so than London?'

'I wouldn't say that exactly, it's probably because in comparison Hong Kong is so much smaller and constantly, no matter what time of the day and night, crammed with people. Frenetic. Do you know, the only time I can honestly say I really like it now is at Chinese New Year; there's always a mass exodus then, with the majority of people leaving to spend the holiday with their relations in China.'

'I'm beginning to get the picture,' Eliza smiled at her, 'and where you live, Wendy? On the Peak? You see, I do know a little bit about Hong Kong!'

'My goodness, no! That's for the seriously rich; my apartment is in what is called Mid-Levels, which isn't too bad. We do have a swimming pool in the complex which is great during the steamy heat of the summer months.'

'And when you get the time.'

'Exactly. Actually, I have some photographs; they were taken a couple of months ago.' she said, pulling out a slim photo album from her bag, 'Here,' pointing to the first one, 'this is the view from the apartment. As you can see,' she added, 'mostly of buildings although if you look between them you will be able to catch a glimpse of the sea!'

Impressive though the view was, Eliza knew she could never live anywhere like that, how did people breathe she wondered. She could make out the sea, but only just, also the coastline of Kowloon, recognisable from seeing similar views from television. She wondered whether Simon had ever been there: for his work perhaps, but she didn't think the environment would suit him either. In spite of his travels he had struck her as a man more comfortable in a quieter and less demanding environment. Who did it suit then? Wendy, according to Simon, had made her life there for the last ten years, which meant she must have adapted to it all. Perhaps ten years was long enough; it could explain why she was ready for a change, apart from extricating herself from a relationship which had obviously gone sour.

'And this one,' Wendy said, turning to the next page, 'it was taken out on my balcony.'

There were three people in the photograph; not Wendy, presumably she had taken it. A woman, around the same age as Wendy, sun-tanned, a mass of auburn hair tied back loosely from her face and with one arm draped possessively around the shoulders of a dark-haired man, also deeply tanned and smiling directly at the camera. The second man, blond and like the other two, smiling. A photograph like thousands of others, of people who knew each other well; friends, enjoying a relaxing time together: an opened bottle of wine on the cane table in front of them, their faces shaded slightly by the canopy of a blue and white striped parasol, but not too much to prevent Eliza recognising the blond-haired man. The man in the pub on Sunday morning! The likeness was uncanny. Everybody, she had often heard, had a double, so surely this must be the case.

'Miranda and Phil, two of my oldest friends and Dan.'

'They look happy.' Eliza said ineptly, unable to drag her eyes away from the photograph. She must be wrong. It couldn't be him. In Meadowbank? Practically on the doorstep of the manor? She could have said something, mentioned the likeness and then the moment passed and it was too late. Something prevented her, some instinct, crazy though it seemed, warned her to say nothing. It did not make sense. Dan, Wendy's boyfriend, lived in Hong Kong. He couldn't have been in two places at once. Could he?

'He's extremely attractive,' she murmured, 'he reminds me of the actor —'

' — Robert Redford.' Wendy finished for her, 'Everyone says that! Younger, of course.' she added with a quirky little smile.

And Eliza managed to leave it at that. They had a second glass of wine and Wendy showed her the other photographs; most of them views: the familiar Hong Kong sights; the Island by night, streaked by the multi-coloured strips of artificial lights; the much-photographed Star Ferry on its way across the harbour towards Kowloon; a Buddhist temple; the street market in Mongkok; the trams in Central and many more. A lovely close-up of Wendy on the top deck of one of the ferries going over to Lantau Island and taken she said by Dan on one of their rare days off; more of Wendy and their friends all wearing the same unmistakable glow of self-confidence she had seen so often among young professionals, especially those enjoying the expatriate lifestyle, but not many of Dan. Eliza tried not to stare, to spend too long each time she saw one of him, at the same time, mentally trying to concentrate instead on the man she had seen in 'The Market Inn', recalling every detail she could remember about him. Although he had not been smiling, quite the reverse, the resemblance was still strong; the way he had been sitting, with his head slightly tilted to one side, identical to Dan in the first photograph, as though listening to something – or someone. She did recall his hands in particular; long slim fingers; clever hands she had thought at the time and she had wondered, speculated as she often did when indulging in people-watching, what he could do for a living. They were similarities, that was all, but it would appear that Wendy's boyfriend did indeed have a double, wishing that Simon could have seen the photograph, but perhaps he hadn't been as observant. He and Brian had been talking for most of the time, not entirely excluding her, about people she had not met, giving her a chance to look round the bar, absorbing her new surroundings. It had been Simon who had first mentioned him, although she had already noticed him, especially how he scarcely changed his position and how withdrawn he appeared from the many customers milling around the bar. Brian had said he'd been in Meadowbank since the previous Thursday, from Singapore he thought. A coincidence? It had to be.

'You've probably had enough of all these,' Wendy smiled, taking the album from her and slipping it back into her bag, 'it's funny, you know, but each time I leave Hong Kong I find myself looking back at it objectively, seeing it properly. It never seems quite real to me then. Perhaps I don't belong there after all.'

'Do you return to England often?' Eliza asked her.

'Not as often as I should.' she said sadly, 'It's ironic in a way, but I had been thinking of making a surprise visit; I hadn't even got round to telling Dan, but then two weeks ago I had to attend a Book Fair in Beijing, this was all at the last minute and I only got back to Hong Kong last Tuesday and I reckon you know the rest, Eliza.'

'You've hardly had time to catch your breath.'

'I know,' she agreed, once again the sad little smile, 'it wouldn't be quite so awful if my father hadn't died in such a shocking way. I believe I could have managed to come to terms with his death, but now. It is all too much to take in.'

'The police don't seem to be much further forward in their enquiries from what I've heard, but maybe you don't want to talk about it.'

'But I do, Eliza!' she said, her voice filled with emotion and for the first time showing a flash of anger, 'Everyone has been treating me as though I should be protected. They all have! Colin, especially. He refuses to talk about that night, but the thing is I want to know! I want to know as much as anyone else does, which probably isn't a great deal.' she added, running out of breath. 'It couldn't have been premeditated. Surely. It must have had something to do with that art collection. It must. Do you know, Eliza, that has, and still is, causing considerable dissention in my family. How I wish dad had never started collecting those damned pictures, because that is what I firmly believe. They are damned. I was glad when I learned he had made arrangements to donate the whole lot to the Tate; I already knew he had lost interest some years ago; he hardly ever went into the gallery, so I wasn't so surprised when Colin told me. He wasn't happy though, nor Nanette.'

'Wanted the collection to remain in the family, I suppose.'

'Perhaps, I don't know. I really do not understand my brother and sister anymore, Eliza. We just don't talk the same language. And then, with dad announcing that he was going to get married again, well, I'm ashamed to say they didn't like that one little bit. Poor woman,' Wendy went on, unstoppable now, 'I felt sorry for her this afternoon, I really did. If she had any doubts about their hostility towards her they would have rapidly gone by now.'

'Oh dear, what happened?'

'Nothing actually *happened*,' she emphasised quickly, 'it was when dad's will was being read out to us. He had made a provision for Maureen's young daughter which I thought was a lovely thing to do, but not those two. I honestly don't know how they could have been so – so rude. And so insensitive. They actually resented her receiving anything!'

'Families.'

'I know,' she agreed, a rueful smile hovering on her lips, 'what must you think of me, Eliza, going on like this.'

'I think you probably wanted to speak to someone.'

'You're right. That's exactly how I felt. You're a good listener and that's a gift.'

'I think you've all had a dreadful shock and maybe when something as bad as this happens, people react in different ways.'

'Possibly, and now I'd better get back,' she said, standing up, 'and it looks as if you have another visitor.' she added, looking out of the kitchen window.

'Really?' surprised; she hadn't heard a car.

'Yes, it's Simon. He must have walked from the mill, probably felt like some exercise.'

Simon Grant must be a mind-reader Eliza thought as she went to let him in. Like Wendy, she also needed to talk, but she thought only to him; there was really no-one else. She wanted to tell him about Steve, get his reaction, and, now, about the extraordinary likeness in Wendy's photograph.

'Ah, Wendy, you've met Eliza. That's good.' he said, following her into the kitchen.

'Well,' Wendy smiled, 'you told me so much about her, I was intrigued. I just had to meet her.'

'I'm glad you did,' Eliza said, 'look, Wendy, do you have to leave? Have another drink.'

'As much as I'd like to, I'd better not. Colin and Rachel are taking me out for a meal this evening; I don't think you know Rachel, but my sister-in-law does not like to be kept waiting.'

'Poor Wendy,' he said, 'you'll be glad to get back to Hong Kong. Too much family, eh?'

'You can say that again! But, it's Eliza you should be feeling sorry for; I've spent the last hour boring her to tears.'

'Not at all,' Eliza insisted, 'in fact, Simon, Wendy has been showing me some photographs of Hong Kong. Have you ever been there?'

'No, I haven't,' he admitted, 'of course I realise how photogenic the Island is, thousands of photographs and reels of film have already proved that, but it never appealed to me. Not my kind of place. Sorry, Wendy,' he added giving her a shamefaced grin, 'I don't mean to offend.'

'No offence, Simon,' she said, 'in fact, Hong Kong has lost its edge somehow for me; I think it's time to make a change.'

'Really? I thought you were quite settled there; your father thought you were.'

'Did he? I hadn't realised, but then how should I. I feel so terribly guilty not making the effort to come back home more often.'

'If it's any comfort,' he assured her, 'he did understand.'

'Good, I'm glad.'

Wendy left soon after, promising to see Eliza again before she finally left England. A nice woman she thought, watching Wendy walk up the drive towards the manor, although realising the description was inadequate. Wendy Tilsly was far more than that. She had insight; she was obviously deeply affected by her father's death, but not only that, trying to sort out her own turbulent private life. Eliza had been there. She knew what it was like to be pulled this way and that, not certain whether the move she finally made would be the right one. There were no guarantees and in the end only one person could make the final decision, but although only being in Wendy's company for such a short time, she felt she would pull through this period, difficult though it may be for her, this thought immediately bringing her back to the photograph. Dan, Wendy's boyfriend; she hadn't mentioned his surname, not that it mattered. If, and Eliza had to admit to herself it was a very large if; if he was the same man they had seen in the pub, his arrival in Meadowbank was no coincidence and that realisation brought a shiver down the back of her spine. She needed a second opinion. Simon's. But first, she must tell him about Steve.

'By the way, Eliza,' he said, walking with her out on to the terrace; the chairs were still wet so, instead, they stood side by side looking across the grounds, the grass glistening greenly in the strong sunlight and the trees edging the drive continuing to drip from the heavy downpour, 'what's happened to your mobile?'

'Oh, no! It's still on charge! I'm sorry, Simon, have you been trying to call me?'

'I have, also Leonora. She sounded worried about you, although I did my best to reassure her.'

'I think she's a bit jittery about me being here, but there is no need for her to be. I'm a big girl now.' attempting a lightness she did not feel.

'I know that, Eliza,' he said quietly, 'and you know that, but I'm afraid your mother doesn't think so.'

'I'll give her a ring; so, she phoned you instead, Simon?'

'No, your father did.'

'Oh!'

'Yes, he had something rather strange to tell me.'

'Yes?'

'It was about Peter from the 'Salmon's Rest'; apparently, he recognised him last night.'

'Danielle's husband? I don't understand.'

'It's rather a long story, but it would seem that might not be his real name. It could be Paul Thomson. Paul Thomson was in Mombasa at the same time as your parents and he was suspected of having something to do with the murder of one of his friends. He had been having an affair with the wife and after her husband's body was found, he did a rapid disappearing act.'

'This is staggering! When did all this happen?'

'About ten or eleven years ago.'

'And the police never found him?'

'No, they didn't; the case is still open. One of their many unsolved crimes, although your father told me there was never any real doubt about Paul Thomson's guilt.'

'Is he sure it's the same person?'

'Oh, yes; he's positive.'

'What is he going to do, Simon? I simply cannot believe any of this, it all sounds so – so incredible.' stumbling over the words.

'He was planning to get in touch with a friend of his who works for the Foreign Office; no doubt they'll take the matter up from there; check into Peter's background, that sort of thing.'

'How unpleasant. If it is true, I feel dreadfully sorry for Danielle.'

And then she told him the visit she'd had from the chief inspector and how she had broken the news to her of Steve. She was all too aware of the flatness in her voice as she recited word for word everything Brenda Masters had said, missing out nothing, even the lingering impression of feeling she was under suspicion. For what? For acting as an accomplice for her ex-husband, enabling him to enter the manor that night and then having something to do with his death? The whole thing was so completely farfetched, she had by now reached the conclusion there was no point in worrying. She knew she was innocent and, in time, surely Chief Inspector Masters would realise this. How many of her other suspects, as innocent as she was, were being subjected to exactly the same aggro?

'And how do you feel about his death?'

'As to that, Simon,' she tried to smile, 'I don't know. Stunned, I suppose.'

'Are you going to tell your parents?'

'It's another 'I don't know', I'm afraid,' she admitted, 'I suppose I should. I wouldn't like them to find out before I had the chance to. The sick irony of this, Simon, is that they were actually there, at the service station, yesterday afternoon not long after – not long after it happened,' struggling to get the words out and for the first time since she had heard the news, trying hard to hold back the tears. Who was she crying for she wondered. Not Steve. While nobody deserved to die the way he did, what she felt for him, was, if she was being honest with herself, nothing. Pity for him, maybe, but that was all. Was she crying for herself? If so, that was a severe case of self-pity, she decided, stifling a sob at the back of her throat.

'It doesn't do to bottle things up, you know, Eliza.' taking both her hands in his. 'Won't you let me help? You know I want to.'

'Yes, I know.' a small voice, not like hers at all.

'Look,' he went on, continuing to hold her hands, raising them to his lips and kissing them gently, 'I'll phone James for you. I'll tell them, also that you're okay. At least that will put their minds at rest about you.'

'But that's me being cowardly.'

'I don't think so. They'll understand.'

It was later, but still daylight, when Eliza told him about Wendy's photograph. Simon had phoned her parents; she had listened to him, standing next to him, as he quietly broke the news, adding that they had nothing to worry about, that he would make sure she was alright. Sweet, reassuring words to her ears, but it would not do to get into the habit of relying on him too much. That would not be fair on him, resolving that once she had snapped out of the way she was thinking at the moment she would be more like her old self: resilient, positive and, above all, optimistic.

'It may be that Wendy's boyfriend has a double.' she said, wondering if, after all, she had been mistaken, but deep down she didn't think so. She felt pretty positive it was the same person, waiting for Simon to come up with some magical explanation.

'It isn't that I don't trust your judgement,' he said at last, 'it's just that if he was here and presumably she would have been unaware of this, there can only be suspicious connotations for his visit to Meadowbank. Do they live together do you know? Dan and her?'

'She didn't say, but I got the impression they did.'

'Brian told us this guy we saw in 'The Market Inn' booked in last Thursday and on the Sunday morning he was still there. So, surely, if he had been out of Hong Kong for that period Wendy would have known.'

'Not necessarily, Simon.'

'Why?' a puzzled frown creasing his forehead.

'Because she was in China during that time and didn't get back to Hong Kong until the Tuesday.'

Chapter Nineteen

'Hell, Colin,' Rachel said when he had finished talking, 'just how did we get into this appalling situation and why the hell have you taken so long to tell me? And don't,' she warned, swivelling round on the dressing table stool, 'say you didn't want to worry me!'

'I wasn't going to. I suppose I thought things might have improved.'

'That's pathetic and you know it!'

'I really thought dad would help out, but as it was, I didn't even get round to asking him on Saturday night.'

'Well you know what a thought did, Colin! This would not have been the first time in our marriage your father has had to bail you out – not to put too fine a point on it! Let's face it, from what you've told me we are on the verge of bankruptcy!'

'It's not as bad as that, Rachel;' trying now to calm her down and wishing he hadn't chosen this evening, less than an hour before they were due to meet Wendy, to tell her. Wendy must never know how dire their financial circumstances were. After all, he did have some pride left. Telling Rachel was one thing, but there was no way he could actually look his younger sister in the eye and confess he had made such a miscalculation and one which was in danger of affecting his and Rachel's lifestyle. 'we'll have to curb our expenses somewhat, that's all. For a while, until my inheritance comes through. I might be able to persuade old Brutton to give me something on account.'

'You really think so, Colin.'

'Yes, it's possible.' ignoring the heavy sarcasm.

'After the way you conducted yourself this afternoon, I very much doubt it!'

'We'll see.'

'And,' she persisted, turning back to face the mirror and running a brush through already immaculately styled hair, 'what sort of expenses were you planning to cut, may I ask?'

'We could, mind you, this is only an idea, I haven't had time to think it through yet, but we could move into the manor –'

'– What?' the hairbrush half-suspended in an arc above her head, her eyes narrowed as she glared at him in the mirror.

'I did say it was only an idea, Rachel, but it would be an answer.'

'And what about this place? Hardly the right time for selling; not that I'm any judge of course.'

'It would only be a temporary measure. We could rent the house out; there shouldn't be any difficulty in finding tenants. At least then the mortgage would be paid and we would be living in the manor rent-free.'

'I thought you said you hadn't thought it through, Colin. It seems you have already decided!'

'That's not true, but think about it, Rachel.'

'I already have,' she said getting up from the stool and turning round to face him, 'and I don't like it. Oh, it would be alright for you; you would still be in the town each day but what about me? Have you considered what I would do buried out there?'

'You have your car, there's nothing to stop you driving into Winchester whenever you want. You wouldn't be a prisoner, Rachel. And, you would have Mrs Plenderneath to do everything for you. In fact, you would have more free time than you have at the moment.'

'That's exactly what I'm worried about!'

'Let's drop the subject for now. It's time we left anyway; we'll talk about it over the weekend.'

'I wish we hadn't agreed to go back to Meadowbank this evening. Wendy could have quite easily have driven into Winchester and we could have gone to one of our favourite restaurants.'

'Be reasonable, Rachel. You don't seem to realise that Wendy has had a gruelling few days, I didn't like the idea of her spending the rest of the day, especially today, on her own.'

'She looked alright to me, too pale of course, but then she never did have much colour.'

Rachel was only half-right he thought; Wendy had looked pale, but it had been so long since he had last seen her he couldn't really remember what she normally looked like. She was taking their father's death badly as he had known she would. It would be some time before she came to terms with it and, much as he looked forward to seeing her again, he thought it might be better if she didn't stay too long. She must be finding it strange to be back in England; it was not as if she had any friends in the area, probably lost touch with them years ago.

'Why don't the three of you decide to sell the estate, Colin. That would be a solution, wouldn't it? It's not as if you have any real desire to hold on to the place.'

'I don't, that's true, but it isn't as simple as that.'

'I don't suppose Nanette would either.'

'But there's Wendy, I know she feels very strongly about the manor; to her, it represents our family history. She's always felt like that, Rachel.'

'Well, in my opinion that is being downright selfish! My God, she was quick enough to leave!'

'Perhaps she was, but I don't think you understand the way she is. The manor has always been there for Wendy.'

'That's no answer and you bloody well know it! There is only one thing for it, Colin; you and Nanette will have to *make* her agree!'

'Easier said than done, Rachel. Come on, it's time we were on our way. And let's try and have a pleasant evening, shall we?'

*

Wendy's mobile rang as she was about to leave the manor. It would be Dan she thought switching it on, but the voice at the other end, a complete and not unpleasant surprise, was Mark Wood; the man she had met on the plane.

'You must tell me, Wendy,' he said, 'if I'm phoning you at an inconvenient moment, I'll understand.'

'Not at all,' she reassured him quickly, 'I'm meeting my brother and his wife for dinner, but I've plenty of time. It's good of you to call, Mark.'

'Has it been pretty grim for you? The funeral and everything?'

'Well, let's say I've had better forty-eight hours, but I'm just trying to accept that dad is no longer here. I'm not finding it very easy.'

'It won't be,' the open sympathy in his voice giving her more comfort than almost anyone else she had spoken to since she had first heard the news, 'it will take time. I know you'll be returning to Hong Kong soon, Wendy, and, well,' he hesitated for a second, 'I was wondering whether there was any chance we could meet before then?'

'I'd like that, but –'

'– let me tell you I'm not usually as impulsive as this and I know we hardly know each other, but I enjoyed talking to you. Made a normally tedious plane journey a pleasurable experience for once. I'm sure you know how it is, often being stuck beside someone you have no wish to speak to for one reason or another and worrying for most of the flight if he or she is going to start up some mindless conversation.'

'Don't I just!' she laughed, 'It's happened to me far too often and the only solution is to pretend to be asleep!'

'Exactly. Look, Wendy, I'm holding you up.'

'No, you're not,' which was not exactly true; at this rate if she didn't leave for the restaurant within the next couple of minutes she was going to be late, but for some reason, uncharacteristically, she didn't care. Talking to him was therapeutic, helping to make her feel her old self again and one she had lost sight of a long time ago, 'as I said, Mark, I would love to see you again. I can't delay returning to Hong Kong for long, as much as I would like to stay on here for a while, so I reckon I'll have to book a flight back no later than the end of next week. Do you want me to come up to London; it would be no problem, I've a hire car.'

'No, that's too much to ask, you just say the day and I'll make it to you. We could meet in Winchester if you like, have lunch somewhere?'

And that was what they arranged to do, fixing on the following Wednesday, Mark leaving it to her to choose the restaurant. She had suggested 'The Green Door' in one of the cobbled streets close to the cathedral. Parking, she warned him, may prove a problem, but he hadn't seemed to mind, saying not to worry he would find a place. Finally, ringing off, locking up behind her and running down the steps to the car she was filled with what she could only describe as a rare sense of anticipation. She did want to see him again. She also wanted to meet him in a totally different environment: not the hermetically concealed cabin of a fully packed plane coursing through the skies from east to west, but in a lively and as she remembered it, sure it would not have altered since she was last there, a popular restaurant in the centre of the city. Perhaps by then she would have resolved what was taking up most of her mind and had been nagging persistently away for several weeks, if not months. To make that crucial step forward, that is, if she finally could pluck up the courage to sever her Hong Kong ties; the ones with the publishing house would not be easy and she knew she would meet with a lot of opposition from the directors, but this, she was fairly confident, would not prove insurmountable. Everyone, after all, was entitled to change direction, move on and seek a new challenge. No, it was when she faced Dan, sensing in advance what his reactions would be. Dan was proud and more than a little vain and it would be more than his feelings which would be hurt, perhaps even offended, and she knew it would be difficult to try to explain to him why she had to take these steps now. Before it was too late.

Colin's BMW was already in the car park when she reached 'The Royal Oak'; an old coaching inn on the outskirts of Meadowbank which she remembered going to almost every Sunday for lunch with the family when the three of them had been children. She wondered whether that was why Colin had suggested it, rather than the ultra-smart and newly vamped 'Salmon's Rest'. Even down-to-earth Mrs Plenderneath had been enthusiastic in her praise for the restaurant although she had freely admitted she had never been there. 'Far too posh for me, Wendy,' she had said before adding with one of her quizzical and enigmatic smiles, 'it is French, you know, and even if I could afford the prices I would never be able to read the menu.' Wendy hadn't pointed out to her that she was sure the menu would also be in English. There would have been no point. Mrs Plenderneath, a country woman, living all her life around Meadowbank, would no doubt have felt out of place in what she had described as a French restaurant.

Although crowded, the first people Wendy saw as she walked into the hotel's lounge bar were Colin and Rachel, noticing also the frown creasing her sister-in-law's usually smooth brow. Oh dear, she thought, going over towards their table, hoping it wasn't going to be one of *those* evenings. Rachel was a force to be reckoned with and up to now, mainly because she had spent most of the time since they were married either in London or in Hong Kong, she had managed to avoid any confrontations with her. Rachel, not only a frightful snob, was an inveterate social climber, but always Wendy had chosen to ignore this, having decided that it would seem Colin managed to cope with her and so far, at least, they were still married.

'There you are, Wendy,' Colin said going up to her and kissing her on the cheek, 'we were beginning to wonder where you had got to.'

'Sorry, Colin,' she said, trying to include Rachel in her apology, noticing the look of annoyance on her face, 'but I had a call just as I was about to leave.'

'On your mobile, I suppose?' Rachel commented, moving her chair to make room for her.'

'Yes, that's right. Can be a nuisance sometimes, but this call was from a friend, so it was good to hear from him.'

'From Hong Kong?'Colin asked, beckoning over to the waiter.

'No, from London actually.' Wendy answered casually, hoping they would take the hint. She was reluctant to say any more. And these two, she thought, at the same time admitting to herself she was being over-sensitive, were about to bombard her with questions about her personal life. Being charitable, she allowed they were probably only being politely interested, but it didn't prevent the impression of being quizzed.

'Really?' Rachel said, 'I didn't think you had kept up with any friends from your London days.'

'A few, Rachel, only a few.' Wendy said casually. Fortuitously, the waiter was at their table and she was able to, as naturally as she could, avoid any further discussion. She ordered a Campari and soda, desperately scrabbling around for a topic, any topic which was less personal and, most of all, nothing to do about family. Not easy, and then she remembered the pleasant hour she had spent that afternoon with Eliza Brent and the strong impression she had had of Simon's attraction towards her.

'I met our new tenant this afternoon.' she said raising her glass to them both.

'What is she like?' Rachel asked.

'Quite lovely; a very together sort of person, if you know what I mean. She is starting up her own jewellery design business.'

'Oh, she's one of those.'

'What do you mean?'

'The cottage industry type. Winchester is full of them, especially at this time of the year; all dressed like gypsies: long floaty dresses, straw hats, clanking bangles and sequined espadrilles. They produce an abundance of wicker baskets that nobody is in the least interested in buying, far less have any real use for, and then there is the jewellery: garish filigree stuff and long shell necklaces. Ghastly.'

'Eliza is a qualified graphic designer, Rachel,' Wendy said, managing to disguise her distaste. Why, she wondered, was her sister-in-law so vitriolic, 'and, until recently, she worked in London, but decided she was tired of city life.'

'Why did she choose Meadowbank, I wonder.' Colin murmured.

'Perhaps Meadowbank chose her, Colin. That can happen, you know. You've made a decision, something you've wanted to do for ages; you want to live in a quieter part of the country, but not too far away from London. You then search through the adverts until you find a place which sounds exactly what you're looking for.'

'As easy as that, eh?'

'I would say so, yes. The most difficult part is making that first decision.'

'Hmmph, you could be right. At least the lodge is being lived in at last and earning its keep.'

As always, the food was excellent. The head waiter, David Johnson, had worked for the hotel for years and came over to their table to talk to them and to commiserate. It was inevitable this would happen each time she saw someone who had known her father and Wendy also realised that each time the deep sadness she was feeling would intensify, but there was no escaping when people, like David Johnson, were genuinely sorry. She had noticed also, earlier at the funeral, not one person referred to how he had died and for this she was grateful. She was finding it impossible to erase the picture it conjured up in her mind.

After they had finished eating they took their coffee outside on to the terrace overlooking the wide sweep of lawn leading down to the river. Incredibly peaceful Wendy thought, leaning back in her wicker chair and savouring the moment. The scent of the honeysuckle and early summer roses filled the air, which after the rain, felt pleasantly soft and cool on her face.

'You must admit, Rachel,' Colin said, 'Meadowbank is lucky having a lovely old hotel like this.'

'There are just as many equally as good in Winchester, you know. Personally, I prefer something with, how would you say, a little bit more panache.'

'Don't be so unkind, the 'Royal Oak' is like an old lady who, although no longer young, has retained her natural elegance.'

'Very poetic! I don't know what's got into you tonight, *darling,* you are not usually so eloquent.'

Undercurrents here, Wendy thought, watching them both: her brother, leaning forward slightly, his hair turning quite grey she noticed for the first time, momentarily reminding her of her father. How odd she thought, she had never seen any resemblance before. Similar characteristics, yes, but not physical likeness. Perhaps, as Colin grew older they would become more prevalent. Rachel, sitting next to him was her normal groomed self: no grey in her hair, the rich copper positively gleaming in the last rays of the sun.

'By the way,' Wendy said, in an effort to change the subject; she did not want to witness any husband and wife wrangle, whatever that may imply, 'did either of you hear about what happened yesterday afternoon; I thought you may have heard about it on the news.'

'No,' Colin said with obvious signs of relief on his face to be distracted from what no doubt he was accustomed to when Rachel got her teeth into anything, 'what sort of thing?'

'A man was shot at the Basingstoke service station; it must have happened as soon as I got there.'

'Dead?' Rachel asked quickly, her green eyes flashing with unconcealed excitement.

'Oh, yes.'

'Did you see him?'

'Only briefly; I was at the cash desk when he was found.'

'My God, Wendy, how dreadful for you.' Colin, openly shocked now, 'You never said anything about it earlier.'

'I haven't told anyone actually, certainly not Mrs Plenderneath, she's had enough to put up with, poor woman.'

'You're right there –'

'– but, Wendy,' Rachel interrupted him, 'what happened then?'

'Oh, well, once the waitress; she was the one who found him, had stopped screaming the place instantly became very hushed and then everyone started talking at once.'

'What did you do?' Colin asked her.

'Well, obviously I couldn't take my coffee and sit down, but the police were amazingly quick to get there, within minutes in fact, and then we were all ushered out to the vestibule and had to wait as they took our names and addresses.'

'No wonder you were so tired. It wasn't just the flight, then?'

'I suppose not, although that had been tiring enough.'

'What about the person who did it?' Rachel persisted.

'I've no idea.'

'And you didn't *actually* hear the gun going off, did you?' she emphasised.

'Honestly, Rachel, you are the limit! I had no idea you could be so ghoulish.'

'I'm not, Colin! I'm interested, that's all. And Basingstoke is practically on our doorstep in case it had escaped your notice! I wonder,' she went on, 'if it was the same man –'

'– please, Rachel, drop it.'

'I'm sorry I mentioned anything about it, I really am.'

'No, Wendy,' Colin said, 'it's not your fault. Anyway, we could have heard about it on the news, but as it happened, we didn't.'

'It was all an unfortunate and unpleasant experience for everyone, especially for the poor waitress. She probably thought the man had fallen asleep at the table.'

'Well, all I can say, for all our sakes, I hope they find the person who shot him!'

'They probably will, Rachel. Eventually.' Colin said quietly.

Chapter Twenty

Sergeant Ash was already at his desk when Brenda arrived the following morning. Saturday morning in Meadowbank was, grumbling to herself, becoming a nightmare, making it difficult to find a place to park. Even the allocated spaces in front of the Station were taken up and she had had to drive around the square twice before being able to slot in between an off-roader and a small Fiat, the latter taking up an unnecessarily large area behind the vehicle in front.

'Alright, Ian,' she said passing his desk, 'we'll go into my office shall we? And you can tell me your latest findings.'

They walked together along the hundred yards or so to her office, Ian Ash taking up his usual position on one of the two chairs at the front of her desk. The air smelt stale, even with the non-smoking ban which by now they were all accustomed to. Frowning, Brenda opened the window. Even the sound of traffic from the road below was better than being suffocated.

'Peter Taylor.' she began, 'What have you on him?'

'So far, ma'am,' he said, 'I've only been able to trace back ten and a half years but before then, nothing.'

'Let's hear what you do have then. It might be best to work backwards, from now until you lost track of him.'

'Right,' he answered quickly, opening his folder and pulling out a sheet of A4, 'as we already know, he and his wife bought the 'Salmon's Rest' and moved in eight months ago, at the beginning of December. Prior to then he was with her in her restaurant, 'Le Bistro', off Bond Street, right up to the time they came to Meadowbank.'

'It wasn't a joint ownership then?'

'No, she'd moved to London from Paris and they weren't married at that time. She'd had the bistro for ten years before finally selling up.'

'Any ideas of why she did that?'

'Apparently the lease had expired.'

'How long have they been married, Ian?'

'Six years, ma'am.'

'Not long. And where was he before he went there?'

'In London as a broker with a firm of financial consultants.'

'For how long?'

'Four years.'

'And when he was recruited he would have had to produce references.'

'This is where it begins to get a bit hazy because, apparently, he had been working as a free-lance consultant. I got the impression it was through one of his contacts.'

'It's not what you know, but who you know, eh?'

'Yes, but,' he went on, 'something interesting did turn up.'

'Yes?'

'I asked them for a list of employees who were there during that period. My idea was to try and find out if he had made friends with any of them.'

'And did you?' the familiar frisson tingled her nerve ends; one seldom experienced in murder enquiries, especially so soon, but when it happened she had learned never to ignore it. It wasn't exactly what Ian had said, but how he had said it. His tone of voice had altered slightly and there was a definite change in his expression.

'It could mean nothing, ma'am –' he hesitated.

'– You're not deliberately trying to keep me in suspense are you, Ian.' she interrupted him, impatient now, wishing he would get to the point. Ian Ash was a good officer, diligent although at times too pedantic for her liking.

'Sorry,' he answered, pulling himself more upright, 'I was trying to make sense of it all.'

'It's alright. I understand. So what was it? It doesn't matter if your supposition is wrong, you know. It is still early days.' but knowing as soon as she uttered the words her supervisor would not agree with her. His silence was beginning to be ominous which she knew from experience meant that soon she could expect a summons to his office.

'Among those names, he went on, 'was that of Alan Jackson, Nanette Tilsly's husband.'

'Now that *is* interesting.' she emphasised. 'How many do they employ? Is it feasible those two may have known each other?'

'I would say so,' he said, glancing down at his notes, 'the firm, I was told, has grown considerably since then, but during the time Peter Taylor was there they only had ten brokers and if you include a supervisor and manager, plus two secretaries and a receptionist, I would say everyone would know each other reasonably well.'

'But not necessarily outside of business hours?'

'Perhaps not. From my knowledge of how these firms operate, the brokers work quite independently, it's a highly competitive business,'

'Yes, I agree, the chief aim to see who can earn the highest bonuses and from what I've seen of Peter Taylor he would, I think, fit quite well into that sort of environment. However, Ian, we cannot afford to ignore a Tilsly connection no matter how tenuous or indeed, at the end of the day, irrelevant it may be.'

'I know and this was why I've been reluctant to put too much importance on what could turn out to be coincidental.'

'Never ignore the slightest piece of information, Ian. We'll find out later, after we've sorted out all the dross, whether it forms part of the picture or not. Meanwhile, I'll get someone from the met. to have a word with Alan Jackson. Quicker than going up to London myself. What I would like you to do is to go back to 'The Royal Oak'. I'm not satisfied with Peter Taylor's alibi. Call it a gut feeling, but it all sounds a little bit too pat. I know he told us he wasn't a regular customer, but I cannot believe there wasn't one member of the staff there on Thursday who didn't recognise him.'

'I suppose, as it was only two days ago, if someone had, it would still be fresh in their minds.'

'Quite. I haven't been to 'The Royal Oak' for a while, but it probably hasn't changed all that much. If I remember rightly the lounge bar leads straight through from reception and from there you can see into the restaurant. It would, of course, have been too early for any of the evening diners, but I would have thought there would have been more than one member of the staff in there, setting the tables and making all the preparations for when they opened. Also, Ian, find out what time the seminar broke up that afternoon.'

'I should get along there straight away, I think.' Ian said, putting the paper back into the folder, 'Being a Saturday, I would imagine they'll soon start to get busy with the lunches. When I've done that, ma'am, is there anything else you'd like me to do?'

'Yes, there is. It's time we heard back on that check we ordered on the car number. He told Melissa when he booked in he was from overseas, so presumably he would have hired the car. Once you've got that, give them a ring; find out how the man paid, we couldn't be so lucky it would have been by credit card, but, so far what he has given the pub is somewhat vague, perhaps it does suggest he was being ultra-cautious. And while you're doing all that, I'm going to have a word with Wendy Tilsly. I've ignored her up to now, but I think it's time I spoke to her.'

Before leaving for the manor, Brenda telephoned Brutton's in Winchester. She was in luck, not really expecting Maureen Summers to be in the office on a Saturday, but she was, and within a couple of seconds she was put through to her.

'Good morning, Chief Inspector,' the same calm, measured tone, 'how can I help you?'

'Good morning, Mrs Summers' equally as formal. For some reason talking to her it seemed perfectly natural and, once again, she was aware of the quiet reserve in her voice. Had she always been like this Brenda wondered. Perhaps as far back, still in her teens, when she had started working for the lawyers, or was it something she had built up over the years; a shield against life and what it had and was still continuing to fling at her. Was it her way of coping? Quietly and with dignity. A woman, she concluded, with enviable fortitude. 'I apologise for disturbing you,' Brenda continued, 'but there is something I would like to ask you.'

'Yes?' encouragingly, no sign of exasperation of again being reminded of the person she had so recently lost.

'You mentioned when we first met that you'd had lunch with Major Tilsly last Friday?'

'Yes, that's right.'

'Did he mention to you a man called Anthony Appleyard who had visited him, twice in fact, to view his art collection?'

'Yes, he did. I remember thinking what an unusual name, not one you could easily forget.'

'According to what we have been able to glean so far about him,' Brenda went on, 'it would seem he had recently arrived from the Far East, booking a room at 'The Market Inn' in Meadowbank and had paid two visits to the manor.'

'Yes, Chief Inspector,' she agreed quickly, 'that's correct, although I don't know about him coming from overseas. Reginald didn't say.'

'Did the major mention to you the nature of the visit, apart that is, from an interest in the paintings?'

'He did. He told me that Mr Appleyard was a university lecturer and was taking a six-month sabbatical to work on a paper focusing on the different techniques and styles of the Old Masters.'

'I see,' Brenda said, 'he didn't happen to mention which university?'

'Once again, Chief Inspector, he didn't. I'm sorry I couldn't have been more help to you.'

'But you have been, Mrs Summers. You see, up to now, although we had already learned that the man had made two visits to the gallery, that was all we did know. We did think when you had lunch with the Major, he may have mentioned the fact to you.'

'I understand. Anything I can do to assist you in finding whoever was responsible is really all I care about, Chief Inspector.'

Brenda, after a few more pleasantries and reassurances that they were doing all they could to find the perpetrator, eventually rang off. It was true the further knowledge she had now did move the case along, but only slightly; not much, but enough to make her want to have another word with the housekeeper.

No sooner had she replaced the receiver than the phone rang again, the desk sergeant telling her it was Chief Inspector Harper from New Scotland Yard.

'Alright,' Brenda said, 'put him through, Sergeant.' waiting to hear the familiar voice. It had been some months since she'd spoken to Mike, the man with whom she had once believed she may have a future, but their careers; equally demanding, working long unsocial hours and with him based in London while she was here, in Meadowbank, eighty-odd miles away, had taken their toll, making it increasingly difficult to find the time to be together.

'Hello, Brenda,' he said, 'how are you?'

'I'm fine, Mike.'

'And now you have another murder on your hands.'

'Yes,' she sighed, 'and, once again, Meadowbank is in the media spotlight.'

'Difficult for you,' he sympathised, 'and no doubt you're expected to solve everything in record-breaking time. Well,' he continued, 'the Steven Blackwood case, Brenda.'

'Yes?'

'There's been a further development at this end; we've been able at last to trace his wife.'

'That's good.'

'Yes,' he agreed, 'they'd only been married for four months, apparently. Karen Martin, as she was called then and the reason it's taken us so long to find her is she'd already left their flat in Bayswater Gardens on the Thursday morning and booked them both into the Hilton at Gatwick Airport for the night and didn't learn of his death until late yesterday.'

'Wasn't she worried when he didn't turn up at the hotel?'

'Not unduly. I've been told by the officer who interviewed her that, to quote him, "she was one tough cookie"!'

'But, Mike, even so, they were booked to fly out to Brazil the following day and she didn't report him missing. Extraordinary.'

'Not really,' he chuckled, 'the Karen Martins of this world are not over keen to call us.'

'They were two of a kind, then.' Brenda said caustically.

'Steven Blackwood and her, you mean?'

'That's exactly what I do mean.'

So, Brenda concluded, when, finally, she had replaced the receiver, it would appear her suspicions of Eliza Brent had been unfounded. Ian would be pleased.

Wendy Tilsly answered the door herself when Brenda arrived, immediately being struck by the slim, fine-boned woman with features her mother would describe as elfin. She would, Brenda guessed, be around her own age, perhaps even younger. She had never known the Tilslys, with only a vague childhood memory of the brother, Colin. He was some years older and went to the same school in Meadowbank, but Brenda was certain neither of his sisters had attended, assuming they must have either gone to boarding school or to one of the schools in Stockbridge or Winchester. Not that it mattered, she decided, following her into the coolness of the hall, fragrantly scented by an arrangement of pink and yellow roses in a tall crystal vase which had been placed on the highly polished table in the centre of the hall, and being led into a sunny room overlooking the lawns. From the window the rear of the Lodge was clearly visible and from where she was standing she could see Eliza Brent on the terrace, also recognising the man sitting next to her. It would appear they had become quite friendly in the short time since Eliza had arrived. She would never have described Simon as a quick worker, quite the opposite. It just shows how wrong you can be Brenda thought with a tiny stab of unaccustomed envy for the older woman, reminding her for a moment how dull her own life had become, especially since her promotion. Too much work and all that, she thought, stifling a sigh and turning away from the window.

'First of all, Miss Tilsly,' she began after refusing coffee, 'I was saddened to hear about your father. In fact, I would say that everyone who knew him is feeling the same way.'

'Thank you.' Wendy Tilsly accepted the condolence.

'I didn't want to disturb you yesterday for obvious reasons, but I feel I have to ask you a few questions, that is, if you don't mind.'

'Of course not, but I don't honestly see how I can be of any help to you over my father's death.'

'It isn't about that, Miss Tilsly. I'm here in connection with another death.'

'Oh dear,' Wendy sighed, 'I suppose you mean that poor man who was shot on Thursday.'

'Yes, that's right. Although Basingstoke is not in my province, I am working closing in conjunction with my opposite number there.'

'Do you mean there could be a connection?'

'We don't know yet, but let's say there are certain – anomalies,' pausing fractionally in an attempt to find the right words without giving too much away; at this stage the least people who were aware that there could be the better. Brenda knew only too well of the ongoing speculation in the town over the murders of Major Tilsly and Len Roberts without introducing a third, 'all of which,' she continued, 'however unlikely, must be followed up.'

'But how can I help? I arrived in the coffee shop after it happened.'

'You saw the body?'

'I couldn't help not see it. When the waitress started screaming I think everyone in there must have looked over at the same time and seen the man.'

'Where were you at the time? Sitting down?'

'No, I was still at the cash desk waiting to pay for my coffee.'

'Did you have long to wait in the queue?'

'No, not really, five, six minutes at the most; there were only two or three people in front of me.'

'You see, Miss Tilsly, we now have the pathologist's report as to the time of death which has been established as no earlier than three-thirty. You may have already entered the restaurant and were waiting to be served before the shot was fired; on the other hand, you may have arrived shortly afterwards. The police received the call from them immediately the body was found and were on the scene within ten minutes – that was at three-forty precisely.'

'I'm sorry,' Wendy frowned, 'I'm not sure where you're coming from?'

'It's like this,' Brenda explained patiently, 'it is possible the killer must have made his escape very close to the time you were arriving at the coffee shop. He wouldn't have remained there and although there are two exit doors at the rear, neither of them had been opened, so he must have gone out the front way. If this had been the case, you may have seen him.'

'What a horrible thought.'

'It's not pleasant, I know, but I would like you to think very carefully. Take your time; think back from the moment you parked your car, walked across towards the main door of the building. And remember, whoever it was, would have been in a hurry.'

'In a hurry?' she repeated.

'I would think so; he would have to get away as rapidly as possible. He would have known that once the call to the police was made it would not be long before the whole area would be cordoned off.'

'You're right it was. I was amazed, in fact, just how quick they were.'

'Can you remember anyone, anyone at all, Miss Tilsly,' Brenda persisted, 'whose behaviour struck you as, let us say, out of the usual?'

'No, I don't think so. I suppose I wasn't really paying much attention. I was feeling pretty exhausted, having only arrived from Hong Kong earlier in the morning and then driving from Heathrow. That was why I decided to call in for a coffee; I hoped it would revive me, keep me going until I got home.'

'What was it like when you reached the main door; were there many people around?'

'No, not that many. Oh! Oh, my God!' Wendy gasped, impulsively putting a hand up to her mouth, 'I've just remembered.'

'Yes?' Brenda prompted.

'As I reached the top of the steps the door was suddenly flung open; it nearly hit me actually, and a man came out, bumping into me! He didn't even stop to apologise. How could I have forgotten something so important?'

'You were tired, perhaps with everything which has been going on recently, there just wasn't room in your mind for anything else. It happens.'

'I suppose so,' Wendy agreed doubtfully, 'but it's not like me at all.'

'This man,' she continued, 'would you be able to describe him?'

'Perhaps if I saw him again, but I'm not sure. It all happened so quickly. He was really no more than a blur.'

'Well, even if it was only an impression, it could help us.'

'Well, he was quite tall, about six foot, not that old, no more than fifty, I would guess. I'm sorry, Chief Inspector; I'm not very good at this.'

'What sort of clothes was he wearing, formal or casual?'

'Dark blue trousers, I remember that.'

'Did he have a jacket?'

'No.' Her response quicker this time as she concentrated. 'A short-sleeved shirt, light coloured; I think pale blue, but it could have been white. I'm sorry I can't remember.'

'Last question,' Brenda smiled at her; she wasn't disappointed with the description, although it could fit any number of men, but it was something.

'Was he carrying anything? A briefcase, or a bag, perhaps?'

'No, except he had a newspaper under his arm, no, I'm wrong,' she added, her words tumbling out now, 'not a newspaper, a magazine. Like one of the supplements you get with a newspaper.'

'Thank you, Miss Tilsly.'

'Not total recall, I'm afraid. Tell me, Chief Inspector,' she added, 'why are you asking me all these questions? I wasn't the only one there and we all had to give our names and addresses.'

'It was mainly the timing of the incident as I mentioned before. Also, we do realise there would have been people who had already left before the body was found, but we won't be able to trace them.'

'I see.' but Brenda could tell by her expression she wasn't entirely convinced by the explanation, but it would have to do. She was not prepared at this point to say anymore, especially not their suspicions that if not a direct link with her father's death, there could be one with Meadowbank itself.

'Finally, Miss Tilsly,' she said, 'at a later date, would you be prepared to attend an identity parade?'

'I would absolutely hate to do that; I've always thought there was a real risk of selecting the wrong person. And, as I've said, I would not be a reliable witness; I only had a fleeting glance of him; I doubt I would be able to remember his features. Also, Chief Inspector, I have to get back to Hong Kong. Next Friday at the latest. I had a call from my boss earlier this morning; he is beginning to get impatient over my absence.'

'I understand. We'll leave it at that, shall we? Before I go, Miss Tilsly, would it be possible to have a word with your housekeeper. It won't take long I assure you.'

'I hope not, she's already been through enough.'

'It's only to ask her a few more questions about someone who visited the gallery. She had already told Sergeant Ash, but I would like to find out a little bit more about him.'

Wendy didn't accompany her to the kitchen where she said Mrs Plenderneath would be working. In any case, Brenda knew the way, assuming she would not want to be present and be forced to listen to whatever she had to say to the woman. She had only met one other member of the family so far; the brother, and although giving every appearance of being shocked when he had heard the news he hadn't struck her as though he was grieving, while she had the distinct impression that Wendy Tilsly was deeply upset over losing her father. It had been apparent in many ways: the most telling was, that throughout the meeting, there had been a number of occasions when her eyes had become almost unfocused as if she was losing concentration and her mind wandering. She really should not be on her own at a time like this Brenda thought. In her career Brenda had seen many people after they had learned of a sudden death, especially of someone close to them, and while each person had their own way of reacting, Wendy's grief had all those signs. She did not have to remind herself that at this moment as she was walking along the passage towards the kitchen that first and foremost she was a police officer and working on a murder case, but it did not alter the fact she was also a woman and she believed there was nothing wrong with going along with her basic instincts. It was not as if she would ever act officially on them, but she had found on previous cases, they had helped.

The housekeeper showed no surprise at seeing her. Probably expecting a visit Brenda thought shaking hands with the elderly woman she had known, although not well, for years. Her plump cheeks flushed from taking out a tray of scones from the oven, she looked pleased to see her; her face no longer bearing evidence of the shock she had experienced so recently.

'I knew you were here.' were her first words, 'I saw you arrive and I wondered if you would want to speak to me again.'

'Why did you think that, Mrs Plenderneath?'

'No reason, I suppose. I hoped, that's all. Do you know yet who did this dreadful thing to Major Tilsly? I cannot believe there is someone around here, in Meadowbank, who could be so wicked. Also, there is poor old Len. Hardly anyone even talks about the way he died, which is a shame. It must have been awful for him, dying like that.'

'Try not to dwell on all of this so much, and,' Brenda added, 'we will find out who killed both Major Tilsly and Len Roberts, Mrs Plenderneath, but there is still a great deal of work to do. We have to keep asking more and more questions until we arrive at the truth.'

'I know.'

'I would like to talk to you about the man who visited the manor last week; I believe he was called Mr Appleyard?'

'Yes, that's right.'

'I realise Sergeant Ash has already asked you about him, but there are one or two points which need to be clarified.'

'I don't know if I'll be able to tell you any more, Chief Inspector.'

'Perhaps not, but let's see. You've already given a very good description of him, but were you able to place his accent? What part of England do you think he came from originally?'

'Oh, he wasn't English,' she answered without hesitation, 'he sounded American, from California.'

'Really, how can you be so sure?'

'Well, you see, Chief Inspector,' she answered, 'my uncle emigrated there when he was a young man. I hardly remember him, but my cousins have often visited our family over the years and Mr Appleyard sounded exactly like them.'

'How I wish everyone we interviewed could be so perceptive.' Brenda encouraged; whether it would help or not she didn't know, but perhaps it added another dimension to the case.

'I understand when Mr Appleyard was here,' Brenda went on, 'he was left on his own in the gallery?'

'The second time, yes.

'He would have had some paperwork with him?'

'He did, yes, also he had one of those laptops.'

'Yes, Sergeant Ash told me. On that day, Mrs Plenderneath, the Friday' Brenda asked her, 'he left before Major Tilsly returned home?'

'Yes, that's right.'

'It was very trusting of the major to leave a complete stranger on his own; didn't you think so?'

'It was, now I come to think about it, but he and Mr Appleyard seemed to get along quite well and of course I was here all the time.'

'And when did the Major return?'

'Just after three.'

'The gallery, Mrs Plenderneath,' she began, 'was it kept locked all the time?'

'Oh, no, the Major was quite particular about that. Although he didn't go in there very often, he told me he couldn't be bothered unlocking the door each time.'

'So when was it locked?'

'Only at night. I wasn't here then, of course, but I assumed he would do that before going to bed.'

'And in the morning? Was the door locked when you arrived for work?'

'No, it wasn't. You see, one of my first jobs each day was to clean in there, not that it ever needed very much. Hardly any dust in fact, probably because the windows were kept closed.'

'You would then have done that as usual the following morning, on the Saturday?'

'Yes, I did.'

'Was everything as usual?'

'What do you mean, Chief Inspector?'

'What I mean is, was everything where it should have been? You must be very familiar with the arrangement of everything in there. Not only the pictures, but also the furniture.'

'Oh, I see.' she said.

'For instance,' Brenda stressed, 'I take it Mr Appleyard would have been sitting at the table for a good part of the time he was in the gallery.'

'Yes, but nothing had been moved. I would have noticed straight away if it had been.'

'You would have noticed then if any of the pictures were out of alignment. That would have been obvious to you?'

'Of course it would.'

'Do you remember at any time having to straighten them, Mrs Plenderneath.'

'I can't say I do.'

Realising she was unlikely to find out any more, not even sure what she expected to learn from her, Brenda made her way back to the car. At least it was beginning to become clear when the three paintings had been replaced. It wouldn't have taken long and Mr Appleyard, if indeed that was his name, had ample opportunity. About to switch on the ignition, her mobile went off.

'Sergeant Ash here, ma'am, we've got a breakthrough on Anthony Appleyard.'

'Fire ahead, Ian.'

'The car was from a firm in Slough; Wilsons Sales and Hire, and he didn't hire it, he bought it.'

'I don't suppose he used a credit card?'

'No, he paid cash, but it's better than that.'

Brenda held her breath as she waited. For the second time during this case she had the impression Ian Ash was deliberately prolonging what he had to tell her, but she could be mistaken.

'Yes?' prompting him, curbing her impatience.

'He paid mainly in American dollars, four thousand pounds altogether and, according to the garage owner, when he was taking the notes from his wallet, an identity card must have fallen out.'

'Did it indeed?'

'The guy didn't notice it until Appleyard had left and as he didn't have any address for him there was nothing much he could do, except wait for him to come back for it.'

'And is Appleyard his real name?'

'No, it's Daniel Browne and, ma'am?'

'Yes, Ian.'

'It's a Hong Kong identity card.'

'Well, well, that is something else! I'm still at the manor, but I'm on my way back, Ian. Don't do any further checking up on this until then; this is going to need some careful thought.'

Assuming Browne and Appleyard was the same person pointed an obvious finger at Wendy Tilsly. It would be a simple and speedy procedure to speak to her again, catch her off guard. Ask her point blank whether she knew Daniel Browne or not, but the time was not right, at least not yet. First, they would find out whether the man had returned to Hong Kong and if so, when. They would get his address and take the enquiry on from there. Was he the man they were looking for? Was he both a murderer as well as an art thief? Brenda remembered what the housekeeper had said: that hardly anyone talked about Len Roberts' death and she had been quite right. He seemed to have been forgotten, his murder becoming less important than the Major's and that now of Steven Blackwood. If Len had been killed because he saw the murderer that night, which had always seemed likely, and knew he could later be identified, it would exclude Daniel Browne; a stranger in the area with the ability to speedily leave the country. Although Peter Taylor had only been in Meadowbank for eight months Len would have seen him around alright. Also, Len was a familiar figure in town and Peter would have known about him. Perhaps Ian had had some luck at 'The Royal Oak'. That alibi continued to bug her; they needed some corroboration before they could dismiss him from their enquiry.

Chapter Twenty-one

'I didn't expect you home so early, Alan. Everything alright?'

'I'm not sure,' he said, shrugging off his jacket and draping it over the back of one of the kitchen chairs, 'where are the boys?' the usual question when they weren't around, but this time side-stepping and delaying the moment when he would have to tell her.

'Watching television; they've already eaten.' she added as though, as she always had the knack of doing, reading his mind, anticipating, but giving him time to collect his thoughts. They had been married too long for her not to have been able to do this. At that moment as he sat down heavily on his usual chair facing out on to the walled garden, resplendent now with Nanette's geraniums, the pinks and yellows merging perfectly with the scarlet buds of the clumps of begonias and running along the edge of their square patch of grass, the sweet peas, early this year, their sad little faces turned up to catch the last rays of the afternoon sun, those thirteen years seemed to stretch out inordinately, making him wonder what his life had been like before he had met her. He was only forty-seven, for God's sake, but he felt twenty years older this evening

'Drink?'

'Please,' he said, 'I'll have a whisky if that's okay with you?'

'Of course it is,' she smiled at him, one of her wide sunny smiles which always had the power to reach out especially to him and make him realise he was important to her. What an idiot he had been, he could have so easily have jeopardised their relationship. At least the first hurdle was over; he had already told her about Peter Taylor. Small comfort he thought, making an effort to return her look of encouragement and taking the glass from her.

'Okay, darling,' Nanette said, sitting down at the other end of the table, 'what's happened?'

'This afternoon, at the office, I had a visit from an officer from New Scotland Yard.'

'In uniform?' Nanette, his wife, ever practical and straight to the point, but he didn't mind.

'No, in plainclothes, but it didn't make all that much difference, Nanette. He had police written all over him.'

'Go on, what did he have to say?'

'It wasn't what he had to say, it was more what he wanted to know!'

'About this blackmailing business?'

'That wasn't the reason, at least not at first, but, I assumed. Bloody stupid of me, but I have such a guilty conscience about it all and I thought – well, I thought they knew.'

'But, darling,' Nanette looked across at him, 'surely you should have realised it wouldn't have been like that. You would have been called into the office.'

'I realise that now, but at the time, well, I guess I panicked.'

'So, can we start at the beginning?'

'He asked me quite a simple question, actually; did I know Peter Taylor.'

'Just like that?'

'Yep, just like that. I tried to stall, to give myself time to think, and said he used to work for the firm and then, this was the stupid bit, I asked him why he wanted to know. As soon as the words were out of my mouth I knew I had quite literally put my foot in it.'

'Were you the only person he wanted to speak to?'

'Once again, I assumed that I was. It wasn't until later; after he'd gone, I found out that it just so happened I was the first. Apparently, he'd been given a list by the manager of everyone who had been there at the same time as Peter, and being a Saturday, there were only a few of us in the office. I'm sorry now I'd gone in this morning, Nanette, but I had a lot to catch up with having lost a whole day yesterday. Mind you, they would only have come back on Monday, so I suppose it was as well to get it over with.'

'Alan,' she said, 'try to relax. Please. It can't be that bad, surely.'

'It's my job I'm worried about, Nanette.'

'But why; has anyone said anything to you?'

'No –' he hesitated.

'- there you go, then.'

'There's time yet, you know.'

'For goodness sake, Alan, you really are looking for reds! Anyway, you haven't told me what you said to him.'

'It could have been a trick question,' he began, 'I did think that until he'd gone, but when I had asked why they wanted to know about Peter, he appeared not to have heard me. He wanted to know where Peter worked before he started with us and when I said I had no idea, that we weren't all that friendly, he asked whether I had seen or spoken to him recently.'

'And?' she prompted, the glass half raised to her lips.

'I should have said no. Of course that was what I should have said, but you see, Nanette, I had already convinced myself that they already knew.'

'I see. And they hadn't?'

'No, I'm sure they had no idea. But then I blurted out that although I hadn't seen Peter recently, we did speak to each other now and again on the phone.'

'And of course they wanted to know why, especially when you had already told them you weren't on very close terms?'

'You've got it.'

'So, that was when you told them about the blackmailing?'

'I told them the lot, Nanette. They say confession is good for the soul, but in this case it certainly was not.'

'What was their reaction? Were they surprised about hearing he was a blackmailer?'

'That's the funny thing; they didn't appear to be all that interested; it was almost as though they expected to learn something like that. And that was when they told me they were trying to get some information about Peter's background in order to eliminate him from their enquiries.'

'I don't suppose they elaborated.'

'No, and that was the end of the interview. They left then, well, after they had spoken to the only two other colleagues who were in the office.'

'It's a pity we didn't speak to Mr Brutton yesterday, Alan. We could have done, you know.'

'After the way that particular meeting went, the way you and Colin reacted to the will and everything it wouldn't have gone down very well with him.'

'Oh, so it's my fault, is it?'

'Darling, Nanette,' he said quickly, 'I don't blame you at all, but we both thought before old Brutton left the manor, the timing wasn't right. Anyway,' he sighed, 'it's too late now. The shit has hit the proverbial fan! At least I expect it will have by the time I get back to work on Monday!'

'But why, Alan? Why should it?'

'Sorry?'

'Think of it logically.'

'That's just what I am trying to do.'

'Look,' she began, pouring them both another drink, 'the reason they came to your office was to find out about Peter Taylor. About his background, you said. If the blackmailing has no connection with whatever case they're working on, there would be no need for anyone else to know and that includes your company, Alan.'

'Yes.'

'Well, the fact that their enquiry uncovered you were being blackmailed because you had provided Peter Taylor with sufficient reason to do so, wouldn't that have made them *more* interested in him, rather than reporting to your boss what you had been up to.'

'Put like that, Nanette, yes.' reluctantly and that reluctance tinged with the first glimmer of what he saw as hope. She could be right.

'And,' she rushed on, 'whatever case they are on, the fact their man was a blackmailer is hardly going to endear him to the authorities!'

'So, in your opinion,' he asked her, 'you don't think I have anything to worry about?'

'Not really. Besides, he started the blackmailing a long time after he found out what you had been doing. I mentioned that to you when you told me about it, if you remember? Surely you realise by now that the man is a shady character.'

'Of course I realise that.'

'So my advice, darling,' she smiled, raising her glass, 'is to forget it. At least now, even if you hadn't finally decided to stop the payments, that decision has been taken out of your hands.'

*

Saturday afternoon; that dead hour between four and five when you thought it would never come to an end. Brenda's office, in spite of the open windows and drawn blinds was stifling, the sun relentlessly pouring into the room and there were still a couple of hours to go before she could finish for the day. She was not only tired – it had been a long week – but emotionally drained, having to hang on and nurture what little energy she had and longing to get home, shower and find something to eat from a fridge which she had not had the time to re-fill. She could eat out; that was always an option, but the idea had little appeal. She had no wish to drive into Winchester. Once a policewoman, always a policewoman, she reminded herself wryly and wondered, not for the first time, whether she should ask for a transfer, or, alternatively, she could move. But, why should she? She had lived in Meadowbank all her life and it suited her. Whether she suited the town and its inhabitants was another issue.

There was no sign of Ian in the outer office, but he had left a report for her, placed neatly in the centre of her desk. Instantly, two points shouted for her attention: Peter Taylor had arrived at the 'Royal Oak' at four-thirty in the afternoon. He'd been seen by the head waiter, David Johnson, who was positive about the time because he had just come on duty and had seen Peter Taylor walking through reception to the lounge bar. Also, the seminar wound up for the day at four forty-five precisely.

So, Brenda sighed deeply, leaning back heavily in the chair, *the alibi is out by several minutes*. If Peter Taylor had arrived at the time he said, at four o'clock, there was no way he would have had to wait to be served because people from the seminar would not have been in the lounge bar, also, neither would they have been when he actually did get there at four-thirty. *It would appear he was not squeaky clean after all* she thought, pulling towards her the faxed report from New Scotland Yard which had arrived minutes earlier. *A blackmailer. But was he also a murderer?*

'Sorry, ma'am,' Ian Ash appeared in her open doorway, 'but I just nipped out for a bite to eat.'

'You don't have to apologise, Ian. That's the drawback in this business. We work such unsociable hours, finding time for a break can become impossible. 'Anyway, thanks for the report.'

'It doesn't look good for him.'

'True.'

'What do you think?' he asked her.

'Apart from the discrepancy in his alibi, not a great deal. There could be other reasons for getting back to Meadowbank later than he said. Another woman, perhaps. Who knows, Ian? We have to continue with our sifting. This has just come through from London,' she said, passing the fax to him, 'it now transpires he'd been blackmailing Alan Jackson.'

'Do you think he knew he was married to one of the Tilslys?'

'Good question. Given the facts we have about the blackmailing, although not many, it would seem unlikely. The two men weren't buddies, so probably not.'

'So, the connection with the family is a coincidence?'

'You know how much I dislike coincidences' she said sharply, taking the sheet back from him and putting it into the folder together with his report, 'but in this case it may be just that. Also, he'd started extracting money before he and his wife had moved to Meadowbank and if we believe he'd never heard of the Tilsly family, and no real reason I suppose why he should have, we could take it the connection was a matter of chance.'

'Unlucky for Alan Jackson, ma'am.'

'You could say that, but quite frankly, Ian, I've no sympathy for him. As much as I detest blackmailers, that extends to those who put themselves in such a vulnerable position through very often their own greed, which appears to be the case here. Now,' she went on', 'those three paintings. I take it they're still there. In the manor, I mean?'

'That's right. No good to the Tate, ma'am.'

'Quite. What do you know about Hong Kong identity cards, Ian?' she asked, trying to ignore the puzzled frown which immediately slipped into its accustomed position, as if she had presented him with a question on which his whole life and future career depended. 'Don't look so worried,' she laughed lightly, regretting now putting him through the agony of trying to answer what, to him, was obviously a tough question. This case was far from easy, requiring more than the usual effort to solve. It was also Ian Ash's first murder case and, so far, she could only commend the way he was handling the various tasks she had given him. She was deliberately giving him more scope, encouraging him to think things through on his own, rather than continually referring to her for guidance. 'I didn't really expect you to know   a great deal about them, especially as the procedure is different from our European neighbours who need to have them. You see, each person who applies has to have their thumb prints taken.'

'Oh, I see. I hadn't realised. You're thinking his prints could be on the pictures?'

'I'd be surprised if they weren't.'

'Do we know yet whether he returned to Hong Kong?' he asked her.

'Yes, Heathrow have already confirmed a Daniel Browne left on Sunday night on a British Airways flight, non-stop to Hong Kong, arriving there at eight o'clock. And he arrived alright, they confirmed that also.'

'So, he couldn't have shot Steven Blackwood. That is,' Ian added quickly as though warding off any interruption; 'if the murders are connected.'

'That's right, Ian and I believe they are.'

Chapter Twenty-two

Eliza and Simon arrived at the 'Salmon's Rest' before Wendy. To invite her to join them had been a spur of the moment decision by Eliza. She had seen the chief inspector's car earlier when they had been out on the terrace, although she didn't think Simon, facing the other direction, had noticed it. She could not explain to herself the empathy she felt with Wendy Tilsly; perhaps it had more than a little to do with her growing animosity towards the chief inspector. There was one thing Eliza had concluded; the visit would not have been a friendly social call. Simon hadn't demurred when she had told him, but neither had he been over-eager.

Eliza sensed he wanted to spend the evening alone with her. It was not as if he said as much, but there was no need. In so short a time their friendship had developed, but she was reluctant for it to move too rapidly or was it, she questioned herself, she was nervous about letting go. Letting go of what? Her independence? Fear of, albeit prematurely, sharing her life with someone else? You are a silly woman, Eliza Brent. You really are old enough not to read too much into a relationship which is still in its infancy. She did feel an affinity with Simon it was true, and she was honest enough to admit it, but Steve, her marriage to him, how it had all turned out and now his death and the manner in which he had died, they were all too close to the forefront of her mind.

They were sitting in what had become their seat: on one of the leather banquettes. Simon had ordered two Campari sodas. It was still early, not yet eight, but already the restaurant was beginning to fill up. Danielle had waved over to them when they came in, but she had been pre-occupied with settling an elderly couple at one of the smaller tables at the far end of the room. She was looking as stylishly elegant as usual Eliza noted, admiring the ankle-length shift; ice-blue linen; its design pointedly understated and undeniably exclusive. Again, she was reminded how out of place she appeared in Meadowbank, even although she had created a new look for the 'Salmon's Rest', which really was a perfect backdrop, but it still wasn't right for Danielle. To Eliza, watching her as she moved from customer to customer, she sensed the smile she had ready for them wasn't natural and she reckoned that once away from her front-of-house duties the expression would revert back to the sulky dissatisfied one Eliza had seen when she had first met her.

'A penny for them.' Simon asked; he had been watching her.

'Oh, I was just wondering about Danielle, that's all. She puts a brave face on things, Simon,' she said, 'but I can't help feeling that the person we see isn't the real Danielle.'

'No, you're probably right. I can't think why they moved here. It wouldn't have been her decision that's for sure.'

'I've still to meet her husband, but from what I've seen so far they do seem to be quite ill-matched.'

'Opposites do attract,' he teased, 'or so I've been told.'

'Touché!'

'I was actually looking at that chap standing at the bar,' Simon said, 'he came in just after us.'

'The one in the white linen jacket and the quaint little goatee beard?' taking her eyes away from Danielle and looking now at the semi-circle of customers at the bar: a young couple, the girl's incredibly short skirt not leaving a great deal to the imagination; a middle-aged couple, rather formerly dressed even for a restaurant as smart as the 'Salmon's Rest'; another couple, much younger, she remembered seeing the other lunchtime when she had been in the 'Market Inn' and finally, the man in the linen suit.

'Yes,' Simon nodded, 'I haven't seen him in Meadowbank before.'

'Do you know *everyone* in this town, Simon?'

'It probably appears like that to you,' he smiled, 'not everyone, it's true, but when they look like him, perhaps I'm not far wrong.'

'Perhaps he's something to do with the press.' Eliza suggested.

'I don't think so,' Simon said slowly, continuing to look across at him, 'they don't normally dress like that, nor do they have such expensive silver cigarette cases! Look at it, Eliza. Nobody these days uses things like that! Not even my father and he's a stickler for tradition!'

'He looks a little eccentric to me.'

Wendy stood for a second in the open doorway of the restaurant, her eyes adjusting from the outside glare, until she saw them. Standing up, Simon waved over to her.

'Hello,' she said reaching their table, 'I hope you didn't mind, Simon, but when Eliza asked me to join you this evening, I thought I might be –' she hesitated, a smile hovering on her lips, '-- *de trop*!'

'Not at all,' he grinned, 'sit down, please. You'll soon be off back to Hong Kong and Eliza and I have all the time in the world for our intimate dinners. Haven't we, Eliza?' he added, turning round to look at her. Ridiculously and something which hadn't happened since she was a teenager, she felt herself blushing.

'And when do you plan to leave, Wendy?' he asked, perhaps sensing her embarrassment, 'or is it too soon for you to have made any plans?'

'I've a flight booked for next Friday,' Wendy answered, pulling out the chair in front of the banquette and sitting down, 'I didn't have a great deal of choice as it happened,' she added, putting her bag on the chair next to her, 'my boss has practically ordered me to get back there.'

'Demanding.'

'Very demanding, Eliza,' she agreed, 'but not for much longer. You see, you were right; these last couple of days have given me the opportunity I needed to think things through and I've decided to pack up over there and come back to England.'

'To Meadowbank?' Simon asked.

'As much as I would like to, it wouldn't be feasible, I'm afraid, so it has to be London.'

'And start all over again?'

'That's right, Simon, as the song goes: 'start all over again'.'

'Do you feel better now, having made up your mind?' Eliza asked her, although she hardly needed to ask the question. There was a difference to Wendy this evening. Not only did she look relaxed; those dark shadows beneath her eyes had gone, but there was a sparkle which lit up her whole face, instantly giving it more colour.

'Oh, yes,' Wendy said, giving an exaggerated sigh, 'heaps! I should have made the decision years ago and not waited so long, but you know how it is, Eliza? You just keep going; you think, no, you really believe, your situation will improve, but you're never quite honest with yourself, because it never does, does it?'

'No,' Eliza said softly, 'it doesn't. But, I'm glad you'll be coming back to England. We'll be able to meet up with you in London.' The suggestion made before she realised with a jolt her use of the word 'we'. She glanced quickly at Simon, but he gave no sign he had noticed. Was she, sub-consciously, already thinking of them as a couple. Surely not. The mind, hers anyway at the moment, was behaving in a very peculiar and uncharacteristic way! And definitely was in urgent need of some controlling.

Wendy also chose a Campari and the three of them sipped their drinks, keeping the conversation, perhaps intentionally, to lighter topics, not wanting to spoil the evening. Wendy was eager to know about her new venture and how she had first become interested in jewellery design. Simon's work, also, intrigued her and she wanted to hear about all the countries he had been to.

'I know you've already told me Hong Kong wasn't among those places;' she put in, 'probably too many photographs have been taken already. After all, when you think about it, what's so special about a load of skyscrapers!'

'Come on,' Eliza laughed, 'Hong Kong's got a lot more going for it than that!'

'You're right, of course,' she smiled apologetically, 'I'm just a trifle jaundiced at the moment, that's all.'

'Eliza was saying you had brought back some of your own photographs' The question, if indeed it was one, was skilfully and adroitly slipped into the conversation and, on cue, Wendy pulled her bag towards her, fumbling inside until she found the album.

'You'll think them all very amateurish,' she apologised, handing it across to him, 'but at least some of them will give you a rough idea of what Hong Kong Island is like, at least from my point of view.' she added, taking a sip of her drink and leaving Simon to look through the album on his own.

Although not watching him as he turned the pages, Eliza knew when he had reached the first group photograph, the one taken on Wendy's balcony. The movement he made was only slight, Wendy wouldn't have noticed, but she had: his hand steadied and remained on the top corner of the page, only for a moment, and she heard the tiny intake of breath he made. And then the moment was gone; he continued through the album, making the odd appreciative and predictable comment until he came to the last photograph.

'They're good, Wendy. You've captured *your* Hong Kong very well.' he emphasised, giving her back the album.

The people at the bar had now been shown to their tables, including the man in the linen suit, when Eliza noticed the cigarette case at the end of the bar next to his empty glass.

'He's left his cigarette case on the bar, Simon.' she said.

As she spoke Wendy turned round in her seat at exactly the same moment as Peter Taylor spotted it, leaning across the bar to pick it up. He must have sensed the three of them watching him because he glanced across at their table, nodding an acknowledgment in Simon's direction, although Eliza could not help noticing it was Wendy he was really looking at, but it was somewhat more than that. The man was positively staring and then he turned his head away, making her wonder if she had imagined it. But, after all, Wendy Tilsly was a lovely looking woman, with an unusual beauty, and although blonde, she didn't look English. Eliza wouldn't describe it as exotic exactly, not even foreign: she just looked different. She watched as Peter came round from behind the bar and walked over to where the man was sitting, two tables away from their own, and handed the cigarette case to him. She couldn't hear whether any words were exchanged, but she didn't think so and watched as Peter, with a brief glance once again at Wendy, returned to the bar.

They ordered their meal: steak for Simon, Wendy and Eliza choosing the lamb cutlets, and she forgot the incident, except she was very much aware of him sitting there on his own, another stranger in Meadowbank, the thought occurring to her, not that he bore any resemblance to the man Simon and Brian had been talking about last Sunday in the pub. Life in London was never like this she concluded. Here, in Meadowbank, where the pace, snail-like in comparison, she was rapidly and surprisingly, without much effort, learning how easy it was to re-adjust from city life; a hectic and relentless pace, to one where she was able to take the time to notice what was happening around her, to see people as individuals, not as one faceless mass.

They took their time over coffee; Eliza getting the impression Wendy was reluctant for the evening to end and it was almost dusk by the time they were ready to leave the restaurant. Danielle brought over the bill, apologising for not making time earlier to talk to them.

'That's alright, Danielle,' Simon reassured her, placing some notes inside the leather folder, 'we understand. You're very busy this evening.'

'Tell me about it!' she pouted, '*Formidable!* There are times when I wonder where all these people come from!'

'You're not complaining?'

'To be honest,' she paused for a moment, 'my head is too full! I just cannot *think* about the restaurant! Too much is happening. Would you believe it, Simon, we have had *another* visit from that high-handed police officer!'

'Brenda Masters.'

'Who else? *Chief* Inspector Brenda Masters. This time she only wanted to question Peter! Peter! *Encroyable!* -'

'- But why?' Eliza asked. The direct question obviously came as a surprise, stopping Danielle in full flow. It was pretty obvious by the glare she was receiving that Danielle objected to being interrupted, wanting no doubt to be centre-stage.

'Why?' Danielle echoed, the dark eyes flashing indignantly. 'How should I know, Eliza? Something to do with a shooting in Basingstoke. Peter didn't tell me the details, but he was asked to give an alibi for Thursday afternoon! That police woman operates in the most *bizarre* manner. What is the expression, Simon,' she turned once more to face him, ignoring both Eliza and Wendy. They were merely an audience to her dramatic display of wrath, whether affected or not was hard to tell. '- a wasp in her bonnet -'

'- no, Danielle,' he provided, suppressing a smile, 'it's 'a **bee** in her bonnet'

'Thank you, Simon,' she said, 'as usual, you help me out, but that is exactly what I meant. That police woman has a bee in her bonnet. Just because we are newcomers to this gossip-ridden town we appear to be at the top of her list of suspects for anything criminal which happens. Now, it would appear, not only in Meadowbank, which was bad enough, but in Basingstoke also! And, please, Simon,' she stressed, 'do not tell me they are only doing their work.'

'I wasn't going to, Danielle,' placatingly and affecting a meekness which Eliza knew perfectly well was only for Danielle's benefit in a valiant effort to calm her down.

'Well, all I can say,' she continued, undaunted, 'it is apparent to me the police believe that the Basingstoke murder is connected to those in Meadowbank last week!'

And with a final flourish she scooped up the folder and taking it with her, walked across to the desk.

'My word!'

'Sorry about that, Wendy,' Simon said to her, 'but once Danielle starts, there's no stopping her. I've found it best to let her carry on until eventually she runs out of steam.'

'Not very tactful of her though.' Eliza added.

'No, tact is something Danielle knows little about.'

'I suppose she does know who I am?' Wendy said quietly. 'I mean as far as I know I've never seen her before.'

'Oh, she would know alright. She might not go around the town talking to the locals, Wendy, but she has staff and they would know of your family.'

'Of course. I hadn't thought of that.'

Danielle sent the waitress over to their table with the receipt, there being no sign of her now in the restaurant.

'Probably in the kitchen,' Simon suggested, 'taking her anger out on the staff.'

'Oh, dear,' Eliza said, 'I wouldn't like to work for her.'

'Neither would I!' Wendy agreed, unable to stifle a quick spurt of laughter. Poor Danielle, Eliza thought, she really is her worst enemy.

A flurry of late customers had arrived in the restaurant which meant Peter's attention was taken up with serving them and he didn't look up as they walked past the bar on the way to the door. Simon had been able to park directly in front of the restaurant, but by the time Wendy had arrived she told them she'd had to find a place at the back, in the restaurant's parking area. They said their goodnights, Wendy thanking Simon for the meal and they watched as she walked up the short distance to the car park. Within minutes she had returned, running towards them.

'What's wrong?' Simon called out to her.

'My car! It's not there! It's not where I left it!'

'Oh, no!' Eliza said, putting a hand on her arm.

'Try not to worry, Wendy,' Simon said, 'some lad may have taken it for a joy ride. It's Saturday night, remember. They just might return it.'

'Do you really think so?' Eliza asked him.

'Well,' he admitted, 'I don't know, but in any case we have to report it.'

'Come back with us, Wendy,' she suggested, 'we'll phone the police from there and I'll make us some coffee. Simon could be right, you know. At least,' she added, 'it's a hire car and not your own, if that's any comfort.'

What an end to an evening Eliza thought as Simon pulled away from the kerb, avoiding those vehicles parked in the square. Half an hour before closing time and 'The Market Inn' was packed; customers two-deep at the bar waiting to order last drinks. Tables and chairs had been brought outside and lined the full length of the pavement extending to include the area directly in front of the two shops on either side of the pub. Melissa, clearing away bottles and glasses from one of the tables, looked up and waved to them as they drove slowly past. A party was in full swing at one of the town houses at the end of the square; the front door and all the downstairs windows wide open; the guests: girls in skimpy mini-skirts and strapless micro tops and as though competing in the youthful fashion stakes, the men, when not in the regimental jeans were wearing baggy cotton trousers, frayed at the hems and threatening to slip down well below their narrow hips, displaying wide expanses of designer boxer shorts, sprawled on the top step and window ledges; a couple glued together, attempting to dance in the only available space left on the pavement to the pulsating and ear-shattering beat of 'Oasis' and still more cars were arriving to join the others and pulling up with a screech of brakes in front of the building.

'Summer comes to Meadowbank.' Simon murmured, changing gear as they approached the traffic lights, accompanied all the way by Liam Gallaher.

'Hell!' Wendy said from the back seat, 'what an idiot! I've left my mobile in the car!'

'Are you sure?' Eliza asked, turning round in her seat, 'it's not at the bottom of your bag?'

'No, it's not. And I remember now, I had it in my hand when I left and I put it on the passenger seat.'

'You're not having much luck at the moment, are you?' Eliza smiled sympathetically.

'You could say that, Eliza.' attempting a smile but it was a poor effort, making it clear to Eliza and probably to Simon that she was under considerable strain. The main thing, she decided, and it was the only help they could offer, was to try and reassure her. It was a pity Wendy was on her own at times like these; she shouldn't have been; the thought instantly acting as a reminder of the boyfriend in Hong Kong. If it had been Dan they had seen, that was something else she would have to face.

They were now approaching the Tilsly estate; the start of the brick wall, interrupted half-way by the gates which Eliza guessed would be open. She wondered whether they were ever closed and if they were, who was responsible for making sure the grounds were secure. It was something which had not occurred to her before. In fact, she still knew very little about how the estate was run and, apart from the housekeeper, whom she had seen arriving each morning; quite early, before eight, and having heard the whine of an electric mower at least one gardener, but that was all. A house and grounds of this size, although the place was now more or less unoccupied must employ more than two people, but then she reminded herself she had only been at the lodge for a week;

incredible though that seemed, considering everything which had occurred in that time.

As soon as they arrived Eliza handed Wendy her mobile, suggesting she might get a better reception out on the terrace. It was too late to phone the car hire people, that would have to wait until the morning, but as Simon told her, they should let the police know as soon as possible. Although he had suggested whoever had taken the car may decide to return it, Eliza didn't think he actually believed it. Also, she wondered how interested the police in Meadowbank would be to turn out late on a Saturday night to try and find what he had described as a joy-rider. In the full scale of things she didn't think so. Judging by the activities going on in the centre of the town it looked as though they would have enough to contend with this evening which gave every appearance of going on well into the early hours.

Eliza went through the automatic motions of making the coffee, Simon helping her by finding mugs and sugar. She wanted to ask him about the photograph, but it wasn't the right time. They would have to wait until they were on their own. First things first she thought, spooning coffee into the cafètiere and switching it on. Wendy didn't take long, coming back into the kitchen and handing her the mobile.

'Thanks, Eliza.'

'And are they going to jump into action?' Simon asked her.

'I don't think so,' she said, dramatically raising her eyes, 'I only spoke to the desk sergeant. I got the distinct impression he gets many calls like mine.'

'Did he say what they would do?' Eliza asked her.

'Not really,' she admitted, 'he took down my details; name, address, that sort of thing. I told him I'd hired the car from Hertz, and that was about all they wanted to know. I suppose when you think about it, there isn't much else they can do, especially tonight. Eventually, no doubt, the car will turn up.'

'But where?'

'Exactly, Simon.'

'Also,' Eliza added, 'in what sort of state will it be in!'

'I dread to think!'

'I would say Hertz will supply you with another car, Wendy.' Simon suggested.

'I know, but I'm really more concerned about my mobile. I reckon I can say goodbye to that.'

Wendy did not stay much longer, only until she had drunk her coffee. They offered to walk up the drive with her to the manor, but she told them it wasn't necessary. She would be alright.

'She's tough,' Eliza said after Wendy had left and, standing on the terrace they watched her until she reached the main door and seen the two carriage lamps come on, also the light in the room with the French windows; 'her delicate appearance is deceptive, isn't it?'

'True;' he agreed, 'she's always been like that. Even as a kid. Resilient, too.'

'But, just how resilient, Simon?'

'You're thinking about the guy in the photograph?'

'Yes. You think it's him, don't you. The man in the pub?'

'Unless he's got a twin, yes.'

'We're in an awkward position,' she complained, turning away from the gardens and facing him, 'what do you think we should do?'

'I don't know the answer to that, Eliza.' he said, 'All I know is we can't do anything tonight and if we did decide to mention the likeness to Wendy, and I'm only saying if, she has enough to worry about at the moment.'

'She's not going to take too kindly to us if we say we think her boyfriend was in Meadowbank last weekend!'

'I know, that would be unkind, but it will have to be said at some point, I suppose it is trying to find the most tactful approach. The thing is though, however we dress this up, Wendy is not stupid. She would be able to see right through us, no matter how we couched our approach.'

'Also,' she put it, 'she's going to wonder why we didn't mention the likeness when we first saw the photograph.'

Chapter Twenty-three

Three cars were reported stolen on Saturday night in Meadowbank, but only one of them was involved in a fatality. In the normal procedure at the station, missing cars, along with the occasional missing person, did not reach the chief inspector's desk, at least not in the initial stages when any of them could turn up within the first few hours and invariably did, but Sergeant Baker, who was on desk duty that night thought differently. Upon receiving the call from Wendy he had instantly become alert to there being a possible link with the much-talked about Tilsly case and made a point of mentioning this to his relief when he went off duty the following morning. Unfortunately, his fellow officer put less importance on what he considered to be just one more missing vehicle on a busier than usual Saturday night and being relatively new to the area knew little and cared even less about the Tilsly family. Also, not long after he came on duty, news of the accident came in. It had happened between the hours of ten and midnight with, at first, only the deeply etched tyre marks on the tarmac on the last bend in the road before it joined the A30 to show there may have been one. The car had been discovered by a woman walking her dog along the river footpath. Once the police and recovery team had arrived, the consensus of opinion was that the driver must have lost control, swerved off the road and somersaulted down the steep incline and, regrettably for him, ending its rapid descent by embedding itself into one of the Dutch elms which lined the bank of the river. It was not until some hours later, when the wrecked car had been pulled free and hauled back up on to the road; they were able to see the number plate.

The driver, young, still in his teens, was already dead when they reached the scene and it did not take long for the pathologist to reach the conclusion, after a brief examination of the man's injuries, that he would have died immediately on impact. And to make their task more difficult, he had no identification on him. They did, however, find a mobile phone on the floor under the passenger seat and this, along with the body, was taken to Meadowbank Police Station.

By the time Brenda Masters arrived in her office shortly after nine, the report, including the pathologist's, was already waiting for her. The desk sergeant was quick to inform her that his colleague, Sergeant Baker, had mentioned to him that Wendy Tilsly was one of the three people who had phoned into the station the previous evening to report their vehicle had been stolen and apologised for not being more diligent in following it up and putting more importance on that call in particular. But what could she say? Also, even if she had been informed, what could she have done? She wouldn't have been able to prevent the accident. It could have been any of the other three vehicles, not necessarily Wendy Tilsly's, but it wasn't until later in the morning when the mechanic's report was faxed into the station she started to view the incident quite differently.

Ian Ash came into her office at exactly the same time as the mobile rang. Glancing up and beckoning him to sit down, she pressed the receive button.

'Hello.' Keep it simple she decided, having no way of knowing whether the mobile belonged to Wendy Tilsly or not.

'Wendy? Is that you? I've been trying to phone you since last night –'

'– no,' she interrupted, 'I'm Chief Inspector Brenda Masters, from the Meadowbank Police Station –'

'– but,' it was now his turn to interrupt, 'I don't understand. Wendy. Miss Tilsly, is she alright?'

'As far as I know, sir, yes.'

'Thank God!'

'You're a friend of hers?'

'Yes, I am.'

'And your name, please, sir?'

'Mark Wood. I'm phoning from London; perhaps you would tell me what's happened and why you have her mobile.'

'Miss Tilsly's car was stolen last night, Mr Wood. Unfortunately it was involved in an accident and the mobile was handed into us at the station.'

'I see. Have you been in touch with her?'

'Not yet,' Brenda said, 'details of the accident have only just come in, but I intend to go along to the manor personally later on this morning.'

There was little more to be said and although she could tell he was distressed by the news, she brought the call to a close. No doubt, she thought, he would find another way to contact her. There was, she already knew, a telephone in the house, but at the moment that was not her concern. As she had told Mark Wood she would be going along there herself. There were a number of questions she needed to ask. The fact Wendy Tilsly had parked the car outside the 'Salmon's Rest' after presumably eaten there last night may now have some relevance.

'An interesting development, wouldn't you say, Ian?'

'In what way, ma'am?'

'You haven't seen the mechanic's report yet?'

'No, I haven't.'

She watched his expression change as she told him about the brakes. Now, since the beginning of this case, she had the feeling they were at last on the same wavelength. Like her, Ian was coming round to the idea that coincidences had no place in this murder enquiry.

'Ian,' Brenda said, taking a clean sheet of paper from a desk drawer and slowly writing the date in the top right-hand corner and neatly underlining it, 'let's spend a few minutes going over this case. The first murder, what do we have so far? And then followed quickly afterwards by that of Len Roberts. As for the suspects, we can, at least for the time being, rule out Daniel Browne, mainly because of the lack of motive.'

'He had already managed to get what he wanted.'

'Quite. So, why return? He had ample opportunity during the daytime, having it would seem, the freedom to spend time on his own in the gallery. He'd managed to create a credible cover-story, remember. At least it fooled the major and anyone else he decided to explain why he was in the area. Mind you,' Brenda went on, 'you could say he was lucky the major was able to leave him on his own, otherwise he may very well have returned later!'

'And,' Ian put in, 'as we've said already, if Len Roberts had seen him that night he wouldn't have known who he was. He'd never seen him before, neither was he likely to see him again.'

'Yes, I think you're right. And, I think that is the key to the first part of this case. So, among those likely suspects, the ones who had anything to gain, I mean by the demise of Major Tilsly, who do we have?'

'Including Peter Taylor?'

'Yes, including him, although his reasons, if indeed he did kill him, would not necessarily have been for the same reason, more for his own protection.'

'Who else do you have in mind, ma'am? The son?'

'Colin? Yes, but also his brother-in-law, Alan Jackson.'

'But he has an alibi,' Ian frowned, 'he was away all weekend on a course. In Brighton.'

'We only have his word for that; also, if we allow ourselves to go off at a slight tangent, we only have his word that Peter Taylor was blackmailing him! Anyway, we should be concentrating on last weekend. We never checked up that he actually did attend the course, did we?'

'No. We should have done.'

'I know; we allowed ourselves to be side-tracked with this man from Hong Kong and, of course, later with Peter Taylor's alibi.'

'I'll check up on the Alan Jackson end, shall I?' he suggested.

'You can try. At least we have the name of the hotel where the management course was being held; his name will be in their register,

239

although it still won't prove if he left the hotel at anytime during the weekend. Brighton is not too many miles from Meadowbank and, given that both murders took place in the early hours, he would not have found it too difficult to slip out and get back to his hotel unnoticed.'

'Someone may have seen him, ma'am. Especially if the hotel had a night porter.'

'There is always that,' she agreed, 'and then, of course, there is our third suspect.'

'You mean Steve Blackwood?'

'Yes, I do and that brings us back once again to Eliza Brent. Oh, I know your views about her, Ian, but there is no room for sensitivity in any of this. She may very well have assisted him. We just don't know.'

'The man is dead.'

'I don't need to be reminded,' Brenda said sharply, 'and I suppose you're going to tell me that dead men can't talk!'

*

Colin Tilsly's BMW was parked outside the Manor when Brenda arrived there shortly before midday. Wendy must have heard the car; appearing on the top steps before she had time to switch off the ignition, followed immediately by her brother, his broad frame, a good head and shoulders taller than his sister.

'I apologise for disturbing you on a Sunday, Miss Tilsly.' were her opening words, although she didn't believe either of them were taken in by the assumed informality. Senior police officers do not investigate missing vehicles and Brenda was under no illusions that both Colin and Wendy Tilsly would be only too well aware of the fact. Judging by their set expressions as she looked up at them, she realised neither of them intended to make this visit an easy one. For the first time she could see through the veneer of ethereal femininity in the other woman to the strength of character which lay within. What you saw, she concluded, was not necessarily what you got. Wendy Tilsly; she recognised as a survivor and although Brenda had never been to Hong Kong, she reckoned to live there, working in what she knew to be a highly competitive and international world it was no place for the faint hearted.

'We were just leaving, Chief Inspector,' Colin Tilsly spoke for the first time, gently pushing his sister aside as he walked towards her, 'I'm taking my sister home with me for lunch.'

'This won't take long,' Brenda said, 'only a few questions I would like to ask you, Miss Tilsly.'

'You've found my car?'

'We have, yes.' Brenda answered, much preferring to talk to her on her own, without her brother's critical presence, but for now, she didn't have much choice, 'Earlier this morning in fact.'

'That's good news.'

'I'm afraid not. You see, the young man who stole it only managed to reach the A30 before running the vehicle off the road –'

'– you mean it's a right-off?' Colin interrupted.

'As to that I can't say, sir,' she said, 'but the driver didn't make it. He was killed outright.'

'How awful!'

'Yes, Miss Tilsly, it was. For him.'

'Who was he anyway?' Colin asked.

'We don't know yet.'

'By that, Chief Inspector, I suppose you mean he didn't have a driving licence?'

'Colin.' Wendy said quietly, warningly.

'He may have had one, all I'm saying is, he didn't have it with him last night.'

'I know for a fact,' Colin went on, his voice rising, 'there have been a number of car thefts in and around Meadowbank over the last six months and I would like to know what the police are doing about them!'

'Miss Tilsly,' Brenda said, ignoring him, 'can you spare a few moments. It would be better, I think, if we went inside.'

'Of course,' she agreed, turning round and leading the way back into the manor. 'We'll use the lounge, it's along here.' she added, opening the first door off the hall.

'We understand you left your car at the rear of the 'Salmon's Rest' restaurant?'

'That's right; there was no space in the square.'

'What time would this have been?'

'About twenty to eight.'

'And you left the restaurant, when?'

'We were quite late, actually. It was almost dark, it must have been after ten, but I can't be sure.'

'I see,' Brenda said, 'and obviously from where you were inside the restaurant it would have been impossible to have seen your car.'

'What does all this matter, Chief Inspector?' Colin Tilsly interrupted again.

'You have been in touch with the car hire firm, Miss Tilsly?'

'I phoned them this morning,' she said, 'they told me they would be sending another one, but not until tomorrow.'

'You must have realised you left your mobile in the car.'

'Yes, that was careless of me. You've found it?'

'Yes,' Brenda said, unzipping her bag and pulling out the mobile, 'here you are.'

'Thank you.' taking it from her and slipping it into the pocket of her skirt, 'I don't feel so cut off now.'

'Chief Inspector,' Colin put in, 'have you quite finished, we'd like to go now. My wife will be getting impatient waiting for us.'

And she wouldn't be the only one, Brenda thought cynically, looking across at his flushed face, whether from the warm morning or suppressed irritation it was hard to tell.

'Miss Tilsly,' once again ignoring him, have you given any more thought to the man you saw on Thursday?'

'Not really, no.'

'A pity.'

'Why?'

'Because we believe,' she went on to explain, 'that encounter, although only lasting seconds, could be important to our investigations.'

'But,' Wendy put it, 'I've already said I didn't look at his face, it all happened so quickly. I was more concerned on trying to keep my balance.'

'But you were able to describe what he was wearing, his height and age, even that he was carrying a magazine, a newspaper supplement you thought. In fact,' she went on, 'your recall was quite a detailed one.'

'What is this?' Colin could no longer contain himself. 'Are you saying my sister is deliberately holding back something? She never even heard his voice!'

'But I did, Colin.' Wendy answered slowly, apologetically as she looked at Brenda, 'I'm sorry, Chief Inspector, I had completely forgotten, but I did hear him speak. He only said one word though which was 'sorry'. That was all.'

'Do you think you would recognise his voice if you heard it again?'

'I very much doubt it.'

'There are times, Miss Tilsly,' Brenda said, 'when the memory plays tricks on us. It can be stubborn until something, often entirely disconnected, triggers it off.'

'For example?' Colin asked, interested in spite of what must be an inbuilt animosity, allowing for the first time his protective guard to slip.

'Well,' Brenda said, turning to face him, 'you may see, come face to face perhaps, with that person and, although you don't recognise his features, in fact are positive you've never seen him before, there can be a glimmer of recognition, a particular mannerism which may have struck you subconsciously as being different from the norm or, as your sister has just mentioned, the voice, which you may hear again, but if that happened, it could be somewhere completely out of context.'

'Do you think this guy came from around here then, Chief Inspector?' Here was a man Brenda decided, who was adept at reaching to the core of the matter and while she had never underestimated his intelligence she hadn't anticipated such a quick and accurate reaction.

'It's possible,' she admitted, 'but so far we have nothing to substantiate this. We need hard facts.'

'Hunches must have some part to play in reaching conclusions though.' a statement, and one not requiring any corroboration from her and nor was she going to say anything further which would enable him to work things out for himself. Although she had nothing personal against Colin Tilsly, until the case was finally wrapped up, he would continue to be considered as a possible suspect.

'Have you booked your flight back to Hong Kong yet?' she asked Wendy.

'Yes, I leave on Friday.'

'I see, well, if anything should occur to you between now and then, I hope you'll call me.'

'Of course.'

'Finally, Miss Tilsly, we shall need your address in Hong Kong. For our records, you understand.'

'That's no problem,' Wendy said, pre-empting her brother's intervention, 'it's fourteen Baxter Mansions, Mid-Levels.'

'Thank you,' Brenda said, jotting it down, 'incidentally, a call came through on your mobile about ten this morning.'

'I was going to ask you that actually, Chief Inspector. I've been expecting to hear from Hong Kong.'

'This was from London; he said he had been trying to call you since last night.'

'Did he give his name?'

'Yes, Mark Wood.'

'Mark?'

'Who's he, Wendy?'

'A friend, Colin.'

'From London?' the man was unbelievably possessive; didn't he realise his sister was an adult and Brenda waited to find out how Wendy would deal with such a blatant intrusion into her privacy.

'Yes, Mark lives in London.'

'I didn't realise you had kept in touch with any of your old friends there.' he said, acting as if they were both on their own, and not with a police officer as an audience. He was entirely oblivious, Brenda decided. His arrogance, his whole manner, verging on rudeness was quite staggering. Also, he had shown no compassion or even interest when she had told him about the accident, brushing off the boy's death as unimportant.

'You've never mentioned him?' peevishness creeping into his voice.

'For goodness sake, Colin,' Wendy snapped, swinging round on her heels to face him, 'will you please shut up! My private life has nothing to do with you! Nothing! I'm sorry, Chief Inspector,' she said, lowering her voice and turning back to her, 'what must you think of us? Squabbling like children!'

'Siblings, Miss Tilsly.' Brenda Master said enigmatically, at the same time suppressing a smile, thankful for once she had been an only child.

*

Margaret Alty

Peter Taylor, pocketing the change for his cigarettes, looked across towards the open door of the stationers as Wendy Tilsly stepped out from the passenger side of a dark blue BMW parked immediately in front of the shop and walked inside, pausing at the magazine rack next to where he was standing. Keeping his eyes averted, he walked past her, close enough to smell her perfume: light and flowery and not one he recognised, at least not one ever worn by Danielle. He crossed the square, waiting until he had reached the pavement outside 'The Salmon's Rest' before turning round, more to have another look at the BMW and find out whether he recognised the driver, than peering into the dark interior of the stationers. And there she was. Framed in the doorway, watching him. For a fraction of a second their eyes locked. So, he thought, opening the restaurant door, he had been right. She remembered him. Anger accompanied this conclusion, anger at himself. For all his experience he had made a complete mess last night. He had allowed panic to dictate. A big mistake. She may not have recognised him at the time, but she sure as hell did now! How long did he have, he wondered, before she said something. To the police? To the man in the BMW or, if it came to that, to anyone. And, where the hell was her car? He knew the job he had done on the brakes had been foolproof. Perhaps the distance between the town and the Manor had been too short; perhaps she had been driving too slowly. How the hell did he know? The main thing was she was still alive!

Peter had the restaurant to himself; Danielle, having decided to spend the hours before they needed to prepare for the evening upstairs in the flat. He needed time to think. And to plan. There were two options. There had always been. This was nothing new. Both were risky, but his whole life had been spent, or so it seemed, on taking risks and, so far, he had emerged relatively unscathed. His alibi for Thursday, planned down to the last detail was watertight. He had made sure of that. Steve had brought things to a head; if he hadn't made that call to him demanding

246

his share from a deal he had done his best to botch up, he would still be alive today. And now it would seem someone else was standing in his way; a woman, until the day before, he had never even heard of. Talk about a loose cannon! This time, he would make sure. And, if in the meantime, she did speak to anyone, she would never be able to prove she had seen him.

The other option and one, because he had used it in the past, would prove much easier. He could leave. Another identity was no problem. He still had the passport he'd had made for such an emergency. He had evaded the authorities before, nothing could have been more hair-raising than extricating himself from the Mombasa debacle and he was capable of doing so again if he had to. But, was his present situation so dire that he was prepared to abandon, not only Danielle, but everything else he had built up over the years, painstakingly creating a new identity and one which no-one had penetrated? Not even Steve had known or even guessed what he'd had to hide.

He poured himself a good measure of whisky, taking the glass out with him to the walled garden and sitting down on one of the wrought iron chairs. It was peaceful out here; no sound of traffic could be heard from the square which even on a Sunday afternoon kept up a constant flow. In spite of not fitting into the social life of the town he didn't dislike living in Meadowbank. He had even begun to feel part of the place, buried, as Danielle had often described it, in the country, but he found it sufficiently far enough away from London to induce a feeling of security. Sipping the scotch, appreciating the familiar soothing effect as the warm liquid coursed through his veins. There was no way he decided, leaning back and stretching out his legs, lifting his face up to the sun and closing his eyes against the glare, was he going to give any of this up. In time, he realised only too well, Danielle would get her way, and they would leave Meadowbank, but not yet. In the final equation he concluded, Wendy Tilsly, like her father, was of no real importance. Neither of them knew what it was like to have to struggle. This was not knowledge he had learned, it was something he knew instinctively. The Tilslys, a wealthy impenetrable close-knit family immediately evoking in him deep-rooted reactions of derision. Who did they think they were anyway? In this day and age! The man had been positively archaic. He had only retired with the rank of major after all. It was not as if he had a *real* title; he hadn't been knighted. Like thousands before him, he had been ex-army. Major Reginald Tilsly. Well, Peter concluded, nobody could pin his murder on him. As much as he had disliked the man, one didn't go around shooting people who insulted you! Tempting though it may be.

If it had not been for Danielle going on incessantly about that damned art collection and complaining how the old boy had refused to talk to her, he would never have known about it. He could have, at any time, quite effortlessly gained entry to the manor, as in fact he had, thanks to the set of skeleton keys he'd held on to for years. And, if it hadn't been for that old fool surprising him at the bottom of the stairs, he would still be alive today!

Peter finished off his whisky and as much as he would have liked another one, decided against it; Danielle would be down soon and he didn't want to do anything to antagonise her. What he had to plan needed his full concentration and would never be accomplished if he had to spend the next few hours parrying words with her. She always won anyway. Thinking about the skeleton keys reminded him once again of Steve and the last time they had both used them. They had carried out the recce together. The property was in St John's Wood, a quiet, tree-lined avenue where everyone minded their own business and even if they saw anything untoward would pretend ignorance and do nothing. They had planned to get in and out as speedily as possible, even although they had known the owners were on holiday in the south of France; they had known exactly what they wanted to pick up: silver tableware; a considerable amount of it, and all saleable; two Paul and John Nash landscapes, a Monet and a Picasso; all genuine and, as with the silver, Peter had the outlets. There had been much more in that house, openly asking to be taken, but that was not how they had planned the robbery. But then, he hadn't taken into account Steve's problem. Greed. He had been motivated by greed, he always craved for that bit extra and that was how, that night, he had overstepped the mark; staying in there for those extra minutes had been his downfall. He had been caught literally red-handed with a clutch of the wife's gold and platinum jewellery which should have been in a safe deposit box, but instead was in one of the dressing-table drawers. Peter, waiting in the car had witnessed it all. Someone must have given the police the tip-off. Perhaps one of the neighbours was more conscientiously concerned than they had bargained for. He had never found out, not that it mattered to him. He had waited across the road until they had taken Steve away before driving in a circuitous route back to Kensington where he and Danielle had lived then. He had learned later through one of his East End contacts that Steve had gone down for eight months and he had assumed, wrongly as it turned out, he would never hear from him again. This was where he and Steve had differed. Steve had been an amateur in spite of having been in the business since a kid. A bloody amateur. Peter had, during the years they had worked together, done his best to try and give him some guidance, but he had been wasting his breath. Steve Blackwood knew it all. He'd had a good run and if it hadn't been for that last fiasco he would never have been banged up, would never have tried to play his last card and paid the ultimate price. He should have known better than to make any demands on him. Well, Peter thought without a trace of regret, too late now. Steve had gambled and lost. Quite simple when you thought about it.

Chapter Twenty-four

At last she was on her own. She thought Colin would never go. While she could understand his reluctance to go home and no doubt be subjected to more haranguing from Rachel, who throughout lunch and even after they had eaten and were outside having their coffee, had not let up on her conjecturing, continuing to harp on about the shooting and doing her best to squeeze out information Wendy had been unable to provide, the way he had prolonged leaving had still struck her as unusual, even for Colin. Surely, she thought, watching the BMW pull out on to the main road, he knew how to handle his wife by now. If not, she decided, it was time he did; she was faced with an awkward decision and Colin would have been the last person she could have turned to for advice. To ask him would have been a waste of time. She knew exactly what he would say. He wouldn't have minced his words either. But whether to get in touch with Brenda Masters was not really a straightforward decision, at least not for her. Could she be absolutely certain Peter Taylor was the same man? Colin would, in his bull-dozer like manner, have told her to let them sort it out, not really caring whether she was right or not. To him, it would not have mattered, but it *did* matter. If she was wrong, the outcome, the questioning, the suspicions, would be worse for Peter Taylor. Was she prepared to take that risk? She'd seen him last night, so why hadn't she recognised him then?

What she needed, Wendy thought, walking back inside, was to speak to someone impartial and that meant not family. Both Colin and Rachel had been right in a way; she had lost touch with the people she had once known and at that moment, staring blindly out of the lounge window across the deserted lawns, she was unable to think of a single person she could confide in, far less hope for any support. Moving to Hong Kong had meant, whether she had intended it to or not, that those ties she'd had; the colleagues and friends she had worked with in London, had weakened until now, after being away for so long, had become practically non-existent. She was still in contact with a handful of them: cards at Christmas, the occasional post card, but that was about all. Most of the old crowd were married now or, like her, had moved on. She then remembered Mark. She hardly knew him. But she would phone him, return his call, and listen to what he had to say. If Peter Taylor was the man who'd barged into her and she even felt sufficiently confident to report this to the police, it would have to be done before she met Mark on Wednesday. It's strange, Wendy thought, not once had she thought of Dan and even considered giving him a ring. Why was that? Was it possible she was not only physically, but mentally, pulling away from him? They had only spoken once since she had come back home; on the Thursday, and she had been tired, not wanting to prolong the conversation. He hadn't given any impression of having noticed and had rung off after five minutes, saying he would call again later in the week. No, it was not Dan she needed to talk to at that moment. He would have been impatient, worse even than Colin, telling her she shouldn't even hesitate to contact the police. She could hear his voice; that laid back drawl which in the early days had fascinated her, overlaid with the faint Californian accent, saying: 'For Christ's Sake, Wendy, tell them. That's what they get paid for!' That wasn't the kind of advice she needed. What then was she looking for? A sympathetic ear? Someone to quite literally hold her hand and make the decision for her? Perhaps, she sighed, that was exactly what she did need. At that moment, emotionally drained, all she wanted was to forget everything; for too long now she had been solely responsible for her life, her decisions, no-one else's, but that was the way she had wanted it. Wasn't it? That was why she had left home in the first place; found a niche in publishing in London and then moving out to the Far East. Each step of the way she had made entirely on her own and she didn't remember pausing for one minute to ask anyone whether they thought she was doing the right thing. Not that she would have listened anyway, she thought cynically. As much as she had loved her father, had enjoyed the cushioned and protected life he had always indulgently provided for her, it had not been enough. She had wanted her independence, craving for something different; to discover what life was like beyond the one she had known. Well, she sighed, you've got what you wanted Wendy, now sort it out. On your own!

She had put the card Mark had given her in one of the pockets of her wallet and, finding it now, was about to key in his number when her mobile rang. She did a rapid mental run-through: Colin with more platitudes; Nanette, wanting a non-characteristic sisterly chat; Dan to ask her when she was going to come back? But it was none of them, although the call was from Hong Kong; Miranda's voice, crystal clear and sounding as if she was in the same room. She should really have given her a call, kept in touch as she had promised and as they always had done. Miranda and she had been friends for years, as far back as those early days in London when they had shared a cramped little flat in Earl's Court, no more than a bed-sit, but it was all they could afford then. As soon as Miranda heard she was going to Hong Kong she hadn't hesitated, immediately resigning from her job as receptionist at the 'Savoy' and travelling with her on the same plane, once again sharing with her a basic and only fractionally larger flat than the one they'd had in London.'

'I'm sorry, Miranda,' Wendy apologised, 'I should be the one phoning you.'

'Don't worry; I know you must be having a rough time of it. I didn't expect to hear from you so soon anyway, but,' she went on, 'it's about Dan.'

'Dan?'

'I hate to add to your worries,' Miranda said, 'but I thought I had better let you know, before you heard from anyone else.'

'Something's happened to him?' immediately suspecting the worse. An accident? He was dead? Another death? Now, holding her breath, she waited.

'He's been taken into custody, Wendy'

'What!' of all the possibilities coursing through her brain that was the last she expected.

'We don't know a great deal, but apparently he was arrested at the airport yesterday and charged with the theft of some valuable paintings in England and, this is the incredible part, Wendy,' she rushed on now, 'each of them had been replaced by a fake!'

'I don't believe it!'

'I know how you feel, Wendy. That was exactly our reaction, but it seems his office was raided early yesterday morning; we've no idea what they found, and it was shortly afterwards he was arrested.'

'You said he was at the airport? I don't understand. Where was he going? I spoke to him on Thursday, he never said anything about going away, but –' she faltered, struck at how quickly she was accepting the possibility that the man she had known for ten years and had lived with for a good part of that time, was not what he had seemed, and perhaps even more significantly, was not the man she had wanted him to be. 'So,' she went on slowly, 'what happens now, Miranda? Will he be tried in Hong Kong?'

'No, we do know that much, Interpol are involved and we heard he would be taken to London.'

'What a mess! Was he doing all this on his own then? But he couldn't have been, could he?' answering her own question, Daniel was no artist; he would have needed someone to help him.

'You're thinking about the fakes?'

'Yes.'

'That's the Hong Kong end and you know what it's like here, Wendy? They'll have to delve deep for whoever else was involved.'

There wasn't much more Miranda could tell her, both of them realising there was nothing to be gained from repetitive and useless speculation and after Wendy told her she would be back in Hong Kong on the late Friday night flight, they rang off. Entirely alone now, she was able to give full reign to the thoughts and emotions which surged through her brain, each of them vying for attention. And all the time, persistently and insidiously, one predominated, demanding an answer. But it was too soon. She wasn't ready yet. It would be too easy to use the shocking news about Dan to influence her. She had always known there could never be any real permanency to their relationship; also that he had not been her sole reason for staying on in Hong Kong for so long. She also knew that if she did decide not to leave, although it would feel strange at first not being with him anymore, she was realistic enough to realise she would adapt to being on her own again. As indeed she would have to if she returned to England.

There was no answer from Mark's mobile. She would try again in the morning. Hours later and unable to sleep, exasperated with continually tossing and turning, trying to find a cool position, she threw back the crumpled sheet. It was no use; sleep refused to come. Each time hovering on the edge of unconsciousness a memory, familiar and at the same time unwelcome, would push through, refusing to be ignored and clamouring for attention. Dan. Always Dan. At the beginning of their relationship; shortly after he had moved in with her, he'd told her not to expect marriage even if his wife did decide to divorce him. Of course he was selfish, but he had never made any attempt to hide the fact from her. There had been another time, about eight years ago when she had made the mistake of mentioning children. It had been her thirtieth birthday when, for the first time, she had become aware of her biological clock ticking. Dan had been quick to squash that idea before it grew into an obsession. He already had a family; she had known that as well, and one he'd had no compunction in leaving behind in California. 'Like wives,

Wendy, my darling,' he had said, 'the older they get, the more demanding!' And that had been that. There had been other examples of his frankness or, as Miranda had once described, his callousness, most of which she had learned to live with. Until recently. And now? It looked as if that particular decision of whether to continue the relationship had now been made for her.

There was no need to switch on the light in the kitchen; a full moon shone through the window. Although there had been a roller blind there for as long as she could remember, the room, facing as it did, out towards the kitchen garden, except during the winter months the blind was never pulled down. Wendy remembered seeing a tin of Ovaltine in one of the cupboards, assuming that Mrs Plenderneath, as she had done since the three of them had been young, made sure there was always some in the event of either Colin or Nanette's children coming to stay. With the tin in one hand and a small milk saucepan in the other the stillness of the night was disturbed by a slight shuffling outside, similar to the sound a dog or cat might make, but there were no pets at the manor, and never had been. She stood there, in the centre of the kitchen, transfixed as she watched the old-fashioned door knob, the engraved wood worn smooth over the years, turn slowly until, silhouetted in the open doorway, was the man she had seen earlier. The owner of the restaurant in Meadowbank. Peter Taylor.

*

Wendy was not the only one unable to sleep, although Eliza's restlessness had more to do with the hot and airless night than to any radical changes she might have to make to her life. Those, she hoped, were now behind her. In spite of the dramatic happenings of the past week she was confident she would be able to settle down to living in the area, not fooling herself that her new friendship with Simon did not have something to do with the way she was feeling. Propping herself up against the pillow she allowed her thoughts to drift, not only about him, but how she planned to expand the business, most importantly, to make it work. Even after so short a time she had already tasted the relative freedom of the self-employed, but realising that the proverbial nut would still have to be cracked. Eliza was determined to make a success of what she had longed wished for, but now she had to turn that old dream into reality. It was a gamble, but a calculated one and she felt stimulated by the challenge. She didn't know how long she would have remained like this, indulging in a kind of self-assessment state, but a change in the light disturbed her. A flickering. There were no drifting clouds to shadow the moon, whatever was causing it had to be something else. And then, pulling herself upright, she realised that what she was looking at was torchlight. Short rapid pinpricks of light threading their way through the trees along the drive; the same trees which had given cover to the intruder the other night she realised with an involuntary shudder.

And, as then, she walked barefoot to the open window, but keeping well back in case whoever was out there happened to glance up and see her. There was more than one torch being used out there; the chilling realisation making her catch her breath. This is weird she thought, looking up the length of the drive to the Manor which, as before, apart from the two carriage lamps outside, was in darkness, and then over towards the rear of the building. More torchlight! What is going on! It looked as if gradually, but systematically, the whole place was being surrounded. She counted, not by the figures indistinguishable even in the moonlight, but by the torches. Puzzled now, she remained there, wondering why they should be using them, and then of course! They were acting as signals! This time, she had to do something! But what? Phone the police? But, perhaps they were the police! And what about Wendy? She must be in there; upstairs asleep and unaware of what was happening only yards away. Simon had already told her to call him if ever she was worried about anything and that it didn't matter what time. He would know what to do and, picking up her mobile from the bedside table, she dialled his number.

It did not take him long to arrive. He had used the footpath linking the two properties and judging by his rapid breathing must have run all the way. She had left the door open for him and without saying anything he took her in his arms, gently pushing damp tendrils of hair back from her forehead.

'I didn't know what to do, Simon.' she said at last, taking his hand and leading him into the kitchen.

'I'm glad you phoned.' he said, following her gaze across to the manor, the lights more solid now, no longer flickering as they formed an arch at the bottom of the steps around the front door.

'I can't help worrying about Wendy.'

'I know.'

'Who do you think these people are?' Eliza asked, 'Could they be the police?'

'There are a lot of them out there, so they can't all be from Meadowbank. I think it must be something quite serious to justify such a turn-out.'

'They must have transport, but I didn't hear anything. I suppose they'll be parked outside the estate.'

'Probably,' he agreed, 'but I don't think there's much we can do. If they are the police, they are not going to thank us for interfering.'

'And if they are not?'

'A good question, my darling. And I wish I knew the answer.'

*

'How did you get in?' Wendy gasped, staring at him in disbelief, 'that door was locked.'

'Put those things down. On the table,' he ordered, his voice harsh, the words staccato-like, 'and stay exactly where you are.'

'You've been here before, haven't you?'

'Be quiet.'

'What do you want?'

But she already knew. This was the man who had shot her father. As she looked into the ice-blue eyes facing her across the room, she knew without any doubt, she was looking at her father's killer. She also knew, sensed, that soon he would deal with her in the same way. As though following her thought process he took two slow steps towards her and with one swift movement pulled out a gun from his jacket pocket. Wendy knew nothing about firearms and it was the first time she had ever seen one. She had no idea of the make, would have found it difficult to describe even, except it was a dark metallic grey and looked incongruously small in his hand. She wanted to take her eyes away from the round black eye of the barrel, but it was not easy. Like a rabbit or some wild night animal caught in the headlamps of an approaching vehicle she was paralysed, unable to move.

'Do you really believe you will get away with this?' she asked, forcing herself to look up at him.

'Like him, you have too much to say for yourself.'

'You mean my father, don't you?'

'Who else?'

'Why did you kill him?' she asked, remembering a thriller she had read where a woman in a similar situation had made an attempt to get her assailant to talk, in particular about himself. Of course in the book the plan had worked, but this was no work of fiction. This was real. The gun was real. The man she knew as Peter Taylor standing in the familiar surroundings of her family home was real. There could be no cheating: she could not turn to the last page to find out what happened.

'I killed him,' he said, slowly, deliberately, 'because he got in my way.'

'What about Len Roberts?' she asked, 'Did he get in your way as well?'

'Of course.'

As he spoke, the two words requiring no response from her, the front door bell rang.

'Expecting visitors?'

'At this time of night?'

'Don't get smart with me.' his body tensing and showing the first signs of unease. This man liked to be in control; not for him, the unexpected. How would he handle this development she wondered? Would he choose to ignore the interruption? He remained in the same position; about four feet away from her, his eyes, unblinking, and never leaving her face and the gun, perfectly still and pointing directly at her. Part of her brain was reacting strangely. Where had she heard that silly expression: 'saved by the bell'? Was it possible, could it really be possible that whoever was outside, could prevent this madman carrying out what to him must be the final stage of extricating himself from whatever he had got himself into? And she waited for him to react. He would have to do something; he couldn't stand like that for ever.

'You will do precisely as I say,' he said, coming up close to her and grabbing her arm, 'one squawk and I'll shoot.'

The irony was not lost on her. How she wanted to say, to remind him, that was his intention anyway. What was this, a stay of execution? Obviously, he wanted to make sure he was in the clear and, once again, she was powerless to do anything. There was no point saying any more. Perversely, this seemed to disturb him; it was plain he was expecting some sort of retaliation.

'We're going out the back way. Now!'

'Where are you taking me?' a useless question and one she hardly expected an answer.

'That needn't concern you. Just shut up and do as you're -'

The magnified and disembodied voice called out, cutting him off, and shattering the silence: 'PETER TAYLOR. THIS IS THE POLICE. WE KNOW YOU ARE IN THERE. PLEASE COME TO THE FRONT DOOR IMMEDIATELY.'

Silence returned, but for how long Wendy thought, holding her breath and feeling the colour drain from her face. He didn't hesitate. With his free hand, his grip tightening, he swung her round until she was in front of him and pushed her forward across the kitchen and into the hall; the cold pressure of the gun pressed hard into her spine, the pain, sharp and intense, making her gasp.

'Open the door and don't try to move.' he hissed, his face so close she could smell his aftershave; sharp, musky and unpleasant. The barrage of lights which confronted her was at first blinding, making it impossible to distinguish properly what must be at least a dozen people down there in the drive.

'RELEASE MISS TILSLY AND STAND TO ONE SIDE.'

'She's coming with me,' Peter Taylor shouted across in the direction of where she could now make out a man in the centre of them all, taller than any of them, a loudspeaker raised high and projected directly towards them both, 'so you have to let me through!'

'YOU ARE IN NO POSITION TO BARGAIN PETER TAYLOR. DO AS WE SAY.'

'And if I don't?' taunting them; is he crazy she thought. Can't he see whatever happens, the outcome is bound to be the same. They'll get him. Was she right then? She now knew Peter Taylor was a killer, but was he also mad?

Was it her imagination, could she be so traumatised by what was happening she was hallucinating, but she was sure the space between the bottom of the steps and the group of officers was narrowing. If so, they were moving in, slowly, the impression if it was one, so slight, to be barely perceptible. Had he noticed? If he had, he showed no sign. The grip on her arm, bent up as it was behind her back had not lessened, neither had the pressure of the muzzle of the gun, the constant pain beginning to make her feel nauseous, so perhaps he was not aware of any difference.

Even if he had, he didn't get a chance to react as a sudden movement in the hall behind them distracted him. Two things happened, both at the same time: she felt his body move away from her as he half-turned and the gun shifted from her spine. Instead of relief at the instant release of pressure, although the pain was losing its intensity, a wave of dizziness swamped her, making her stumble. She heard the sharp crack of gunfire as she fell full-length on to the top step before losing consciousness.

*

'I don't believe Meadowbank will ever be the same again.' Simon commented after they had all gone; Peter Taylor, belligerently confident right up to the end, handcuffed and seated in the back of the black Mercedes, flanked on either side by a police officer. Chief Inspector Brenda Masters and Sergeant Ian Ash had left at the same time as the police team from Winchester, but not before she had introduced Jonathan Brothers, one of Interpol's senior officers, to them. He had walked back with the four of them to the Lodge and stayed long enough to explain his involvement; how they had been shadowing Peter Taylor, following him that night to the Manor and fortuitously, due to Peter's own carelessness, one of the officers had been able to gain access simply by walking in through the open back door. Jonathan Brothers also mentioned to Eliza if it had not been for her father recognising Peter Taylor, alias Paul Thomson, as the man they had been looking for, it may have taken another eleven years before the file on the murder in Mombasa and one which had shaken the entire expatriate community, could have been closed. Eliza stopped him as he was leaving to mention the cigarette case he had left on the bar in the restaurant, suggesting he had done so on purpose to enable them to take Peter Taylor's fingerprints. 'I must be losing my edge!' Jonathan had smiled at her, making him look more like someone's favourite uncle than a key man from Interpol.

'You're probably right, Simon,' Wendy said quietly, 'but thank God it's all over.'

'Are you sure you're alright?' Mark asked her, his eyes dark with concern. 'You look so pale.'

'I'm always pale. Always have been.' she smiled shakily at him.

'If you're sure?'

'I'm sure.'

'I just cannot get that picture out of my mind,' he went on, including Simon and Eliza, looking across the table at them, 'arriving at the same time as the ambulance and to see Wendy lying like that. On the top step. She was so still. I –' he faltered, his voice trembling, 'I thought she was dead.' he finished and for a few seconds there was silence in Eliza's kitchen as each of them considered what might have been.

'That police officer will be okay, Simon, won't he?' Eliza was the first to speak.

'Apparently only a flesh wound.'

Dawn was breaking and they were still there. More coffee had been made and Eliza had cooked large platefuls of scrambled eggs and along with the hot buttered toast all helped to revive them. Mark had already, as soon as Wendy had regained consciousness, explained why he had made the journey from London in the middle of the night. Earlier in the day, after speaking to Brenda Masters and trying a number of times to telephone Wendy throughout the day, even the number he had found for the Manor in the directory, he had become more and more concerned, but it was not until much later that night, unable to sleep, he finally decided to get in the car and drive to Meadowbank.

Eliza then told Wendy and Mark about Steve, painful though she found it to even mention his name, but she thought it only fair they should know that she had once been married to him. She felt, although he never said anything that Jonathan Brothers had understood. He may have noticed her sharp intake of breath when he was telling them earlier why Steve was murdered. Simon had. He had taken her hand, slowly stroking each finger, as though trying to erase the memory.

'What a can of worms,' Mark said, 'to think that one man could destroy people's lives the way Peter Taylor did and continue, outwardly at least, to live a normal one himself. It does make you wonder, though, doesn't it,' he went on thoughtfully, 'however innocently you may conduct your own life that at any moment that can be taken away from you.'

Other titles by Margaret Alty:

Tangled Web – ISBN: 978 1 84549 422 3

Jenny – ISBN: 978 1 84549 442 1

Camouflage – ISBN: 978 1 84549 478 0

All published by arima Publishing.